The
Seven Fabulous Wonders

For more information about Katherine Roberts, visit
www.katherineroberts.com

First published in Great Britain by CollinsVoyager 2002
CollinsVoyager is an imprint of HarperCollins*Publishers* Ltd
77-85 Fulham Palace Road, Hammersmith
London W6 8JB

The HarperCollins website address is:
www.**fire**and**water**.com

1 3 5 7 9 8 6 4 2

Passages from Heraclitus, translated by Richard Geldard
from *Remembering Heraclitus*, copyright © 2000 by Richard Geldard.
Reprinted with permission of Lindisfarne Books
Illustrations by Fiona Land

ISBN 0 00 711280 7

Printed and bound in England by
Clays Ltd, St Ives plc

Katherine Roberts

THE AMAZON TEMPLE ·QUEST·

An imprint of HarperCollinsPublishers

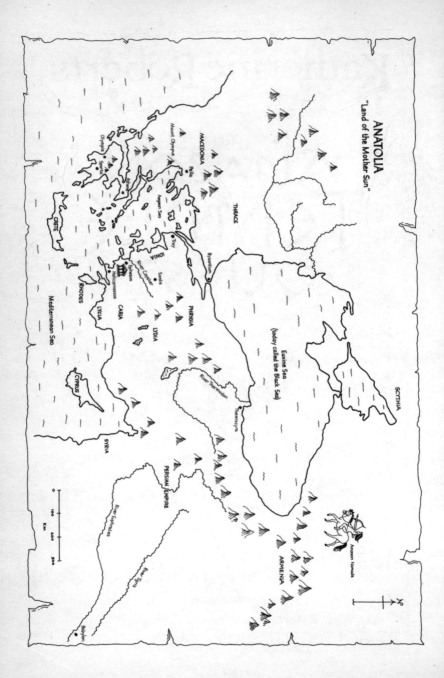

ANATOLIA
"Land of the Mother Sun"

MACEDONIA
Mount Olympos
Olympia
Sparta
Athens
Pella
Aegean Sea
CRETE
Troy
IONIA
River Caïcus
Ephesos
Halicarnassos
Sardis
RHODES
LYCIA
CARIA
LYDIA
PHRYGIA
CYPRUS
SYRIA
Mediterranean Sea
THRACE
Byzantium
River Thermodon
Themiskyra
Euxine Sea
(today called the Black Sea)
SCYTHIA
PERSIAN EMPIRE
River Euphrates
River Tigris
Babylon
ARMENIA
Amazon Nomads

0   100   200   300
Km

N

Seven are the signs of a true Amazon:
the yellow glare,
the sleep that heals,
a fighting spirit,
a blinding shield,
birth without man,
death without pain,
and the power to command a gryphon's flame.

Chapter 1

ARGUMENT
We should not act like the children of our parents.

The argument was so silly.

It would never have happened if Lysippe and Tanais had been back home on the steppe – or, at least, there it would never have got past the first few angry words. Lysippe would simply have ridden Northwind towards the horizon until the wind blew the bad feelings away. Then she'd have returned to the tents and said she was sorry. Her sister would have hugged her, and everything would have been all right again. But they were alone together in a cave halfway across the world, their mother and the rest of the tribe had been gone since before dawn, and they were starting to worry.

The unfamiliar feel of the rock pressing all around her made Lysippe irritable and scared. She longed for the others to return. Yet that would mean riding further into this rocky, hostile land, when all she really wanted was to go home. She rubbed harder at Northwind's neck with a handful of grass she'd picked from the mountainside, and the seeds poked him in the eye. The sturdy little horse, who had been leaning against her enjoying the attention, snorted in surprise and nipped Tanais' mare. Sunrise squealed. Tanais hurried over to separate the two animals. Northwind laid back his ears, and Tanais gave him a gentle slap on the nose.

"Don't hit my horse!" Lysippe said.

"Then control him!" Tanais snapped back, which showed how tense she was because she never normally raised her voice around the horses.

And that was the start of it.

In fact, the argument had been building ever since their mother Queen Oreithyia had found this cave, raised the ancient gryphon-shield of their tribe, and spoken the secret words of summoning. Lysippe remembered how they'd all held their breath, but nothing seemed to happen. Then their mother had vaulted on her horse, looked sternly at her and Tanais, and told them they had to stay in the cave. Apparently, she'd summoned a spirit called an oread to protect them while she led her warriors down to the city. Tanais hadn't wanted to stay behind, and neither had Lysippe. She'd much rather see the fabled city of their ancestors than be stuck in a cave with an invisible spirit.

"It's not Northwind's fault. He doesn't like it in here. Nor do I." Lysippe pushed past her sister and went to the cave mouth. She stared down the empty trail until her eyes hurt. "How much longer are they going to be? What if they don't come back?"

"Don't be silly. Of course they'll come back."

"Do you think they'll find the Stone?"

Tanais looked at her over Sunrise's withers. "No."

"What do you mean?"

Her sister frowned. For a moment, she looked as if she was about to say something else. Then she sighed. "Themiscyra's the first city we've tried. We're unlikely to find one of the Gryphon Stones so soon, that's all."

"Then why's it taking so long? Something might have happened. We should go down there and look for them."

"No. You heard Mother – it might be dangerous. We're to stay in the cave."

Lysippe clenched her fists. "I've got a bow. I can fight!"

But Tanais shook her head. "And what would you do if we were attacked? You can't even bear to bring down a bird. I know you too well, little sister! I've even seen you put Northwind's ticks back in the grass instead of squashing them. We'd have left you back on the steppe if there was anyone to leave you with."

Lysippe blushed because, deep down, she suspected this was true. The older members of the tribe had discussed it at length when they'd received the invitation to join King Philip's army, eventually deciding that seven fully-trained Amazon warriors ought to be able to protect two youngsters who were, after all, on the verge of adulthood. But she was still feeling too prickly to say sorry.

"They'd have left you, too," she mumbled.

"No, they wouldn't. I'm nearly old enough to fight."

"Bet you couldn't kill a man!"

Tanais pressed her lips together. "I'll do it if I have to. We're supposed to be going to Macedonia to join an army, after all. That's what armies do. Fight and kill people." But she looked uncertainly at the cave mouth.

"If you're such a great warrior, then why did Mother leave you up here with me?"

Her sister gave her an exasperated look. "To look after you, what do you think? Sometimes, Lysippe, you're quite impossible! Be sensible and come back inside."

Lysippe set her jaw. "She summoned an oread to do that."

"Don't be so stupid!" Tanais snapped. "There's no oread or any other type of spirit in here, can't you see that? Cave-spirits and water-spirits and all the rest are just legends like our Gryphon Stones. They don't really exist. They never have."

Lysippe blinked at her in surprise. When their mother had explained that they couldn't see the oread because they didn't have a Gryphon Stone yet, Lysippe had believed her. She'd thought Tanais had believed, too.

"Then why—?"

"Why's Mother down in the city looking for a Gryphon Stone? Because she knows it'll make our enemies weaker if she wears one in battle, that's why. No point trying to kill someone who carries a Stone that can ward off death, is there? I wouldn't be surprised if she doesn't bring some old piece of rock back up the mountain and pretend it's magic. It's what people believe that matters. I expect that's why she told us there was an oread in here and did all that stuff with the shield – so we'd feel safe."

Lysippe blinked again. "Mother wouldn't lie to us."

"No?" Tanais gave her a pitying look. "She's been lying to you every day of your life, little sister."

Lysippe's heart lurched. "What do you mean?"

Tanais pulled a face. It was as if she'd only just decided something and she didn't like what it was. She squatted by their smouldering fire. The pile of wood they'd collected last night was nearly gone, but she pushed another branch into the ash and muttered, "You've no more got pure Amazon blood than I have. Everyone knows Mother lay with a Scythian man to get you, same as she did to get me."

Lysippe stared at her in amazement. Her eyes filled with furious tears. "You take that back!"

Tanais shook her head. "Take what back? The truth? Do you really believe your father was a god who visited Mother in the middle of the night? Grow up, Lysippe! Things just don't happen that way. Why do you think our race is dying out? I'd have thought you were old enough to have worked it out for yourself by now."

The shadows inside the cave were a blur. "I hate you!" Lysippe reached for her bow, but Tanais was right about it being useless in her hands and she hated the way it bounced on her shoulder when she was carrying it. She knocked it aside and whistled for Northwind. He trotted across the cave and blew through his nose in sympathy. She vaulted on his back and urged him out into the sunlight, blinded by tears.

"No, Lysippe!" Tanais called after her. "I'm sorry, I didn't mean it... Come back! It's not safe to leave the cave!"

"Doesn't matter if there isn't an oread here, does it?" Lysippe shouted over her shoulder, too upset to care.

There was a strange sparkle at the entrance, as if she were riding through thick mist. Then Northwind's hooves rattled over the rock, drowning Tanais' reply.

Lysippe was aware of riding too fast for the terrain. This was no level steppe with soft, forgiving grass; it was an alien mountainside littered with loose white rocks. But her fleeting worry that Northwind would sprain a tendon passed as he galloped down the trail. He was the most sure-footed horse in the whole world, and she'd trust him with her life. All the same, her sister was right. Riding off alone and unarmed into strange hills was a stupid thing to do.

She slowed Northwind and wiped her nose on her sleeve. "I am a real Amazon," she whispered under her breath. "I *am*. Tanais is just jealous because her father was a Scythian. The Gryphon Stones are real, as well. When Mother gets back with one, Tanais will have to believe." As if in answer, Northwind tossed his head and whinnied. Lysippe laughed, and some of the hurt faded. "You understand, don't you, my friend?"

The sunlight and pure air, cool with the scent of the sea, cleared the final echoes of the argument from her head. She was about to turn back to the cave, when Northwind whinnied again. The little horse's neck arched, tight as a bow, and his small ears pricked as he stared down the trail. Lysippe caught her breath. The light reflecting off the rocks was bright, but she could make out another horse and rider coming round the bend below in a cloud of white dust.

Her heart pounded with joy and relief. She pushed Northwind into a trot. "Mother! Did you find it...?"

Her words trailed off as the rider came into focus. Instead of the tightly-braided hair of the Amazons, the rider's head was encased in a helmet moulded to look like a face with two slits for eyes and a blue crest on top. He wore a dusty cloak thrown back over one shoulder to reveal a tunic belted at the waist. A sword swung at his hip.

While Lysippe stared in surprise at the rider's hairy legs, he stared back at her through the eye slits of his helmet, taking in her close-fitting Amazon leggings and her hair that she liked to wear loose to show its unusual golden highlights. Still staring, he reined in his horse, untied a little pouch from his belt, and signalled to someone behind him.

Lysippe saw movement out of the corner of her eye and turned Northwind, suddenly uncomfortable. She'd ridden a lot further down the mountain than she'd intended. But the rider's eyes, cold and blue through his helmet slits, held her gaze. By the time she'd completed the turn, there were several men on foot between her and the cave, moving faster through the rocks than a horse could safely go.

She wheeled Northwind off the path to get round them. But the helmeted man shook some green powder from his pouch and threw it towards her. The air sparkled, blinding Lysippe, and another bare-legged man rose from the rocks right in front of her, his sword flashing through the air. The flat side of the blade hit Northwind on the muzzle. Surprised and dazzled, the little horse reared and lost his balance on the steep scree.

Lysippe's first memories were of sitting on her mother's horse in the safe circle of Oreithyia's arms. She'd had Northwind since her legs grew long enough to ride astride and he was an unbroken colt. In all those years, she'd fallen off just a handful of times. So her first reaction as she tumbled over his shoulder was to blush with shame at falling off her horse in front of a stranger. But there was no time to be embarrassed. As she scrambled up to remount, a heavy weight knocked her flat again. Before she'd recovered her breath, her arms were pinned behind her back and a cord wound tightly about her wrists.

"What are you doing?" she said, more surprised than anything. "Let me go!"

Her captor lifted her to her feet and chuckled. He said

something in Greek to the helmeted rider, too fast for her to follow, and the rider replied in the same language.

"...should be another one... check up there..."

Lysippe's breath was returning, and with it her senses. She waited until her captor relaxed his grip, then sprang away from him.

"Tanais!" she shouted. "Tanais! Watch out!"

She twisted her hands as she fled, trying desperately to get the rope off, but the knots were too tight. She could barely see what was happening through her mussed hair and wished she'd let Tanais braid it for her. But from the shouts behind, she knew others had joined the chase. Northwind was back on his feet now, snorting and shaking his head. She took a run downhill at her horse and vaulted as high as she could.

It wasn't easy with her hands tied behind her, but she would still have made it if the helmeted man hadn't urged his horse past her and grabbed Northwind's dangling rein, dragging him round in a tight circle and making her miss her jump. Lysippe's ankle turned on a loose stone and she fell awkwardly, her bound arms trapped beneath her. The helmeted man jumped down from his horse and put one foot on Lysippe's chest.

"That was stupid," he said, speaking slowly and clearly in Greek, as if to a small child. "No one likes a stupid slave. Apologize to your new master, and maybe he'll be kind."

As she stared back at him in horror, the man she'd got away from earlier came over, dusting himself off. He had brown, curly hair and green-flecked eyes. He slapped the helmeted man on the shoulder and chuckled as he looked down at Lysippe. "An unexpected bonus thanks to you, my friend! Not pretty, and those yellow eyes don't do her any favours. But she's plenty young and strong enough for the silver mines if no one wants her for a house slave. Tall, too. Some people like that. Let her up, Alchemist, and let's go see what other booty we've caught today."

The helmeted man removed his foot. Lysippe rolled on to her side and climbed stiffly to her knees, watching him warily. Northwind had been caught by one of the other men. The rest had gone on up the trail with their leader. As Lysippe was struggling to her feet, there was a sudden rumble above, and dust and small stones rattled down the hillside. She sprang towards the cave in sudden fear for Tanais. But she'd forgotten her injured ankle. It buckled under her, and the white rocks and sun swam together in a blaze of pain.

When she could see again, the frightening helmet with its eye slits was a hand's span from her face.

"Don't know when you're beaten, do you?" Her captor pulled her into a sitting position and propped her against one of the white boulders. Through a gap in the hills, she could see the sea, wave-tossed like the way she felt inside.

She took deep breaths as her captor crouched before her and removed his helmet. He had pale silver hair and grime on his cheeks where dust had built up under the bronze. A jagged scar split his forehead above his left eye. Most unsettling of all, he had no eyebrows or eyelashes so there was nothing to soften that cold, blue glare. Lysippe made herself meet his gaze, though she still felt queasy from the pain in her ankle, and the bruises she'd suffered in her fall were beginning to hurt.

He fingered the worn leather of her leggings. "Where are you from, slave? Where did you steal that horse?"

"I'm an Amazon!" Lysippe said, trying to sound braver than she felt. She peered past him to see what had happened to Tanais. "Northwind's mine – I didn't steal him. And my mother and all her warriors are on their way back, so you'd better let me go!"

The men who had stayed behind laughed.

"Don't lie to me, slave!" her captor growled. "Everyone knows Amazons are extinct." But his thin lips twisted up at one corner, as if she'd merely confirmed something he already knew.

A flicker of doubt went through Lysippe. The noises up at the cave had ceased, leaving an ominous, sun-glaring silence. Then there was a crash that echoed round the slopes, and the men who had gone with their leader came running back down the trail, pointing wildly up the mountain. One had blood running down his arm. Another was limping. "It's crazy!" they screamed. "It's after us!" Their leader's curly hair was covered in dust. He drew his sword and barked out orders, and the men crouched down behind the rocks.

The man he'd called 'Alchemist' jammed his battered

helmet back on and hauled Lysippe to her feet. She cried out as her weight pressed on her injured ankle. Then she heard it, too. Hoof beats, rattling down the trail above them. Her heart lifted as a horse rounded the bend, its rider controlling it with her knees so she could hold her bow with an arrow on the string.

"Tanais!" Lysippe cried. "Careful, they — "

With a silent glitter, her captor's sword appeared at her throat.

Tanais brought her mare to a halt in three strides. She paled when she saw Lysippe, and her knuckles tightened on her bow.

"What are you waiting for?" Lysippe shouted hoarsely. "Shoot them!"

Tanais shook her head, and her bow lowered. Lysippe's heart sank. She might have known her sister wouldn't have the courage when it came to it.

"Throw your weapon to me," instructed the dusty-haired leader, emerging from the rocks. "And get down off your horse."

"No, Tanais!" Lysippe cried in Scythian, tears in her eyes. "Don't! They're trying to make us into slaves."

Tanais' dark gaze met hers. There was such fear and love in that single look, Lysippe's heart twisted. Why had she provoked her sister into that stupid, stupid argument?

"Be brave, little sister," Tanais replied in the same language. "I'll be back with the others as soon as I can."

Lysippe saw the way her sister's toe pressed behind Sunrise's elbow and how her weight shifted in preparation for the leap off the path. Her heart twisted a second time. "No, not that way!"

Her warning came too late. The slavers pulled the same trick they'd used on Lysippe. As the helmeted man cast his green powder, they rose from the rocks and sliced at the mare's legs to bring the little horse to its knees. Tanais dropped her bow and clung on valiantly with both arms around Sunrise's neck. But the men pulled her from the mare's back. Poor Sunrise, suddenly unbalanced, somersaulted and slid all the way to the bottom of the slope. Lysippe gritted her teeth and kicked backwards, aiming for her captor's shin. But her ankle betrayed her again and a red mist swam before her eyes. That was when she knew the injury was serious. From a long way off, her sister was shouting something. Lysippe couldn't see what was happening. A horse cantered away. She hoped it was Northwind.

"Tanais!" she sobbed, frightened now, fighting the dizziness and what she knew would follow. "Tanais, don't leave me..."

Her captor sheathed his sword and hissed into her ear. "Don't worry, slave. You and your sister are going to be very close indeed until we reach Ephesos."

He shoved her forwards, and Lysippe's full weight fell on her injured ankle. There wasn't time to wonder how the men had known where they would be. Her natural Amazon defences took over, carrying her softly into the place where there was no pain.

Chapter 2

HERO
Some he makes slaves, others free.

Lysippe's world had turned upside down. Clouds floated at her feet, rocks blurred above her head, and mountain peaks hung in the sky. The whole vista was jolting up and down, accompanied by the smell of sweaty horse and an endless, chinking shuffle.

A dream, she thought. Except there were no dreams in the Amazon healing-sleep. She closed her eyes again with a moan.

When she next came to herself, the world was the right way up again and the stars were in the sky. She lay on her back without moving, staring up at a dark cliff. There was soft breathing nearby, the sound of a horse's teeth tearing grass, and another of those strange chinks.

Tanais' face blotted out the stars, her dirty hair escaping from its travel braids and a new bruise on her cheek. "About time!" she said in a funny little voice. "I thought you were going to sleep all the way to Ephesos!"

"Ephesos?" Lysippe frowned. The name was familiar, something she ought to remember.

"Slavemaster Mikkos thought you were faking it and threatened to leave you for the wolves if you didn't wake up. I was terrified he would do it and I wouldn't be able to help you. But the Alchemist said to tie you on the donkey, and then if you were pretending you'd soon decide to be sensible because it hurts to travel that way..."

Tanais' voice broke. As she moved, something long and heavy wriggled across Lysippe's shoulder. Lysippe was too confused in the aftermath of her long sleep to work it out.

"Oh, little sister! We'll be rescued soon, I know we will! Mother and the others are following us – I think I heard horses behind us yesterday. They'll kill Mikkos and that horrid Alchemist and free us all, and then we'll go back and find Sunrise, and— Lysippe? Don't go back to sleep, *please*. They don't understand how it is for us."

The desperation in her sister's voice was nothing compared to the shivers that were rippling up Lysippe's spine and the cold sweat that suddenly broke out all over her body. Everything was coming back now. Her tearful ride down the mountain, the helmeted man with his cold blue eyes, Tanais being dragged off her mare and Sunrise rolling down the scree... The heavy thing on her shoulder was a length of chain. It ran through a manacle that encircled her wrist, linking her to Tanais and to several unfamiliar boys and girls sleeping in a huddle nearby.

They were penned in a cleft of the cliffs. Guarding the narrow entrance were two of the slavers who had captured them, playing some sort of game that involved throwing a stone and picking up small bones. Out in the valley, Northwind had been tethered to a stake next to a strange black horse and the donkey Tanais had mentioned. Lysippe looked anxiously to see if her horse had been hurt, but he seemed happy enough grazing the short mountain grass. To her relief, she couldn't see the animal the helmeted man had been riding. The rest of the slavers slept nearby, rolled in their cloaks with their weapons close at hand. There weren't as many of them as she'd thought. In a bundle next to the men's packs, she recognized their bows and arrows and the spare axe Mother had left them in case they needed to chop more wood.

"I'm sorry," Lysippe whispered, fighting off the last of the sleep. "Next time I'll listen to you, I promise."

Tanais smiled sadly. "Don't make promises you can't keep, little sister. It was as much my fault as yours. The important thing is we're still alive and together. We'll get out of this, somehow."

Lysippe struggled into a sitting position. "What happened at the cave? I remember there was an avalanche, and the men were shouting about a monster..." She felt a glow of excitement and hope. "Did the oread come? Did it kill the Alchemist? What's an alchemist, anyway?"

Tanais put a warning hand on her arm as the guards looked round. "Shh, little sister, or they'll separate us. The Alchemist isn't here tonight. He rides off every few days to buy things from the towns. I don't think he's one of Mikkos' men. As far as I can work out, an alchemist is a sort of Greek magician. The other slaves are terrified of him. They say he uses human blood in his experiments, but I think that's just a story like our spirits and things."

"But there must have been an oread! The avalanche—"

Tanais frowned. "There was a rock fall, that's all. Some of the men got crushed in it. I was lucky to get Sunrise out, and now she's gone. I think she was lame, but at least she got away." She smiled bravely. "They caught Northwind, though. They've been making him carry the packs while you were on the donkey. Does your ankle still hurt? You broke it. That's why you've been in the healing-sleep so long. They let me bandage it, but you'll have to walk now you're awake. Mikkos thinks it's just a sprain."

Lysippe took deep breaths and her shivers eased slightly. She wasn't alone. Tanais was looking after her, as she had done all her life. Even though she knew it would have been better if Tanais had escaped and gone to find the others, she was selfishly glad to see her sister.

She tried her weight on her bandaged ankle while she looked more closely at their fellow captives. They were all young, scruffily dressed in the same fashion as the men and bare-legged under their tunics. Some were barefoot, too. They looked as if nothing short of an earthquake would wake them. But one of the older boys was staring at them intently with his black eyes.

"Where are we?" Lysippe asked, tempted to use Scythian so he wouldn't understand, except she guessed Tanais was speaking Greek to hide their identity.

"I don't know," Tanais said. "Somewhere in the mountains still. We left the sea behind ages ago, but we're supposed to be heading for another coast. I think it must be a different sea, or maybe we're taking a short cut..." She sounded vague, as if she were thinking of something else.

"They're keepin' us off the main trade routes, you mean," said the black-eyed boy. He eased the chain aside and sat up carefully so he wouldn't attract the attention of the guards. "Slavers don't like to be seen about their work. We'll have to climb every last mountain between here and Ephesos, you'll see. It's called takin' the wings off our heels, so none of us'll have a scrap of energy left to make a run for it when we reach the market block. Get more for well-behaved slaves, don't they?" When they didn't react, he flapped his hands. "Wings? You know? Like the messenger-god Hermes has on his heels to make him fast?"

Tanais scowled at the boy. But Lysippe wriggled closer. "How do you know so much?"

The boy grinned at her. He'd lost two of his front teeth. "I'm pretty much stone deaf, but I can tell what people are sayin' if I can see their lips. I don't let on, though. It's funny what people say when they think you can't hear. Most of 'em assume that because I'm deaf, I'm stupid as well."

"They're right," muttered Tanais, but the boy didn't react.

"What's your name?" Lysippe asked, careful to let him see her lips.

"People call me Hero." He stared curiously at Lysippe's eyes. "Did you know you've got the gryphon's glare? It's supposed to turn your enemies to ash."

Lysippe's stomach jumped. "What do you know about gryphons?"

The boy grinned. "I know they're half-lion and half-eagle and very fierce – least, their statues are. No one's ever seen a real one. They're supposed to live in Persia. Is that where you're from?"

Tanais pushed him away. "Shut up, Hero. Gryphons aren't real, everyone knows that. Lysippe's been ill. She needs to rest, not listen to your stupid stories."

"I don't need rest. I've been asleep for ages!" Lysippe massaged her ankle. She wanted to ask Hero if he knew any more about gryphons, but other things were more important. "Are we going to escape now?" she said. "I can run."

Hero gave her an amused look. "Run? On your bad ankle? You'll have a hard enough time walkin' on it tomorrow."

"But it's—"

Tanais gave her hand a warning squeeze. "Mother's following our trail," she said firmly. "Be patient. She'll make her move soon. Then we can run."

Hero looked up at the stars past the dark cliffs and hummed faintly to himself, as if he'd been through all this before.

"But we can't just do nothing!" Lysippe said fiercely. The rocks further up the mountain were sparkling in a strange way. She hoped she wasn't going to slip into the healing-sleep again.

"The others are coming," Tanais repeated. "They won't abandon us, don't worry."

"What if they think we're dead?"

Her sister blinked at her. "They won't. They'll have gone back to the cave, and—" She broke off, as if she'd only just realized what the Amazons would think when they found the cave where they'd told them to hide choked with recently-avalanched rocks.

Lysippe set her jaw. "I can't believe you haven't tried to escape yet."

Hero broke off humming and watched them with interest.

"I was looking after you," Tanais said. "You were hurt."

Lysippe shook her head. The rocks were still glittering at the edges of her vision. "Well, I'm going to escape right now!" she said, lifting the chain that ran through their manacles and examining it. One end was fixed to the manacle of a small girl with untidy golden hair who slept curled into a ball, sucking her thumb. The other was looped about a stake near the guards. There were seven children between the small girl and Hero, then Tanais, and finally Lysippe. A bar locked the end.

"Won't slide through," Hero said, seeing her look. "Not until they take off that bar, and Mikkos keeps the key around his neck. It's one of those newfangled metal locks from Persia, so it won't come off without it." He gave her a speculative look. "Plannin' to steal it off him, are you?"

Lysippe considered the Slavemaster. If they all crept to the mouth of the cleft together, maybe the small girl at the end could reach Mikkos before he or any of the other slavers woke up. But there were the guards to get past first, and they both had swords... She shook her head.

Hero laughed softly. "Thought not. Punishment for tryin' to escape is bein' tied upside down on the donkey for a day without food or water. An' if you don't keep up, the rest of us have to drag or carry you – so don't try it, huh, Lysippe? It's hard enough climbin' these goat paths chained together as it is."

"What if we all refuse to march? They can't put us all on the donkey."

"They can still starve us." Hero gave Mikkos a dark look. "The others like their food too much, and they're scared of bein' sold off cheap to the Alchemist if they misbehave. You'll never get everyone to agree. Besides, where would we go? We're days away from the nearest town. We'd be caught long before we got out of these mountains. Are you goin' to be responsible for little Timareta over there? Not me!"

Lysippe eyed the small girl sleeping at the end of the

chain. Timareta couldn't have been more than six years old. She clenched her fists in frustration.

One of the boys turned over with a groan and jerked on the chain. "Cut it out, will you? Some of us are trying to sleep here."

Tanais repeated what she'd said about waiting for the Amazons to catch up with them. But Lysippe bit her knuckles and pulled at the manacle. "I can't," she whispered. "I just can't. This is horrible! How can you let them do this to you? There must be *some* way we can escape!"

"Well, there ain't," Hero said with a note of finality. "Not up in these mountains with the Alchemist around. Give it up, Lysippe. Your sister's right. We got to wait."

By the time they stopped well after sunset on the following day, Lysippe had a better idea of why the others were so resigned to their fate. They'd been climbing all afternoon, shuffling in the dust behind Mikkos' black horse with the end of their chain secured to a strap about its neck. Since that morning, all they'd been given to share between them was a loaf of hard bread and a few swallows from an amphora of bitter-tasting water to wash it down. Lysippe's throat was so dry, she could have drunk an entire river. Although her ankle had mended, she felt dizzy and faintly sick. As they marched, she thought she glimpsed faces sparkling at the corners of her eyes, watching them from the cover of rocks and trees. But when she turned her head, there was nothing to be seen except dust and sunlight.

They camped that night in a pass so high, Lysippe was sure she could have reached up and touched the stars if she'd only had the energy to try. It was cold enough to see their breath. They got more bread, this time supplemented by a few olives and berries, and another swallow of water from the amphora. Then the captives curled up around each other, jostling for a position that meant they weren't lying on the chain or exposed on the windward side of the huddle. Lysippe had meant to stay awake and ask Hero more about gryphons, and she wanted to ask Tanais if she'd seen anything strange in the hills. But as soon as her head touched the ground, it seemed the slavers were kicking them awake again.

Mikkos occasionally left them chained in a cave or crack of the cliffs under guard, while he took the rest of his men on foraging missions. The others were glad of the chance to rest, but Lysippe grew to hate these stops. Mikkos brought back several more slaves this way. Each had their hands tied behind them and was dirty, dishevelled, and sobbing with the shock of their capture. But as soon as they were chained, they seemed to accept their fate and fell into the routine without complaint.

Tanais grew quieter the further they marched. Every time they stopped, she stared back the way they had come. "Mother will be here soon," she assured Lysippe each night as they lay down to sleep. "She will." But she sounded less and less sure of herself.

"I don't think they're coming," Lysippe said eventually one night after their meagre supper, knowing she risked another argument. "I think it's the oread, following us. I keep seeing strange sparkles in the rocks."

Tanais stroked her hair from her cheek. "No, little sister. There's no oread. You're just overtired. We all are. If you did see anything, I expect it's that horrid Alchemist – remember how he threw that powder when he captured us?"

Lysippe's stomach knotted and she shifted closer to her sister. She eyed the rocks with new trepidation. "We *have* to escape before we get to Ephesos," she said. "We can't let Mikkos sell us! What if he sells us to the Alchemist?"

"Shh," Tanais said, still stroking her hair. "If Mother doesn't come, we'll think of something, I promise."

"But it'll be too late when we get there!"

Hero, who had been following their conversation with his usual curiosity, sighed as if he'd come to a decision. He edged closer and mouthed, "There is a chance at Ephesos. Trouble is, it's almost as bad as bein' a slave. But if you're desperate..."

"What chance?" Lysippe sat up so sharply, the guards looked round.

"Get some sleep, you!" they called. "Long march tomorrow. That's *sleep*, Cloth-Ears, sleep!" They mimed lying their heads on their hands for Hero's benefit.

Tanais pulled Lysippe back down. Hero made a rude sign at the guards, which made them chuckle, put his hands behind his head and stared up at the stars. When the guards had gone back to their game, he spoke very quietly into the night.

"There's this big Temple at Ephesos. Belongs to a Greek goddess called Artemis. Any rate, once you're past the Temple gate and on sacred ground, no one's allowed to drag you out again till you're ready to come out yourself. That's no one. Not kings, not generals, not the Ionian Satrap, not even the Emperor of all Persia. Certainly not Mikkos and his common slavers."

"You sure?" Tanais frowned. "What's to stop them coming in after us and taking us out by force?"

"Sanctuary, of course," Hero said with a long-suffering sigh. "Holy sanctuary. They're too scared of the goddess, aren't they?"

"Why didn't you tell us this before?" Tanais said, still frowning.

"Didn't know if I could trust you, did I?" Hero grinned. "But I reckon you're as desperate as you look – we'll have to work together, though. No good one person runnin' if the others don't, not with this here chain on our wrists."

Lysippe listened with fresh hope. It would mean staying a captive as far as Ephesos, and they'd have a long ride back again to find the tribe. But it might be better than trying to escape before then and getting recaptured, punished and sold off cheap to the Alchemist. The very thought of being the Alchemist's slave made her shudder, even if the rumours about human sacrifice weren't true.

"Why are people so scared of the goddess?" Lysippe asked.

Hero sighed again. "Do I have to explain everything? Where are you two from? The wilds of Scythia, or something? Your clothes are pretty barbaric, come to think of it, and you muddle up your words when you speak Greek. Even Spartan girls don't wear those things on their legs. You look like Persians, only dirtier." He reached over and fingered Lysippe's leggings. "Are these made out of *skin*?"

"It's horsehide," Lysippe began. "And we're—"

"There's no need to be rude," Tanais said stiffly, giving her a warning look. "And you're no prince yourself. Your accent's terrible."

Hero bared his broken teeth at her. "What do you expect? I'm a poor deaf boy, ain't I? It's hard learnin' to talk proper when you can't hear nothin'."

Tanais snorted and turned over. She put her arms around Lysippe and whispered into her hair. "Sorry, but that boy's unbearable! You haven't had to put up with him for as long as I have."

"He seems pretty knowledgeable," Lysippe whispered back. "Do you think it's true, what he said about the Temple?"

"About as true as our legends," Tanais said after a pause.

"Do you think Ephesos could be one of the old Amazon cities?" Lysippe asked excitedly. "Hero might know something about our Gryphon Stones!"

Tanais stiffened. "Don't you go telling anyone who we are, little sister! The Slavemaster and his men probably wouldn't believe us, anyway, but I'm not so sure about the Alchemist. And I don't trust that boy Hero – he knows far too much. I know your ankle's nearly better, but keep your bandage on and limp a bit tomorrow. If they think you can't walk very well, we'll have an advantage when the time comes to run. No sense letting them know how quickly Amazons heal until we have to." Her arms tightened, enfolding Lysippe in their first real hug since their argument in the cave. "Don't worry, little sister," she whispered. "We won't have to rely on Hero's Greek goddess for sanctuary. Mother will rescue us long before we get to Ephesos."

But the Amazons still didn't come, and late on the fifteenth day since Lysippe had woken from her healing-sleep, they crested a ridge and saw the sea ahead of them. The clear, turquoise water formed a wide bay between the mountains, dotted with small islands. Buildings gleamed on the river-plain, their white walls tinged pink by the setting sun.

They all stopped to stare, and Mikkos reined his horse to a halt. "That's where you're going," he said, his voice carrying on the evening air. "Civilization! Those of you who don't sell in Ephesos will sail across that sea to Athens." His gaze moved down the line, lingering a little on Tanais and Lysippe and finishing at Hero. He frowned and urged his horse forward.

They camped too low to see the sea that night, but the scent of it was in the air and no one slept much. Mikkos had hidden them in a glen beside a muddy yellow river that Hero said flowed into the bay at Ephesos. After they'd crossed it, they would ford a second river near the Temple of Artemis to reach the city. That was when they'd have their single chance. Tanais was still convinced that Hero's story about holy sanctuary was a lot of nonsense, but she agreed something must have happened to delay the Amazons and they had no choice now. Lysippe felt like a horse bursting to gallop, that had been held on a tight rein far too long. She barely noticed the leafy beauty of their surroundings, nor the fact they were all given extra food and water that night. Nothing mattered except the second river, the Temple, and freedom.

But persuading Tanais was one thing; persuading the other captives proved to be quite another. Most of the others didn't even seem to *want* to escape. The older ones mumbled things about regular meals and a slave's life not being so bad if you behaved yourself and worked hard. Some even seemed quite excited about crossing the sea to see Athens, and one boy quoted examples of slaves who had worked their way into positions of power and become richer than their masters. Lysippe stared at him in disbelief. "That's a load of horse dung!" she shouted, making the guards look round. But the boy just shook his head and said she didn't understand. The extra food they'd been given that night didn't help matters. A full belly appeared to have made everyone forget the days and days they'd marched under the hot sun with dust in their mouths and nothing to eat but stale bread.

Lysippe snatched at the chain, dragging it through the others' manacles until she had length enough to sit with her back to them. She wrapped her arms around her knees and stared, hot-eyed, through the olive blossom at the swirling river. Her feet hurt. Her boots had holes in them. The bandage about her ankle was filthy, and her wrist itched where it had been rubbed raw by the manacle during the day and then healed overnight into a ridge of scar tissue. She'd been dirty most of her life, often smelling of horse and smoke, but this was different. This dirt was inside her, and it wouldn't come out. The river glimmered with reflected stars that almost looked like a woman's face... Lysippe closed her eyes before she could start seeing things again.

Hero edged across. His task had been to watch the guards and make some diversion if they showed too much of an interest in what their captives were saying. But Mikkos and his slavers seemed pleased to have reached the river, and were laughing and talking loudly as they passed round an amphora of wine one of the men had collected from a village earlier that day. Lysippe wondered if they'd stolen it the same way as they stole people. She scowled at them, then eyed Hero speculatively.

"They won't get drunk," Hero said. "Mikkos watered it, I saw him."

Lysippe sighed. "Why are the others so *stupid*?" she mouthed.

Tanais was still trying to persuade the other captives to see sense. She was talking about fighting units and combined strength, but it was obvious none of them understood. They'd come from isolated farms and bee-keepers' huts, and although their country had been a battleground for various skirmishes over the past hundred years, they'd not taken much notice of the soldiers. Timareta was already asleep, licking her lips as if dreaming of food.

"They're Phrygian peasants." Hero shrugged, as if this explained everything.

"And you're not, I suppose?" Lysippe was pent up with nervous energy. "Are *you* going to help us when we get to the Temple, Hero? Or are you more interested in your belly, too?"

Hero drew patterns in the mud, avoiding her eye. "I'll help you get inside the Temple. But I'm not stayin'."

Lysippe seized his arm. "What?"

Hero shrugged her off. "You heard. I'm not stayin' in there with you."

"But you'll be sold as a slave if Mikkos catches you again!"

"Slaves can run away. I done it before."

She stared at him. Hero gave her a tight smile and pulled his tattered tunic off his shoulder to show her his back. Lysippe's stomach churned at the sight of the white lines that criss-crossed the boy's flesh. "You'd see it anyway, tomorrow. They'll strip us an' make us wash in the river before we get to the market block at Ephesos. Take a good look, everyone! This is what they do to slaves." Still with a tight expression, he pulled the tunic back to cover the scars. He shrugged. "Could've been worse."

By now, all those awake were staring at Hero. Some people looked as if they were about to be sick.

"Why didn't you tell us you'd been a slave?" Tanais demanded.

"You didn't ask."

"That's how you know so much, isn't it? Because you've travelled this route before?"

Hero nodded, but his eyes slid away from hers.

Lysippe shook her head. "You were stupid to get caught again."

The boy scowled. "Crept up behind me, didn't they? Didn't hear them comin' with these Olympic-grade ears of mine."

There was an embarrassed silence.

"Maybe it would be a good idea to try this Temple," said one of the boys, at last. "I don't fancy stripes like that on my back."

"He wouldn't have got beat if he'd behaved himself!" said the girl chained beside him. "They only do that if you try to escape."

"How would you know?" Hero shot back. "Not been a slave before, have you? If you don't obey your master's orders, you get beat. Don't matter if you don't hear 'cause you're deaf, or asleep, or in the next field. If you get sold to the silver mines and try to run away, I heard they do worse than beat you. They break your ankles so you don't ever run again."

A cold ripple went down Lysippe's spine, and the others muttered uneasily. The word "Temple" was mentioned several times, and hastily shushed as people cast anxious glances at the guards. But their captors weren't interested in the conversation of slaves. The Alchemist had left them two days ago, and spirits were high. At the mouth of the glen, the men burst out laughing at some coarse joke Mikkos had cracked.

"Aren't you afraid of what they'll do to you if you try to run away again?" another girl whispered, staring at Hero.

"I don't intend to get caught next time," Hero said. But he looked away, and only Lysippe saw the pained expression in his eyes.

Someone mentioned the Alchemist in a nervous tone, but Lysippe pointed out that they couldn't get sold to anyone if they escaped and made sure they didn't get caught again.

"None of us will get caught," Tanais said firmly. "Not if we all stick together and keep to the plan."

Chapter 3

SANCTUARY
We cannot step twice in the same river.

There was a new tension among the captives when the men roused them the next morning. It was later than usual. Despite what Hero had said about Mikkos watering the wine, some of the slavers definitely had sore heads.

Lysippe was worried that they would suspect something. But the men must have assumed it was the washing in the river that was making their merchandise so jumpy. They laughed and joked as they made their captives pull their tunics over their heads as far as their manacled wrists and pushed them, one by one, under the cold water. They confiscated Lysippe's and Tanais' leggings, leaving them only the short skirts of their tunics for modesty, and they made Lysippe remove her bandage. Without it, her ankle felt weak, and she shivered with the unfamiliar feel of air on her bare legs.

Tanais put a hand on her arm and whispered, "It doesn't matter. We'll get some more clothes once we're in the Temple."

After they were all washed and dressed again, and had been marshalled into a line along the river bank, Mikkos mounted his black horse and surveyed them critically. "Mmm," he said. "Some of you might fetch a good price, after all. Now remember what I told you. Behave yourselves on the market block, and try to smile. It makes all the difference, especially for you girls. Not far now. Let's march!"

They shuffled forwards, heads lowered, casting furtive glances at one another. Lysippe made sure she limped heavily, leaning on Tanais. Hero assumed a deep sulk. The girl at the back took Timareta by the hand and whispered to her as they walked. Lysippe watched the pair, uncomfortable. After Tanais had explained her plan to the others the night before, Timareta had been gently woken and told what was going to happen. But although Timareta seemed to understand the need for secrecy, she couldn't hide her excitement as well as the older ones.

"Help us, First Mother," Lysippe whispered, feeling slightly foolish to be praying like their mother might, but beginning to understand why she did.

As they crossed the bridge over the yellow river, a breeze blew around Lysippe's bare legs and the sun sparkled on the water, making her feel dizzy again. She looked down between the cracks in the planks – and there under the bridge not an arm's length away, staring up at her, surrounded by swirling blue hair, was a face.

Definitely real. No question.

Lysippe stared. The luminous eyes stared back. Then the chain jerked, and one of the men shouted at her to get a move on. Lysippe blinked – and the face was gone.

"Did you see that?" She turned excitedly to Tanais. But her sister was frowning at Mikkos' back, obviously rehearsing in her head their plans to unhorse him. Lysippe bit the words off. They had other things to worry about.

After the bridge, they joined a well-used road that followed the contour of the mountain and opened on their right to a marshy plain. Wild flowers showed where the sun broke through the mist, bees hummed nearby, and little blue butterflies kept fluttering in front of Lysippe's nose, making her jump. They met a cart rumbling in the opposite direction, and the men herded them all to the side of the road and exchanged jokes with the driver. The carter looked down at the chained slaves as he drove past, but only as he might have looked at a flock of sheep. As the mist burnt off, a twin-peaked mountain became visible in the distance with a great white city shimmering on the plain before it. The second river Hero had mentioned wound like a bright snake ahead of them, leading towards a single hill that stood out of the plain. Nestled among the bushes on its slopes were several curious thatched huts where the bees hovered, but there was still no sign of anything that looked like a temple.

The captives were beginning to look round nervously, when a horse came trotting up the road ahead of them. Its rider wore a battered helmet over his face and sat the jolting pace with an arrogance that would have been recognizable anywhere.

Lysippe's stomach fluttered, and she felt the unease pass down the whole line. She grabbed Hero's elbow. "The Alchemist's here!" she hissed. "Where's your Temple?"

"Get back in line," Hero hissed back. "You'll give us away."

"If you're lying—"

"Get off!" Hero shoved her so hard, her ankle gave way and she nearly fell.

She recovered her balance and glared at him, but Tanais whispered, "Shh."

The Alchemist exchanged a few words with the Slavemaster and walked his horse slowly down the line, looking at the slaves as he passed. He gave Lysippe a long stare through his helmet slits, glanced down at her ankle, then leant over to ruffle Hero's hair and rode on. Hero scowled.

The captives stiffened as the Alchemist took up a position at the rear of the column. Lysippe's back prickled as the chain jerked them forwards again. They hadn't counted on him being around when they made their run for the Temple, but there was no time to change their plans now.

As they drew closer to the hill, sounds carried across

the plain – loud voices, the bellow of an ox, horses whinnying, cart wheels rumbling on stone, splashing water, laughter, flute music, and someone singing in a pure voice. Clouds of scented smoke coiled around the hill to meet them, making Lysippe dizzier than ever. But as the road rounded the hill, the smoke cleared and everyone stopped to stare.

It was like when they'd crested the pass and first seen the sea, only even more breathtaking. Out of that golden, scented haze rose a building larger than any Lysippe had ever seen. Their tribe's tents, pitched in a circle Amazon-style, would have fit inside it a hundred times over. Rows of brightly-painted columns held up a soaring, gilded roof that towered over the smaller, six-sided buildings that huddled in the courtyard around it. The Temple seemed to float on its clouds of incense above the marsh where the river met the sea. But it must have been built on land because beyond it, piercing the haze, were the masts of an anchored ship. They had come upon the Temple complex from the rear, where a low wall separated the courtyard from the river. The activity they could hear was happening out of sight around the other side of the building.

Lysippe let out her breath very slowly. Beside her, Tanais was as rigid as a foal which has just been haltered for the first time. Whispers of amazement rippled down the chain as the captives stared in awe – with the exception of Hero, who was scowling at the great Temple as if it were the ugliest building on earth.

Lysippe measured the wall with her eyes. Low enough for Northwind to jump easily. Low enough for even the younger ones to scramble over. The road they were following forded the river close by the trees, and from there it didn't look far to the gate where the crowds were gathered around the front of the Temple. She started to feel a bit better. This might be easier than they'd expected.

Another cloud of incense drifted towards them, and one or two people sneezed as it got up their noses. The singing suddenly stopped. There was a heartbeat of silence, then an animal shriek, followed by a cheer from the unseen crowd at the front of the Temple. Timareta, who had been one of the people sneezing, clutched at the legs of the girl who usually carried her and burst into tears. "I don't want to run away in there! I'm frightened!"

The slavers, who had also been looking at the Temple, turned to frown at their youngest captive. The Alchemist's blue eyes narrowed behind his helmet and he motioned to one of the men. The slaver tried to pull Timareta away from the older girl, who backed to the edge of the river, her eyes wide. She glanced over her shoulder at the Temple.

"NOW!" Tanais shouted, grabbing Lysippe's hand and dragging her towards the ford. "Run, everyone! NOW!"

They'd planned to get across the river first and wait until the road met the Sacred Way in front of the Temple, where they'd be in full view of the city when they made their break for freedom. They'd planned to take Northwind with them and snatch their weapons from his packs. None of this happened. There was a moment of stunned terror. Then people ran in all directions, trying to remember their tasks. The boy at the front of the chain grabbed Mikkos' foot and hung on, trying to pull him off the horse. The girl chained behind him got hold of its bridle as planned, but the other new girl in front of Lysippe froze in panic.

Lysippe pushed her aside and leapt clumsily on to the black horse's quarters behind Mikkos. The Slavemaster twisted round in surprise. He had drawn his sword, but was hesitating to use it on the boy clinging to his foot. Lysippe fumbled for the key around his neck, and Mikkos made a blind swipe behind him. Her weight unbalanced him, and they both fell off the horse. The Slavemaster immediately rolled to his feet, but the chain got tangled around Lysippe's leg as she tried to follow him, and her ankle – her stupid, stupid ankle – turned sideways in the mud.

Someone dragged her up and pulled her away from Mikkos. The horse galloped off, but fortunately the girl at the front had managed to unbuckle the strap that held the chain around its neck in time, and the chain clanked into the mud. The captives cheered and splashed into the river, still linked together, led by the boy at the front. The manacle about Lysippe's wrist jerked, and her ankle blazed with pain as she was dragged in after them.

Behind her, Tanais was yelling. Other people were shouting, too. Water filled Lysippe's mouth and nose. The river was deeper than she'd thought, or maybe they'd missed the ford. She struggled to keep her head above the water and shouted, "The key! Get the key!"

About half of the captives were in the water. The other half were still on the far bank. The Alchemist had hold of Timareta, who was screaming and kicking his shins, while the others at the back of the chain tried to make him let her go. Northwind and the donkey trotted loose on the bank, having been abandoned by the slavers in favour of trying to stop the rest of their merchandise from jumping into the river. Thankfully, the men's swords were still in their scabbards – either it was too much of a muddle for them to draw their weapons, or Mikkos had ordered them not to. The Slavemaster was on his feet, muddy and furious, shouting orders. His men seized the rest of the captives who had not yet managed to jump into the water. The chain tightened, and those floundering in the river were held fast, though the first boy had managed to scramble out on the far side and was clinging to a branch within touching distance of the Temple wall.

"Fight!" Tanais yelled. "Don't give up now!"

Lysippe's head swam with the first warnings of the healing-sleep. She stumbled and scraped the skin off her elbow on a submerged rock, but hardly felt the pain.

Then Tanais' arms were around her. "You can't sleep yet, Lysippe!" she shouted in her ear. "Just hold on till you get over that wall, do you hear? Then you can heal for as long as you want. I've got to go back for the others."

"No!" Lysippe tried to stop her going. But Tanais pulled herself back along the length of vacant chain between the recaptured children and the free ones and scrambled out on the far bank. She whistled, and Northwind trotted obediently across. As Tanais struggled to free the Amazon axe from his pack, Lysippe saw the Alchemist pass Timareta to one of the other men and run towards her sister, drawing his sword.

"Tanais! Look out!" Lysippe let go of the root she'd caught hold of and slid back into the water. The dizziness came in waves. She fought against it. In the water nearby, Hero was yelling a warning. She didn't know if he was shouting at her or at Tanais. Her sister got the axe free just as the Alchemist reached her and raised his sword. There was a flash of sun on metal and a sudden slackening of the chain as Tanais brought the axe down, severing the links with a single blow their mother would have been proud of. But the Alchemist's sword came down at the same time, and Tanais screamed and tumbled into the water. Blood swirled around her body.

"No-o-o!" Lysippe fought her way towards her sister. "Help her, someone!"

Hero got his arm around Tanais' neck and started to swim sideways towards the Temple bank, dragging the unconscious girl with him. Losing the support of the chain, Lysippe went under again and got a mouthful of mud and bloody water. She came up, spluttering and disorientated, to find herself face to face with the most beautiful creature she had ever seen.

Its hair floated on the water, delicate shades of mauve and pale blue that sparkled with stars. The river showed through its ghostly body, which shone so brightly that Lysippe could hardly bear to look. She had an impression of webbed fingers and toes, glittering scales, and pale arms and legs. The creature looked vaguely human, but was clothed in silver light. Its luminous eyes held Lysippe's, and she thought she saw the ghostly lips move.

"Help my sister," Lysippe whispered. "Please."

The creature glimmered and vanished. There was another glimmer near the ford, where Mikkos had sent some of his men into the water after Hero and Tanais, then a yell as the men abandoned the chase, turned and ran for the bank. Blue-silver light followed them, partly hidden by another cloud of incense. The Alchemist shouted something, and there was a green sparkle in the air on the far bank.

Lysippe squinted at it, trying to make out what was happening.

"This way, Lysippe!" Hero surfaced beside her, breathing hard. "Leave the others. We can't do anything for them now. Over the wall! Quick!"

She splashed after him in a daze. "Tanais?" she whispered. "Where's Tanais?"

"I've got her. Just a bit further, that's it."

There was a strip of grass, and then the wall. It might have looked low before, but in her weakened state it was like scaling a mountain. Someone boosted her up. She clung to the top, wriggled across, and fell on hard stone, which jolted some of the dizziness and strangeness from her.

She pushed herself to her knees. Tanais was already lying in the Temple courtyard, frighteningly still. Hero crouched over her, coughing up water. The others who had escaped stood round them in a silent circle, dripping mud on the beautiful white marble. Only half of them had made it. The boy and two girls who had been ahead of Lysippe on the chain, another boy who had managed to evade the men in the confusion when the chain had snapped, herself, Hero, Tanais. Around them, a hazy crowd was forming – people in colourful robes sewn with glittering beads, gold in their hair and grease on their fingers, who seemed exciting and alien and terrifying all at once. Some clutched pieces of meat, which they must have been eating when the refugees arrived.

"Tanais!" Lysippe pushed Hero aside and touched her sister's pale face. There was blood on her sister's tunic and in her hair.

"Tanais!" she screamed.

Hero gently pulled her back. "The Alchemist stabbed her twice. She didn't even try to defend herself. She cut the chain with the axe so we could escape. Craziest, bravest thing I ever saw."

"No... Tanais..."

Hero glanced round. "I got to go now, Lysippe. The chief priest's coming."

"No, Hero... please stay! Where's Northwind? Got to get Northwind... horse for Tanais... so we can go home..." She tried to whistle for her horse, but didn't have the breath.

Hero shook his head, then stiffened, caught on his knees, as the crowd parted. Still half in a dream, Lysippe saw long, orange and white robes swish across the marble out of the incense clouds towards them. For a moment, she thought it was another spirit like the one she'd seen in the river. But the robes were ordinary human clothes, and a large man wearing golden sandals with upturned toes and an elaborate golden headdress stopped before them. His head and face were entirely smooth of hair, and his eyes were dark almonds outlined with black paint. He wore a belt hung with heavy plates of red-gold embossed with bees which chinked as he moved.

Everyone in the courtyard fell silent. Even the slavers' shouts on the other side of the wall had stopped. The priest's gaze passed over the bedraggled refugees with the manacles still locked on their wrists, lingered on the unconscious Tanais, paused at Lysippe, and finished at Hero. For the first time, his almond eyes showed a flicker of surprise.

"Herostratus," he said in educated Greek. "I might have known if there was trouble, you wouldn't be far behind."

Hero hadn't moved, though his fingers tightened on Lysippe's shoulder. As they did so, she lost a little more of her grip on the world.

The priest turned to the refugees. "I assume you're claiming sanctuary?" he said, and a sigh rippled through the spectators.

The others nodded, casting nervous glances at the wall, beyond which Mikkos had remounted his black horse and was waiting outside with a look like thunder.

"And you?" The priest's almond-shaped eyes rested on Hero. "Do you claim sanctuary, too?"

Hero still hadn't moved. Lysippe shook off the dizziness. "Of course he does!" she said, making the priest look sharply at her. "And I claim it for my sister Tanais!" She pointed.

The priest looked at Tanais and all the blood. "You can't claim sanctuary for the dead," he said emotionlessly.

Lysippe pushed Hero away and struggled to her feet. She fixed the head priest of the Temple of Artemis with a glare. "She's – not going – to – die," she said, having to concentrate on each word.

The priest frowned and reconsidered the motionless Tanais. He looked at the Slavemaster, still waiting outside the wall, and tightened his lips. He lifted one large, beringed finger, and six white-robed priestesses appeared from between the huge columns of the Temple. They lifted Tanais on to a litter and helped the other refugees across to one of the smaller buildings in the

Temple grounds. Two of them brought a second litter across to Lysippe and tried to force her to lie down. She pushed them off and hopped after Tanais, pulling Hero with her.

"Steady!" Hero grunted. "They're only takin' her to the Blood House. Don't worry, the Megabyxos won't let Mikkos have her now."

Behind them, the large priest Hero had called the Megabyxos was telling Mikkos and his men to go on their way. The crowd lost interest and began to disperse, some returning around the front of the Temple to their interrupted ceremony, others leaving by a small gate in the courtyard wall. Lysippe stiffened, expecting Mikkos to order his men over the wall to seize the refugees as soon as the crowds had gone. But the Slavemaster wheeled his horse and splashed back across the river, where he'd left the exhausted, wet, recaptured children under the Alchemist's guard. Lysippe saw one of the men lift Timareta so they could continue their journey to the harbour, and hesitated.

"She'll be all right," Hero said, seeing her look. "No one sends a little girl like that to the mines. We did what we could. Block your ears, now—"

Lysippe still felt bad about the ones who hadn't made it. But they'd reached the door of the building Hero had called the Blood House, and Tanais was already inside. It was a lot larger than Lysippe had thought, with six mud-and-stone walls and a tiled roof. It smelled of herbs and more incense. As Lysippe and Hero stumbled through the doorway after the priestesses, a sonorous blast echoed around the mountains, making the birds fall silent and the entire plain of Ephesos vibrate. The blast was repeated seven times.

The last of Lysippe's strength left her with the final fading note. She staggered, and Hero grimaced as he caught her. "That's the Sanctuary Horn," he said. "Even I can feel the vibrations – only time I'm glad I can't hear nothin'! You'd better get used to it. They blow the thing every time someone claims sanctuary here."

Smyrna speaks...

So it is true, this incredible tale my sisters whisper throughout the land! The Amazons have indeed returned to the cities of men. But what sort of Amazons allow themselves to be captured and treated as slaves? It is a disgrace to our ancient name.

I helped them, of course. The young one with the gryphon's eyes commanded me to do so, though I doubt she realized what she was about. If she were my daughter... but no, that time is past, and I must look to the future now. I would rather work with the elder sister. She proved herself a true warrior during the struggle at the river, in spite of her diluted blood. But because of that blood she will lie long in the healing-sleep, so it is the younger one I must use for my purpose.

Little point expecting the child to understand the old ways. But she will do what I ask, once I tell her what my sisters in the ocean have seen. The young are vulnerable and easily moulded, particularly when they are alone and frightened and in a strange place.

I, Smyrna, will be her mother now. I will teach her. And before the summer ends, the gryphon will fly again.

Chapter 4

BLOOD HOUSE
Those who sleep also share in the work of the cosmos.

Someone was singing as they gently unwound the bandages from Lysippe's arm. For a moment she didn't know if she were asleep or awake. The singing stopped abruptly, and there was a catch of breath.

"Look, Melissa." A soft finger ran over Lysippe's elbow. "It's like the skin was never broken!"

"Let me see."

A shadow blocked the light, and Lysippe smelled wild flowers. She breathed in the perfume, reluctant to open her eyes. She was lying on something soft and she felt pleasantly dreamy. She couldn't remember when she'd last been this comfortable or relaxed. But she was hungry, and there was something dark lurking just beyond the dream.

"Mmm," continued the second voice. "That new batch of silphium stalks must be good. Either that or it's your singing, Annyla. Maybe we should get you to sing to all the terminal cases."

"But she's not—"

"I know. I'm just teasing. I don't think it's the silphium. There's something strange about this girl. And her sister ought to be dead twice over. In all my years at the Temple, I've never seen anything like it."

A pause. The singer's voice dropped to a whisper. "Maybe it was the Alchemist's magic. Did you see those strange lights over the river when the slaves made their escape? Everyone's talking about them."

A cool hand rested on Lysippe's forehead.

"There's no such thing as magic, you know that, Annyla," the second voice said in a reproving tone. "The goddess' incense makes people see strange things. Besides, where that boy Herostratus is involved, anything can happen! He's got some cheek, I must say, coming back here and claiming sanctuary. But I'm more worried about the time this one's been asleep. If she doesn't wake up and take something to eat soon, she'll die, healed or not. The other girl, the same."

Lysippe's pleasant dream faded. She sat up and fought the cover wrapped around her legs. "Where's Tanais? Let me see her!"

"Steady!" The older priestess, who had been examining the elbow Lysippe had scraped on the rock in the river, jumped back and transferred her attention to Lysippe's eyes. Like the head priest, she wore an ankle-length white robe with a lozenge pattern of orange and gold bees worked through the hem. In places, however, her robe was stained by old blood. Her dark hair had been braided and pinned on top of her head. The younger one – the singer, Annyla – had unruly red hair which escaped its pins in curls of fire, and she'd hitched her long skirt into her girdle so it cleared her knees. She looked about the same age as Lysippe and she, too, was staring at Lysippe's eyes.

"Melissa!" she said. "She's got—"

The older priestess put a warning hand on Annyla's shoulder. "How are you feeling?" she asked Lysippe. "Your arm's much better, and your ankle will be as good as new, given proper rest."

"There's nothing wrong with my ankle," said Lysippe, gazing round.

They were inside the Blood House. She remembered following the litter that carried Tanais, fighting off Hero and stumbling through all the white-robed priestesses to her sister's side. There had been voices, hands pulling her away, something bitter to drink, and Hero trying to explain something. She didn't remember what. She supposed they must have carried her to bed. The Blood House had a high ceiling supported by marble columns, and would have been one large room except that the individual beds were screened by curtains, blocking her view of the other patients. Low moans came from behind the curtain on the left side of her bed; silence from the other. Lysippe stared at the rich patterns in the curtain weave, afraid to look behind it.

"There isn't now," Annyla said with a shy smile. "Melissa Aspasia reset it for you. You shouldn't walk on it until—"

Lysippe got the covers off and darted through the curtain before either surprised priestess could stop her.

Tanais lay on a bed in the shadowy alcove on the other side, her chest wrapped in bandages, her dark hair brushed loose and fanned over the pillow. Her eyes were closed. She was breathing very deeply and very slowly. Lysippe sank to one knee and touched her cheek. It was warm. She let out her breath in relief. "Sleep, sister," she whispered. "Heal. I'll look after you."

When she turned, Annyla was standing with her hands over her mouth, staring at Lysippe's ankle in disbelief. The older priestess shook her head at a dark-skinned man armed with a spear, who had come running when Lysippe sprang through the curtain. "It's all right," she said. "Go back to your post. I'll handle this."

The guard nodded and returned to the door of the Blood House.

Aspasia dropped a hand on Lysippe's shoulder. "Come," she said gently. "Since you're obviously healed, there's no reason for you to stay here any longer. I want to talk to you before you see the Megabyxos."

Lysippe shook her head. "I'm not leaving Tanais."

"She's perfectly safe in here. The other Melissae will look after her. Come on, Lysippe. I know you've been through a lot lately, but no one's going to hurt you now. I expect you're hungry."

As if in answer, Lysippe's stomach rumbled. She flushed as Annyla giggled. "How do you know my name?" she demanded, getting to her feet.

"The boy you were with – Herostratus – told us."

"Where is he?" Lysippe looked round at the rich curtains, which rippled gently in the breeze that came through the door. "What happened to poor little Timareta and the others? They didn't get sold to the Alchemist, did they? We'd have been all right if he hadn't come back..."

"Not here." Melissa Aspasia's voice was firm. "The sick need their rest. We can talk outside."

Reluctantly, with many backward glances, Lysippe allowed herself to be led from Tanais' side. They passed more of the curtained alcoves, behind which unseen patients moaned in their sleep. Priestesses strode back and forth carrying amphorae of strong-smelling unguent, bowls of water and bandages. They nodded to Melissa Aspasia, who exchanged a few words with them on her way out. Annyla followed shyly, still staring at Lysippe's ankle. As if it could feel the girl's puzzlement, her foot began to ache. Lysippe fought an urge to limp.

They emerged into bright sunshine and the clamour of many voices, which made her pause in surprise. The vast Temple courtyard, which yesterday had been shrouded in incense, was filled with market stalls and thronged with people dressed in colourful robes. A fountain sparkled in the sunlight and several small, very wet children were playing a game of chase beneath it.

Beyond the fountain, the altar area where yesterday's crowds had been gathered was deserted except for a dark-haired boy sweeping out a mixture of dung, bones and ashes.

Lysippe's gaze, which had been drawn onwards to the Temple itself, swung back. "Hero!" she called in relief.

He didn't look up from his broom. At first she thought he was deliberately ignoring her. Then she remembered he couldn't hear her.

She wanted to rush across and ask him all the questions that were racing round inside her head, but Melissa Aspasia had other ideas. Firmly, she shepherded Lysippe and Annyla through the crowds and stalls to another six-sided building within the courtyard walls. This one was smaller than the Blood House and part of a group that fitted together like a honeycomb. A delicious smell came from the open door that made Lysippe's stomach rumble again. Inside, three-legged tables were laid with olives, bread, goat's cheese and some white meat wrapped in leaves. Couches were positioned near the tables, and brightly-coloured rugs decorated the floor. There was only one person in the room when they entered – a young priest with a shaven head, who got hurriedly to his feet when he saw Melissa Aspasia and snatched a handful of olives before darting out the door.

"Priests!" Aspasia said with a sigh, pushing Lysippe down on one of the couches and pouring her a cup of water. "Lazy, the lot of them. Nothing to do all day but tend the bees and count the Temple silver. Now then, Lysippe, eat! We can talk while you get your strength back." She reclined on the couch opposite, unwrapped one of the leaf parcels and smelled the meat appreciatively. "Mmm – from the River Selinus, I believe. Try some, Lysippe. It's our sacred fish. Some of them are as big as a man."

Lysippe stopped darting glances at the door and stared at the priestess. A shiver went down her spine as she remembered the creature she'd seen in the river. "You caught this in the river?" she said. "What did it look like?"

Aspasia's eyes narrowed slightly. "I'm much too busy to sit fishing on the river bank all day. But some of the priests enjoy it – gives them an excuse to be lazy without being told off by me for lounging about in here." She smiled at Lysippe. "Now, why don't you tell me where you came from and how you ended up in old Mikkos' slave chain? I'm particularly interested to know how you broke your ankle and how come you're walking around the day after I reset it, when any normal person would still be lying in their bed with their foot in the air – to say nothing of your elbow that was scraped nearly to the bone yesterday, but now looks as good as new."

Lysippe took a tentative bite, still thinking of the water-spirit. She'd never eaten fish before and was surprised how good it tasted. But it didn't make her forget Tanais' warning.

"I heal fast," she mumbled.

Melissa Aspasia shook her head. "I've worked in the Blood House since I was a little girl. Refugees from all over end up at the Temple of Artemis, fleeing one war or another. If it's not Athens and Sparta at each other's throats, or the Persians extending their empire, it's some new tyrant setting himself up as king and raiding his neighbours. I've seen every sort of wound and broken bone known to man. I've seen people recover, and I've seen them die. But never have I seen anyone who heals as fast as you! Who are you, Lysippe? Where did you come from?"

Annyla curled on another couch, sucking an olive and watching the exchange with her bright, curious eyes.

"I... we..." Lysippe glanced at the door again. It was still open. Her ankle was mended. She could run. Except Tanais still lay in the healing-sleep in the Blood House, and for all she knew Mikkos was still waiting outside the gate for his runaway slaves to emerge. She shook her head. "I don't know how I heal so fast, I just always have. We were on our way through the mountains when Mikkos captured us."

"Where were you going?"

"To Macedonia."

Melissa Aspasia's eyes narrowed again. "To the tyrant Philip? Why?"

Lysippe bit her lip. "I don't know..."

She flinched as the priestess suddenly got to her feet. "All right, Lysippe, finish your meal. I'm going to tell the other Melissae they might as well get rid of your sister's body. There's no point us keeping it here if she's not going to recover. We're not allowed to keep the dead inside the Temple grounds, and we need the bed for more deserving patients – don't we, Annyla?"

The girl stiffened on her couch. "But—"

Lysippe choked on the fish and leapt to her feet. "But she's not dying! She's only sleeping! You promised me she'd be *safe*!"

"That was when I thought you two might be special. In my experience, people with wounds like your sister's don't recover. And since you insist you don't know any reason why she should heal, I don't see why we should waste any more time on her."

"Tanais isn't going to die!" Lysippe shouted. Fists clenched, she glared at the priestess. "She's in the healing-sleep! It's natural for us..." Her voice trailed off. Melissa Aspasia was looking at her with half a smile.

"Go on."

Lysippe sat down. "We're Amazons," she said, staring at the table top.

Annyla caught her breath, but the older priestess showed little surprise. "And that's why you were going to Macedonia?" she said. "To fight for King Philip?"

"Yes."

"Just the two of you?"

Lysippe shook her head. "Mother... that's Queen Oreithyia and the others... went looking for something in Themiscyra. They left us in a cave where we'd be safe." She closed her eyes, and once again relived that stupid argument with Tanais. She squeezed the cushions until her fingers hurt.

Melissa Aspasia sighed. "Amazons!" she said, half to herself. "I didn't think there were any left in the world. This is fascinating. Do you always heal as fast as that? Do you all have the gryphon's glare? Do you eat anything special? We must talk more, Lysippe. But it might be best if this doesn't go further than this room for now. The Megabyxos gets so worked up about his Temple funds. If he thinks he's got a pair of real, live Amazons sheltering in his Temple, he'll find a way to make a profit out of it somehow."

Lysippe looked sharply at the priestess. Aspasia had tricked her, yet she seemed to be on their side. And Tanais would need all the professional care she could get. "You promise you won't throw Tanais out?" she said in a small voice.

Melissa Aspasia smiled and patted her hand. "I promise. I wouldn't really throw a patient out, don't worry, but I needed to know what you were hiding from me. I'm going to look after both of you. It's not every day we get real, live Amazons visiting us!" She brushed fish crumbs off her robe. "Annyla, you stay with Lysippe today. Show her round the Temple and where to sleep and everything, and tell her the rules. Then after she's seen the Megabyxos and been presented to the goddess, we'll speak again. Let's have another look at that ankle, Lysippe." She went down on one knee, took Lysippe's foot into her lap and unwound the bandage.

She probed with gentle fingers around the ankle bone. "Does that hurt?"

"A little," Lysippe admitted. "But it's not as bad as when I was walking on it in the slave chain."

Aspasia pulled a face. "I'm not surprised it hurt. It had set as crooked as a tyrant's smile! Those slavers need lessons in looking after their merchandise." She replaced the bandage. "No jumping or running on it until it stops aching," she warned as she left them to finish their meal. "I don't think even Amazon ankles are made to be broken more than twice in the same month."

Chapter 5

TEMPLE

If we do not expect the unexpected, we will not discover it.

The Temple of Artemis had looked impressive enough from the outside. Inside, it was a maze of shadows, drifting incense, and gilded marble that glimmered in the soft glow of thousands of lamps. Great columns rose on all sides like the trunks of a gigantic forest, the base of each sculpted with life-sized people and animals painted in bright colours. Overhead, in a haze of dusty sunbeams that shone through openings in the pediment, elegant double-spirals at the top of the columns supported the roof beams. A wooden gallery ran around an upper level, hung with musical instruments and paintings.

As Lysippe twisted her head, trying to see everything at once, Annyla tugged her down a double row of columns and through a high, narrow door into an inner sanctuary. "Artemis Ephesia!" she announced proudly, stopping at last. "Our goddess."

Lysippe caught her breath. At the far end of the chamber, shrouded in incense and illuminated by rainbows that shone through panes of coloured glass set in the roof above her head, was the statue of a winged woman flanked by two half-seen creatures. Lighted candles glimmered around the goddess' feet, and she was knee deep in offerings of fruit, amphorae, carved wooden animals, quivers of decorative arrows, loaves, honey-cakes and little ivory dolls. Her robes were of silk and embroidered with gold, and her golden arms reached out as if ready to receive those who came through the door. Without knowing she had moved, Lysippe ventured closer, staring up at the statue in amazement. Little animals seemed to be carved into the goddess' body – lions, stags, bees and stranger creatures Lysippe could put no name to. More of these creatures peered out of the goddess' hair, and the entire statue was wreathed in strings of beads made from amber and coloured glass that glowed in the rainbows and the light from the candles. Then the incense swirled to give her a proper look at the creatures that flanked Artemis, and she staggered backwards, suddenly dizzy.

The goddess' guardians were the size of horses with eagles' beaks and necks, and the bodies and claws of lions. Their eyes were pieces of amber. Wings, frozen in marble, half-lifted from their backs, and their tails curled upwards. The pose was different, but they were unmistakably the same creatures as the one on Oreithyia's tribal shield.

"Gryphons…" she whispered, and tripped over the offerings, scattering candles. As the goddess' robes flared and crackled, a strange whispering filled Lysippe's head as if all the stone creatures had started talking at once.

She closed her eyes, no longer sure where she was.

"Hey, steady!" Annyla beat out the flames, guided her safely away from the candles and lowered her to the floor. "Is it your ankle? I'm sorry, I shouldn't have made you walk so fast. Sit down a moment. Lean against the wall, that's right. Now, take deep breaths and put your head between your knees. Better? Here – have something else to eat. I'm not surprised you're feeling faint. You didn't eat at all for three days, not since you came out of the river." She selected a loaf and a handful of olives from among Artemis' offerings and dropped them in Lysippe's lap, then splashed some wine from one of the amphorae over the goddess' singed robe.

Lysippe stared warily at the gryphons. But the whispering had stopped, and Artemis kept smiling – only a statue, after all.

She relaxed slightly as the dizziness passed. So she'd been in the healing-sleep for three days? She shuddered to imagine what Mikkos and the Alchemist might have done to her and Tanais in that time, had the escape failed. She sucked an olive from its stone and considered the red-haired novice. On their way through the Temple, she'd glimpsed the white and orange robes of other priests and priestesses in the forest of columns, but they seemed to be alone in the sanctuary.

"What did you see in the river when we escaped?" she asked softly. "I heard you telling Melissa Aspasia about strange lights."

"That's what I wanted to ask you!" Annyla glanced round, too. "I was watching the sacrifice with everyone else, so I didn't see how it started. But when we got to the back court, there were these lights sparkling all around you like stars! Then some of the slavers started screaming, and the lights seemed to follow them. They ran off into the marsh. The Alchemist shouted after them, but they didn't come back. Then the Megabyxos gave you sanctuary, and the Melissae carried you into the Blood House and I had to come to help, so I couldn't go and see what was in the river. But I think it had gone by then, anyway, whatever it was." She glanced round again to check no one was at the door and whispered, "Was it your Amazon powers?"

Lysippe sighed. "I haven't got any powers. I wish I had! Then maybe Tanais wouldn't have got hurt."

"Oh, come on, Lysippe! You must have seen something – you were right in the middle of those lights! Did the Alchemist do some magic, after all?"

Lysippe bit her lip. "I think I saw a water-spirit in the river." She peered sideways at Annyla. "I know it sounds silly, but we have legends about them. Back at the cave, our mother was supposed to have summoned an oread to look after us. I never saw the oread, but a rockfall killed some of Mikkos' men and I kept seeing strange sparkles all through the mountains. Then when I was in the river,

I definitely saw something. She was all blue and silver and shining. I think she helped us escape."

Annyla's eyes sparkled. "You saw a naiad? Really?"

Lysippe looked at her in surprise, and Annyla laughed.

"You're not the only one with legends! The Greeks call them river-nymphs. There's supposed to be sea-nymphs, cave-nymphs and tree-nymphs, as well. They're mentioned in some of the scrolls we've got in the Temple library, only Melissa Aspasia thinks they're just stories. She says things like that are illusions. She says it's like when the Megabyxos does things with incense and the angle of the sun and a statue of the goddess to make it look as if Artemis herself appears on the roof of the temple during sacrifices. But that really is just a trick. I know how that's done. I'll show you, if you like."

Lysippe closed her eyes again. "Tanais thinks the spirits are just stories, too. And everything else that's in the old legends." She opened her eyes and looked at the statue of the goddess with her two guardian gryphons, shivering a little. "Annyla?"

"Mmm?" The girl was looking up at the gallery, obviously still thinking about the trick with the statue.

"Are there other scrolls in here? With other stories in them?"

"Thousands!" Annyla said with a smile. "People are always bringing them here and dedicating them to Artemis. They come from all over the world. Even an immortal goddess would never have time to read them all!"

Lysippe breathed out very slowly. "Is there anything about us? About Amazons, I mean?" She looked again at the gryphons and lowered her voice. "Do any of the scrolls mention Stones... special Stones that fell from the sky and have power?"

She was surprised again when Annyla laughed and waved a hand, scattering olives. "You don't need a musty old scroll to tell you that story!" She sobered and frowned at Lysippe. "I thought everyone knew about the Sanctuary Stone!"

"Tell me." Lysippe struggled to her feet.

The girl smiled. "It's the reason you're safe in here, and the slavers didn't come in after you. They don't dare test it out, see? Everyone believes in the Sanctuary Stone, or pretends they do, even Melissa Aspasia." She pulled a face and added, "Except I think she only says that so the Megabyxos won't give her job to someone else."

"What does it look like?"

Annyla smiled again. "No one knows. But it's supposed to have fallen from the sky long ago, before the Temple was built. People worshipped it. The story goes that if they slept near the Stone, they would be safe from all harm. It was even supposed to bring the dead back to life – only if it was used to do that, it lost its power. That's why we're not allowed to keep dead bodies inside the Temple grounds. When the Temple was built, the Stone was hidden inside so anyone seeking sanctuary here would be safe."

Lysippe's heart beat faster.

"Where's it hidden?" She stepped cautiously towards the statue and looked more closely at the beads. Some were the size of her fist, others tiny and delicate as the glow-flies that lit the marshes at night. One piece of amber had a bee trapped inside it. Tentatively, she stood on tip-toe and reached up to touch it.

Annyla came to join her and nibbled one of the goddess' honey-cakes. "No one knows, exactly, which is probably just as well... What are you doing?"

The bead was cold. Nothing happened when she touched it. Lysippe withdrew her hand, slightly relieved. She frowned at Annyla. "You don't believe in the Stone, do you?"

"Well..." Annyla avoided her gaze. "Sometimes it doesn't work. I've seen refugees dragged out of the Temple, and nothing happened to stop them being taken. Maybe it was used to bring too many people back from the dead, and its power is all gone."

Lysippe touched another bead, a glass one with green swirls. "Hero said not even the Emperor of all Persia would dare come in here uninvited."

Annyla snorted. "Huh! You don't want to believe a word that boy says! The slavers didn't come in after you, that's the main thing."

"But hasn't anyone ever tried to look for it?" she asked.

Annyla sighed. "Not as far as I know – oh!" She giggled as Lysippe ran her fingers across a large red bead. "I know what you're thinking! Some of the priests think it's hidden among her jewellery too. But that's silly. If the stories are true, the Sanctuary Stone's much too dangerous to leave lying around. It's supposed to be so powerful, it turns those who touch it into ash. Imagine, if every time they had to dress the goddess, the poor priestesses chosen to serve her disintegrated!" She giggled again. "Come on, let me show you the Amazon statues on the pediment. They'll make you laugh. Back when the Temple was built, they had a sculpture competition to see who could do the best Amazon, but the sculptors were quite wrong about you – they only gave you one breast. Come and see!" She took hold of Lysippe's hand.

Lysippe pulled back. "I'd rather see what the scrolls say about us."

"But the statues are far more interesting. You can look at the scrolls any time – it'll give you something to do while you're waiting for me to finish my duties."

"I can't read," Lysippe admitted.

The girl paused. "I'm sorry, I didn't think... oh, all right, we'll go to the library first. But I'm not reading to you if there's a lot of nosy priests up there."

They worked their way around the great columns to a staircase that spiralled up to the gallery. The stairs were of old cedar and creaked. As they climbed, Lysippe caught glimpses of more white and orange robes and hoped none of the priests and priestesses had overheard their conversation. On the way up, Annyla chattered about the goddess, the Megabyxos, her work in the

Blood House, and the strange things she'd seen in and around the Temple. Lysippe only half listened.

The Sanctuary Stone had to be one of the Amazon Gryphon Stones. If she found it, their mother would be pleased and maybe she could use it to help Tanais. But what if the things Annyla had said were true? *Turns people to ash.*

They had reached the gallery under the roof, where it was lighter and airier than below and they had a better view of the sunlit windows in the pediment. Annyla explained that the goddess made her appearance in the centre one. "You interrupted the trick, you know," she said. "The Megabyxos had a white stag on the altar, and the goddess was supposed to appear to bless its transformation from life to death. But just as he got to the bit about the stag's death giving us life, you lot came over the wall. You should have seen his face! It was quite funny, really."

"Not for us," Lysippe said.

"No." Annyla touched her arm. "I'm sorry, it must have been awful for you. I don't know what I'd do if anyone ever tried to make me into a slave. I'd rather be dead."

"No, you wouldn't. I thought so too, at first. But Tanais said we had to stay strong so that when the time came we could escape..." She broke off, eyes pricking.

"And now your sister's hurt." Annyla sighed. "Don't worry, Lysippe, Melissa Aspasia's the best healer in Anatolia. She'll make her better, if anyone can."

They had reached a dusty room at the side of the gallery, where scrolls were stacked to the eaves. The sunbeams picked out a pile that had been carelessly scattered across the floor. They heard a soft curse from inside.

Annyla dragged Lysippe down and cautiously raised her head to peer through the lattice-work. She stiffened. "It's one of the merchants! How did he get in here? How dare he mess with Artemis' library?"

She started to get to her feet.

"I wouldn't let him see you, if I were you," a boy's voice said behind them.

Annyla whirled with a little scream that was cut off short as the owner of the voice clamped a hand over her mouth. Lysippe whirled as well, even as she recognized the cheeky tones that had accompanied them through the mountains. "Hero! What are you doing up here?"

"Shh!" he mouthed, releasing Annyla and signalling they should follow him.

He led them round the gallery to a triangular alcove in the pediment, where the roof sloped down to meet the eaves. Because of the brightness shining through the windows, the alcove was invisible until they were on top of it. There was just room to squeeze in and sit, though Lysippe had to pull her knees to her chest and bend her head.

"I used to fit in here better when I was younger," Hero said with a grin. "Good place to watch all the goings on." He waved a hand at the nearest window, which gave a bird's eye view of the courtyard, the altar, and the deep blue of the bay beyond.

Annyla glared at the boy. "You're not supposed to be in here, Herostratus! What are you doing, creeping around the roof giving people frights like that?"

"I thought you weren't staying?" Lysippe added, with a rush of confused emotions.

Hero scowled. "Mikkos' ship is still in harbour, ain't it? I'm not goin' nowhere till it sets sail." He caught Lysippe's arm. "But listen, I been looking all over for you! I saw the Alchemist at the gate earlier, talking to that man you saw nosin' around the scrolls. Some gold changed hands. Look out for the Alchemist, Lysippe. I think he means you and your sister some harm."

A chill went down Lysippe's back. She glanced at Annyla. "If he ever lays a hand on Tanais again, I'll kill him," she said.

The other two went quiet. "Don't worry, he can't touch you in here," Annyla said. "Once the Sanctuary Horn has been blown for you, you can stay as long as you like. What was the Alchemist doing in the courtyard, anyway? I thought he wasn't allowed in the Temple any more?"

"He disguised himself as a beggar," Hero said. "But the guards soon kicked him out again."

"See?" Annyla said. "We'll look after you, Lysippe, don't worry."

Lysippe glanced back at the library, where the flicker of the merchant's lamp could still be seen. "What's he looking for?"

Hero shrugged. "Only the goddess knows. He's been in there ages."

"Then we must tell the Megabyxos!" Annyla scrambled out of the alcove. "The public aren't allowed up here!"

Hero grabbed her wrist. "The Megabyxos knows."

"What do you mean, he knows?" Annyla frowned at the boy. "How do you know?"

"I read lips, remember? I don't need to be close enough to hear a conversation. I saw them talking earlier, when I was sweepin' out the altar. The merchant's from Macedonia, which means he's probably a spy. Everyone knows King Philip ain't friendly with Athens or Persia. I reckon something political's going on, and the Alchemist is up to his neck in it. If I were you, I'd be very careful what you say to the Megabyxos."

Lysippe hugged her knees and stared out of the window as a new chill went through her. Macedonia, where they'd been going when their mother disappeared and the slavers captured them. The brightly-dressed crowds outside suddenly seemed threatening. Beyond the altar court and the Temple gate, the city was caught between the mountains and the sea. This place was starting to feel like a trap. She longed to be back on the steppe with only the wind to fence her in.

"When will Mikkos sail?" she asked.

Hero shrugged again. "Soon, I expect. He won't wait much longer, or he'll miss the big slave market in Athens."

Lysippe didn't want to be reminded of what was going to happen to the other captives. She chewed her lip. "I've got to find my horse," she said.

The other two exchanged a glance. Annyla shook her head. "Lysippe, I know you must miss your horse, but be sensible."

"Someone's probably caught it and sold it by now," Hero said more forcefully. "You've been in the Blood House three days, you know! And you can't leave the Temple grounds. Once you're on the other side of that wall, you're no longer protected."

Lysippe set her jaw. "Northwind will come to me. I have to get Tanais out of here. If the Alchemist can get in, she's not safe."

"She certainly won't be safe outside!" Annyla said. "She's very sick. The Melissae can't take care of her if you leave. Even if Mikkos sails, there are plenty more like him out there in the mountains. Are you going to fight your way back home with an unconscious patient single-handedly? I know you're an Amazon, but—"

"You're a *what*?" Hero's black eyes were suddenly fierce.

Annyla flushed, her hands to her mouth. "I'm sorry, Lysippe, I didn't think."

But Hero bared his broken teeth. "That explains it! Normal girls don't do the sorts of things you did when we were in the slave chain, and I knew you weren't Spartans or Thracians. So *that's* why the Alchemist is so interested in you!" He whistled. "Amazons, wow!"

"Herostratus, if you dare tell anyone..."

He grinned at Annyla. "Think I'm completely stupid?"

"Yes, I do!" The young priestess glared at him again. "You're sneaky, and you're always around when there's trouble. Look what happened last time you were here!"

Hero's grin vanished. "Didn't have no choice, did I?"

"Ha!"

Lysippe was still trying to work out how she was going to get Tanais out of the Temple before it was too late. But Hero's defensive tone distracted her. "What happened last time you were here, Hero?" she asked.

The boy scrambled out of the alcove and glowered at Annyla. "You wouldn't understand. I got to go back and finish muckin' out the altar before the Megabyxos comes to check on me. Don't say I didn't warn you, Amazon-girl! If you go outside with the Alchemist still snoopin' around out there, you deserve all you get."

Chapter 6

SMYRNA

We have as one in us that which is living and dead.

Lysippe lay awake in the Novices' Sleeping House, staring at the stars through the small window-hole above her bed and trying to summon the courage to move. Annyla's shadowy form breathed deeply on the pallet beside her, and forty-three other girls, including those who had escaped the slave chain, slept in rows on either side. Unlike the Blood Room, there were no privacy curtains – just the bare walls and a low table in the centre with a hydria of water and some plain cups in case anyone got thirsty in the night. The door was closed and guarded by a man with a spear, whose job was to protect the innocence of Artemis' young priestesses and refugees. She hadn't counted on the guard, but she dared not wait much longer.

At sunset, she and the other refugees had been interviewed by the Megabyxos and officially presented to Artemis. The head priest had seemed distracted, and had appeared happy enough with Lysippe's tale that she and Tanais were Phrygians like the others. But he'd frowned at her eyes. It was only a matter of time before he suspected what Melissa Aspasia already knew.

She rolled off her pallet and got silently to her feet. Her tunic and underclothes were folded at the foot of her bed, together with a cloak Annyla had found for her. It was too short, but Lysippe pulled it on. She picked up the sandals Annyla had given her to replace her ruined boots, hid them under the cloak, and tiptoed to the door. One of the girls from the slave chain moaned in her dreams and opened a sleepy eye. Lysippe crossed her legs and pulled a face. The girl grimaced and rolled over, tucking her head under her blanket.

Lysippe rapped softly on the door. The guard opened it a crack.

"I need to go," Lysippe whispered, crossing her legs again for effect.

"How many times have I told you girls to make sure you do what you need to before the door's shut for the night?" the guard muttered. He peered closer at Lysippe, and his tone turned more sympathetic. "Oh, you're the one who's been in the Blood House, aren't you? All right, I suppose you weren't to know. But be quick."

Lysippe flashed him a grateful smile and hurried along the side of the building into the shadows, where she'd seen the other girls go. The guard watched her. As soon as she was out of sight, she paused to put on her sandals and ducked around the back. The guard was still waiting for her to emerge from the other side. She raced across the empty courtyard into the shadow of the great Temple. Heart thudding, she crouched by the steps and checked again. A pair of guards patrolled the courtyard, their spears glinting in the moonlight. A priest was coming out of the Temple, some scrolls under his arm, muttering to himself. Lysippe froze, and he disappeared into the priests' complex without seeing her. She tensed, ready to run as soon as the guards passed out of sight. The moon bathed the white marble between her and the wall, but once she reached the river bank, she'd have plenty of places to hide.

She glanced back at the Sleeping House, where the guard was still peering into the shadows after her. Taking a deep breath, she pulled the cloak over her head, ran for the wall and quickly scrambled over.

Her ankle jarred as she landed, but it held. Bent double, she ran alongside the wall until she reached the ford. As she splashed into the water, she risked a low whistle for Northwind, and a shadow moved on the bank under the olive trees. She stared at the spot, her heart lifting. "Northwind?" she whispered. "Come on, boy!" But the shadow was too small for a horse and disappeared with a rustle.

Shivering a little, Lysippe moved faster. Even at the ford, the water was deep and running fast. As she fought to keep her balance, there was a glimmer at the corner of her eye. Her head spun, and she missed her footing and sprawled full-length in the river. By the time she regained her feet, she'd been carried downstream of the Temple – and seated on a rock in the shallows, with her silver-blue hair swirling around her, was the naiad she'd seen before.

"*Took your time, didn't you?*" The words formed inside Lysippe's head. "*I've been waiting for you.*"

Lysippe stared at the creature in disbelief. Had a spirit really spoken to her? "Wh— what?" she stammered.

"*You're the last Amazon. It's up to you now.*"

"What... what do you mean?"

The naiad swirled her hair. "*I do hope you're not going to turn out to be stupid. I helped you get into the Temple, remember?*"

"Yes, but spirits don't speak to the living." Lysippe closed her eyes and took three slow breaths. I'm dreaming, she thought. I only imagined I got out of bed and sneaked out of the Sleeping House. This is a dream.

"*You're thinking I'm a dream, aren't you?*" said the naiad, making her start. "*Yet you know I'm not. You saw me before, and you saw my sisters in the mountains and in the yellow river. The oread back at Themiscyra told us about you. She can't leave the cave where her blood was spilled, but she warned us you were coming, and so we watched out for you.*"

Lysippe's heart leapt. "Then Mother was telling the truth about the oread! Are the Gryphon Stones real as well? Did she find one?"

There was a pause while the naiad sparkled a little.

Then she said, *"Of course they're real! What sort of upbringing have you had?"*

"Wait!" Lysippe said, struggling through the water towards the shining silver being. "Why do you call me the last Amazon? I'm not the last. There's Mother and the others, and Tanais—" A chill went through her. She stared back at the Temple, silent and ghostly in the moonlight.

The naiad swirled her hair out of Lysippe's reach. *"Careful. You can't touch me while you're still in that form."*

Lysippe hesitated. "What do you mean, in this form?"

"Your lessons have been seriously lacking, it seems. Didn't your mother tell you the legend of how our race began? How the First Mother Harmonia slept with the war-god and gave birth to the first Amazon?"

Lysippe's breath caught. "It's true, then? I always said it was! Only Tanais—"

"And how the gryphons are our blessing and our curse?"

Lysippe frowned. "Curse?" she whispered.

The naiad sighed. *"She didn't tell you the whole story, did she? It doesn't surprise me. These days, it seems Amazons prefer to mix their blood with mortals than accept their destiny."*

Another shiver went through Lysippe. "What destiny?" She clenched her fists. "If you're trying to scare me, it won't work. I'm going to pinch myself now, and when I wake up you'll be gone, and I'll be back in the Sleeping House."

She pinched herself hard on the arm.

When she opened her eyes, she was still standing thigh-deep in the river with the moon shining silver over the water and a spirit frowning at her.

The naiad brightened and rose from her rock. Standing, she was very tall and terrible. Her hair swirled against the stars.

"*Listen and learn, young Amazon! I am Smyrna, Queen of my tribe. They named a district of Ephesos after me – it's right over there, between the hills.*" She pointed. "*My tribe built the first Temple to the Mother here, long before men raised that marble monstrosity to house the goddess they call Artemis. And for our efforts, the men of this land betrayed us. We fought them here, on the shores of the Selinus. It was a bloody battle, but we were outnumbered. My blood ran into the river. As a pure-bred Amazon, I transformed. But they took my daughter, who should have assumed the leadership after me, into the hills where I could not help her, and they took our... Stone into their Temple where I could not reach it. It still has power. You can see and hear me because you have been close to it. But without it, I cannot leave the waters of this river. I can go no further than where the fresh water mingles with the sea, and I can travel upstream only as far as the Selinus Spring in the mountains. Such a small river they bound me to, and so cruel a prison! I've watched men fight for my city and die, and other men come from the east and fight, and die and again come. I've watched them destroy and rebuild the Temple seven times, but always the Stone remains out of reach. For hundreds of years, I've been waiting for a pure-bred Amazon to free me and my tribe. And now you're here, you turn out to be little more than a child who doesn't know the old stories and who let herself be taken as a slave! You have much to learn.*"

Lysippe had been listening with a mixture of excitement and disbelief. But when Smyrna called her a child, the old rage rose.

"It wasn't my fault!" she said. "The slavers jumped me, and the Alchemist did some magic."

"*The oread told us you rode off alone and your sister had to leave the cave to try to rescue you. Is this true?*"

Lysippe hung her head.

Smyrna sighed. "*I see that it is. And, of course, you and your sister were taken, and your sister was almost killed in my river. Find my Stone, young Amazon! Find it and bring it here, and I'll heal her for you. It's the only thing that can help her now.*" She swirled faster, her hair sparkling in excitement. "*Bring it soon! Otherwise your sister will die.*"

Lysippe stared at the naiad until her eyes hurt, trying to see the expression on her face. It was impossible. Smyrna was so bright, it was like trying to look straight at the sun.

"Will it bring you back from the dead?" she asked, starting to suspect what the naiad wanted.

Smyrna stopped swirling. "*Where did you hear that?*"

"Annyla said the Sanctuary Stone, which must be the

one you lost, could bring people back from the dead. And she said if it was used to do so, it lost its powers. You're a dead Amazon, aren't you? You're a kind of ghost. So if you want to be free of your river, then that means the Stone must have the power to transform you back to life. And if it's used to do that, then it won't work on Tanais, will it?"

The naiad sparkled towards her. Her luminous eyes stared straight at Lysippe, turning her cold. "*It's my Stone,*" came the whispered words in her head. "*I should know what it's capable of.*"

"But Annyla said—"

"*The girl's not even a Melissa yet, and you'd take her word over mine? I, who have been on this earth for hundreds of years!*"

"It doesn't matter, anyway," Lysippe said, trying to sound as if she didn't care, though her thoughts were churning madly. "Because no one knows where the Sanctuary Stone is. Annyla thinks it's probably buried in the foundations, and I can hardly dig up the whole Temple! Or do you know where it's hidden?" She held her breath.

Smyrna backed off and considered her, swirling gently again. "*Unfortunately, I don't. But men have tried to find it over the years. Some of them left their secret writings in the Temple so others of their kind could continue the quest. It's known to them as the Philosopher's Stone. They think it bestows the gift of immortality, and the alchemists among them believe it*

87

can transform worthless metal into gold. That's nonsense, of course. The power of the gryphon transforms, but not in the small way their minds think. Their scrolls might help you, though."

Lysippe thought of the Alchemist, and how he had not seemed surprised when he'd captured her and Tanais at Themiscyra. A chill rippled through her. He must have overheard their mother and the others discussing the Gryphon Stone while they were down in the city. That was why he'd guided Mikkos up the trail to the cave. He had been in search of hostages, not slaves.

"Is it true you can talk to other Amazon spirits, all over the world?" she asked.

"*Yes.*" Smyrna swirled a bit faster.

"If I agree to find your Gryphon Stone for you, you have to find out something for me."

"*What?*"

Lysippe drew a deep breath. "I want to know what happened to Queen Oreithyia and the others. Why didn't they rescue us after we were taken by the slavers?"

Smyrna smiled. "*Easy. They couldn't.*"

Lysippe's stomach churned. "Couldn't? Why not?"

"*Men were waiting for them in Themiscyra. They were tricked on board a Macedonian ship, which set sail before they realized what was happening. The oceanids' songs were full of it for a while. How your mother and her little tribe fought to make the ship turn back, but were overpowered and taken to an island, where they were imprisoned while the Macedonian Queen sailed from Pella to speak to them."*

Lysippe's knees turned weak. She clung to a submerged rock, the water tugging at her cloak.

"Imprisoned?" she whispered. "Are you sure?"

"Oceanids see a lot. The sea is large and touches many lands."

"But how do you know they didn't go willingly? We were on our way to Pella to fight for King Philip! Why would he imprison his own allies?" But she supposed it would explain why their mother hadn't tried to rescue them from the slave chain.

"The oceanids say your mother and her tribe have yet to leave the island," Smyrna said. *"My guess is that the Macedonian Queen has her own agenda, and for some reason she's interested in you. Probably trying to work out the secret of Amazon healing... more fool her."*

"No..." Lysippe splashed out of the river, away from the naiad. She slipped to her knees in the mud and scrambled on all fours up the bank, tears blinding her. "I don't believe you! We were on our way to join the Macedonian army! Why would they hurt us? You're lying so I'll do what you want!"

Smyrna came after her, a lightning streak of silver and blue.

"Quiet, foolish young Amazon! Someone will hear you. When you find the... Stone, don't let it get hot. This is important, do you hear? Keep it cool and bring it to me. Then I'll be able to help you and your sister. Now ride!

Your horse is here, but so is the Alchemist. I cannot protect you once you're out of the river."

Lysippe looked round in alarm. Her heart leapt as she saw Northwind trotting up the bank from the Temple harbour, a frayed rope dangling from his halter. But the Alchemist was running towards her from the opposite direction, squinting at the water where the naiad sparkled. He was not wearing his helmet, and his silver hair and strange, lashless eyes reflected the blue light. He didn't seem able to see Smyrna, but he had seen Lysippe.

His lips twisted into a thin smile and he drew his sword from under his cloak. "So, you followed your boyfriend, did you?" he said, advancing on her slowly. "That was a mistake, slave."

Lysippe backed away from him. Boyfriend? What was he talking about? She whistled, and heard Northwind break into a canter behind her. She listened to his approaching hoof beats... one-two-three, one-two-three... she spun on her heel and vaulted blind. Her injured ankle sent a spear of pain up her leg, but she'd timed it perfectly and landed on the little horse's back as he cantered past. She rode straight at the surprised Alchemist, hoping he didn't have any of his green powder ready. The Alchemist's eyes widened. He fumbled at his belt. But before he could get the pouch untied, a familiar, curly-haired figure darted out of the trees and barrelled into him. Lysippe had a glimpse of Hero's black eyes and the Alchemist's furious expression as he flung the boy aside. Then Northwind was clearing the wall in one bound. Only when his hooves clattered safely in the Temple courtyard did she risk a look back.

"You can't hide in there for ever!" the Alchemist shouted after her. "Mikkos might have given up on you, but I'll have you in the end. Both of you."

Lysippe's heart pounded. But Hero had made it over the wall too. She slipped off Northwind and staggered. The Alchemist looked crazy enough to come in after them, but the guards had heard the commotion and came running. The Sanctuary Horn sounded in the night, and the doors of the Sleeping Houses burst open. Before she knew what was happening, she and Hero were surrounded by anxious priestesses and priests, barefoot and in their night clothes, all asking questions at once. Annyla came out with the other novices, confusion in her eyes. As soon as she saw Lysippe, she rushed across and put her arms around her.

"You're soaking wet!" she exclaimed. "What on earth happened?"

"I found my horse," Lysippe said, her teeth chattering with reaction.

Annyla looked at Northwind, unimpressed. Then she saw the muddy boy standing behind the horse.

"Herostratus!" she said. "I might have known this was your idea. All that for a stupid horse – you're crazy, Lysippe! Anything might have happened to you out there."

Lysippe blinked at Hero, who stared back with his black eyes. There was something unreadable in them, and she wondered exactly what he'd been doing outside the Temple. Had he seen the naiad? And what was the Alchemist up to, out on the river bank at night?

She plucked at a guard's sleeve to warn him. But when she pointed to the wall, the Alchemist had gone.

Chapter 7

TROUBLE
Dogs bark at strangers.

There was trouble, of course. But it was Hero, not Lysippe, who got punished for waking everyone in the middle of the night with the blowing of the Sanctuary Horn. Although Lysippe protested, everyone seemed to assume the same as Annyla – that the boy had somehow persuaded Lysippe to sneak out of the Temple to look for her horse, then irresponsibly left her behind when she fell in the river. Nothing would change their minds, despite denials on Lysippe's part that she wouldn't be so stupid. Besides, what could she tell them? The truth was crazier than the story they'd invented.

She couldn't make up her own mind about what had happened. Believing the old legends around the camp fire back on the steppe was one thing; actually speaking to a naiad in a starlit river on the other side of the world, quite another. And all those things Smyrna had told her...

they couldn't be true, could they? She didn't want them to be true.

Everything was still churning around her head the next morning, when Melissa Aspasia called her over to the Blood House for a check-up on her ankle. She bore the priestess's probing fingers and stern words in silence.

"If you want to be walking on this when you're a woman, you're going to have to start looking after yourself," Aspasia said, applying a tight bandage that matched the tightness of her lips. "And don't give me any nonsense about Amazons not getting crippled! Healing fast is one thing, but there comes a point beyond which a body cannot heal itself. Amazons die same as anyone else, if they're injured badly enough."

Her words brought back what the naiad had said about Tanais. As soon as the priestess released her ankle, Lysippe rushed through the curtain to check on her sister.

"Don't worry, your sister's not dead yet," Melissa Aspasia followed, her tone softening slightly. "At least she can't run around, undoing all my work. Now, get out of here – it's time for me to change her dressing, and I don't want you breathing down my neck and getting dirt into the wounds."

The Megabyxos had stern words for Lysippe too. "Those who seek sanctuary in the Temple of Artemis Ephesia are expected to observe our rules," he said. His robes, stiff with gold embroidery, glittered in the shadows of his private room as he folded his arms and considered Lysippe. "One of those rules is that no one should wander about the Temple grounds at night without my express permission. The sacred law of sanctuary forbids me to throw a refugee out if they disobey, but things can be made uncomfortable for you in here. On the other hand, if you don't like the rules, no one will stop you leaving. Just ask your friend Herostratus."

Lysippe had been standing quietly with her eyes downcast, as Annyla had advised. But at the mention of Hero, she raised her gaze. "What did you do to him?" Last night, all she remembered was the Temple guards escorting Hero one way, while she was hustled back to the Sleeping House by the priestesses. "Where did you put my horse?"

"The horse has been stabled in the altar stalls for now. It'll have to be moved before Artemis' Birthday celebrations, but for the time being it gives the boy something to do to keep him out of trouble." The Megabyxos' almond eyes were almost amused. "He has expressed a wish to stay with us, even though your slavers have sailed for Athens."

"They've gone?" Lysippe's heart lifted, then fell again. "When?"

"Yesterday, on the evening wind. So you see, you and your sister can leave us without fear and go back to wherever you came from."

Lysippe considered the priest. How much did he

know? Annyla, who was waiting near one of the carved column bases, flashed her a warning glance.

"We can't leave yet. My sister's still too sick to travel," she said carefully, thinking of Northwind in the altar stalls. All she had to do was get Tanais out of the Blood House and lift her on to the horse. But they still had to get past the Alchemist. And how would Tanais survive, if Smyrna was telling the truth about the Stone being her only hope?

"So Melissa Aspasia tells me." Again, the Megabyxos smiled in his stiff manner. "But if you're staying, you'll have to work. We can always do with extra hands during the big festivals. You can help Novice Annyla and the other girls with the decorating. Artemis' Birthday is quite an occasion. You should enjoy it. All right, you can go."

"Phew!" Annyla said, once they were out of earshot. "You got off lightly, I think. And isn't it good the slavers have gone? You're free now! They won't come back this way until next spring."

Lysippe shook her head. "They haven't all gone."

"What do you mean?"

"The Alchemist. He was out there last night, by the river. He tried to grab me – would have, too, if Hero hadn't stopped him getting his magic powder out." She shuddered in memory.

Annyla clutched her hand. "You're cold!" she said. "The Alchemist has a laboratory somewhere near here, so I expect that's why he hasn't gone to Athens with the others. Forget him, Lysippe. He didn't catch you, that's the main thing."

"But he must have been waiting for me out there."

"So? He'll give up eventually, don't worry. And he's not allowed in the Temple grounds any more, not after what happened last time."

"What did happen?" Lysippe asked.

"Oh, he and the Megabyxos fell out. The Alchemist used to come here a lot to use the library, but then there was some trouble over one of the goddess' necklaces. Hero was mixed up in it too. That's when he ran off – and now he's back. Can't get rid of a bad coin, Melissa Aspasia says."

Annyla was already pulling her across the courtyard, where the merchants were beginning to set up their stalls. Some of the younger Melissae had spread a cloth on the ground and were laying out tiny silver statues that glittered in the sunlight. Annyla laughed and snatched one up. "Look, Lysippe! It's the goddess! People come from all over the world to buy them. They think if they take one home, Artemis will protect their families the same way the Sanctuary Stone protects us. We don't tell them any different – the goddess' statues fetch a lot of funds into the Megabyxos' bank."

Lysippe wasn't listening. She pulled Annyla away from the other girls, who wanted to know what the Megabyxos had said to Lysippe, and how she'd managed to fall in the river last night. Annyla only just managed to put the statue back in time. "Where are you going?"

"To see my horse." Lysippe didn't say any more until they were safely in the altar court at the front of the Temple. As she'd hoped, it was quiet inside the enclosure. Northwind had been tethered in one of the stalls meant for the animals brought to the Temple for sacrifice. He was happily munching his way through a pile of cut grass, his snorts muffled by the wooden stall and the earth underfoot. A stone ramp opposite the stalls led up to the altar itself, which had been scrubbed clean but still bore the dark stains of old blood.

Turning her gaze from the bloodstains, Lysippe slipped into the stall with Northwind. As she ran her hands down his legs, he whinnied and rubbed his head against her arm. Satisfied at last that he was all right, she put her arms around his neck and buried her face in his familiar horse-smell. His stiff mane scratched her cheek, transporting her back to the last time she'd turned to him for comfort, in the cave above Themiscyra on the other side of the mountains and the coast of a different sea. As she hugged her horse, the strain of the month-long march in the slave chain and everything that had happened since emerged as a huge sob. She struggled to hold the tears back.

"Oh, Northwind!" she sniffed into his mane. "Mother's been captured, and I think Tanais is dying! I don't know what to do!"

Annyla's gentle hand touched her shoulder. The girl began to sing softly, even as she'd sung to her in the healing-sleep. Lysippe squeezed her eyes shut, then opened them and took a deep breath. "I'm sorry, it's just..."

"It's all right," Annyla said. "Take your time."

Lysippe wiped her face on the sleeve of her tunic. "I'm so scared, Annyla! I've never been alone like this before."

"You're not alone, silly. I'm here." Annyla's arms slid around her and held her silently. Out in the main courtyard, there were shouts and the sound of running feet. Annyla looked up with a frown, but the excitement passed the altar court without anyone coming inside. As the shouts faded, she asked, "What really happened last night?"

Lysippe sighed. "I spoke to the naiad. She's called Smyrna, and she said..." Suddenly, without meaning to, she was telling Annyla everything. All about the march through the mountains, and how Tanais had looked after her, and what Smyrna had said about the Gryphon Stones and the Macedonians betraying Queen Oreithyia and the others, and her own suspicions about the Alchemist being a part of it.

When she'd finished, Annyla was silent. They were sitting between Northwind's feet. The little horse dropped his head to nuzzle Lysippe's hair, but he wouldn't step on them. No Amazon horse ever would.

"And do you believe this naiad?" Annyla said seriously, as if it had been a living person Lysippe had spoken to last night.

"Yes," Lysippe whispered. "I think I do."

"But Tanais is still alive. So you're not the last Amazon."

"I lied to you," Lysippe sniffed. "Tanais is only my half-sister. Her father was a Scythian, which means she's only half Amazon. She's never been hurt this bad before. I don't know if the healing-sleep will work for her."

Annyla's hand squeezed hers. "Melissa Aspasia says she's got a strong heart. She won't die while the Melissae are looking after her."

Lysippe took a deep breath. "I have to find Smyrna's Stone. It's the only way to help Tanais."

"What about Smyrna?"

Lysippe sighed again. "I don't know. She went all secretive when I asked if it would bring her back from the dead and lose its powers. But I don't know how to use the Stone myself, so I'll have to give it to her... unless the scrolls she mentioned contain instructions. Do you think they do?"

Annyla shook her head. "Even supposing you find the Stone, it might not work. It's very old, remember. I expect that's why our sanctuary fails sometimes."

Lysippe scrambled up, eager to make a start. "I have to try! Will you help me? Do you know the scrolls Smyrna means?"

Annyla hesitated before she mumbled, "There are all sorts of obscure texts buried in the library. But we're supposed to be preparing for the goddess' Birthday. We're going to be very busy."

"Please, Annyla. Help me. I need you to read the

scrolls for me, remember?"

The girl bit her lip and looked up at the Temple roof, which was visible above the altar wall. "I'm not sure about this," she admitted at last. "If the Stone really does have power, and you take it out of the Temple, then no refugee will ever be safe in here again. It's like... a betrayal, somehow. Artemis will be angry."

Lysippe experienced a flash of guilt. She hadn't really thought about the Temple and its law of sanctuary. But if the Stone had power and she took it away, people like the Alchemist would be able to rush in and drag out anyone they wished. "It's all right," she said quickly. "You don't have to help if you don't want to. I'll find someone else to read the scrolls." Except she didn't know who. Maybe Hero? Could he be trusted? Could he even read?

Annyla gazed up at the Amazon statues on the pediment of the Temple and bit her lip again. "You'd have to promise to give it back afterwards."

"I promise! It wouldn't really be mine, anyway. It's Smyrna's."

"And promise not to tell anyone where it came from. Otherwise people will stop believing."

"I promise."

"Not that it's likely to still be here, anyway," Annyla said, looking more cheerful again. "Someone probably found it ages ago, if they were really looking for it like your naiad said."

"Let's go and look at the scrolls now!" Lysippe said, not

KATHERINE ROBERTS

wanting to consider the very real possibility that the Stone might have already been found and removed without Smyrna's knowledge. She couldn't stop thinking about the Macedonian spy they'd seen in the library yesterday, the one Hero said had been talking to the Alchemist.

They left Northwind munching happily on his grass. But they never got as far as the library. As they emerged from the altar court into the main courtyard, they saw an excited crowd gathered around the Temple gates. Some people had climbed on the wall to see better, and on the Temple steps behind them, young priests and Melissae in their honey and white robes were standing on tip-toe trying to see what was going on. Lysippe didn't have to. She could see over most people's heads.

A great ship had entered the narrow inlet that led to the Temple harbour. The ship was too large to negotiate the shallows, and the sailors were struggling to bring down the crimson sails and throw out the anchor stones before it ran aground on the harbour steps. They were hampered by a phalanx of soldiers on deck, who wore full-face, crested helmets as if for battle and crimson cloaks with the same design as the sails – a gold star with sixteen slender points. Each soldier carried a long pike twice his height with red ribbons tied beneath a functional-looking spike. In front of the phalanx, standing at the bow-rail, was a tall young woman with an ocean of golden hair twisted into a ruby tiara. She was wearing a crimson himation worked with golden thread over her dress, which billowed about her in the breeze like the wings of an exotic butterfly but could not disguise the fact she was heavily pregnant.

"That's the Royal Star of Macedon!" Annyla breathed, scrambling up on the wall to see better. "That woman must be the Queen of Macedonia herself! I wonder what she's doing here?"

Lysippe stiffened as a great bubble of hatred rose in her throat. But before she could move, the crowd around the Temple gates parted to allow the Megabyxos through. In full ceremonial dress and carrying his bee-staff, he strode down to the water's edge to meet the landing party. Everyone fell silent, waiting to hear what the priest would say.

"What is the meaning of this?" the Megabyxos demanded, but with a curious lack of surprise. "How dare you bring armed soldiers to the Temple of Artemis Ephesia?"

The pregnant young queen raised her chin and stared stonily down at him from the deck of her ship. "I'm here for Artemis' Birthday celebrations and to ask the goddess' blessing for my child. These men are my bodyguard – they'll wait outside the gates while I'm staying with you. Sound the Sanctuary Horn!"

The Megabyxos frowned, and the crowd began to mutter. Once it became clear the Macedonians weren't invading, more people ventured out from the city, until every stretch of land between the Temple and the harbour, every wall, and every statue plinth, was thick with men, women and children come to catch a glimpse of the tyrant's Queen from across the sea.

"You're claiming sanctuary?" the Megabyxos said stiffly, jolted out of his calm.

The Queen laughed. "Don't act so surprised, Megabyxos! How else am I supposed to guarantee my safety and the safety of my unborn son, here on your barbarian shore?"

The crowd muttered again.

"The Satrap will hear of it," warned the Megabyxos, regaining his composure.

The Queen laughed again. She had a pretty, silvery laugh, but it sent shivers through Lysippe. Macedonians, she kept thinking. They betrayed us. Because of her, Tanais is dying.

"Of course your dear Satrap will hear of it!" the Queen said. "But unless he's a complete idiot, he won't dare violate your sacred law of sanctuary. In fact, I can't wait to meet him. My husband, who sadly cannot be here because he's too busy conquering other lands, has a message for your Satrap's masters in Persia. So, are you going to let me in? Or shall I return to Pella and tell my husband how the Megabyxos of Ephesos keeps pregnant woman standing at his gates?"

She pressed a theatrical hand to her forehead, cast her pretty smile around the assembly, and cleared her throat. "I, Queen Olympias, wife of King Philip of Macedon and mother of his future heir, claim sanctuary in the Temple of Artemis Ephesia!" Her voice echoed in the hills. Even Hero must have been able to hear it. "Now then, priest," she said in a quieter tone, fixing the Megabyxos with a glare. "Sound the Sanctuary Horn."

There was a moment of perfect silence. The ribbons on the soldiers' pikes fluttered. The sea lapped the white steps. The anchor ropes creaked under the strain of holding the heavy Macedonian ship. A bee, heavy with pollen, buzzed past Lysippe's nose on its way to the hives on the Sacred Hill. Then the Megabyxos turned on his heel and strode back to his Temple. On his way through the gate, he flicked a finger. A priest ran to one of the great bronze horns, and the familiar sonorous note echoed in the hills.

Lysippe's stomach clenched uncomfortably as the Macedonian Queen's gaze roamed the crowd, turning her way for the first time. Olympias' eyes were amber. She had the gryphon's glare.

Smyrna speaks...

I am not often surprised these days. In my centuries of existence I have seen most things, and mortals have become sadly predictable with their petty wars and political games. But it seems there is more to this matter than my sisters suspected. The Macedonian Queen has Amazon blood, and she is carrying a child!

The Queen's tale of seeking the goddess' blessing is obviously an excuse, but her pregnancy explains her interest in the Amazons. The question is, how much does she know? She could frustrate all my plans, particularly if she discovers the young Amazon and her sister are here in Ephesos.

The young one is cleverer than I anticipated. This will make my task more difficult. Yet it has certain advantages. At least she has sufficient imagination to be afraid, and I know I scared her with my sisters' tales. Perhaps she will be clever enough to stay out of sight until the Queen leaves? For her sake as well as mine, I hope so.

Chapter 8

PHILOSOPHER'S SCROLL
Nature prefers to hide.

Queen Olympias managed to upset just about everyone by sunset on the first day of her arrival. Although the Megabyxos insisted she leave her armed bodyguard outside the Temple gates, she brought in all seven of her female attendants and one huge, black-skinned male slave who followed her around everywhere with folded arms and a permanent scowl. To Lysippe's relief, the young Queen refused to sleep in the common Sleeping House with the other refugees, and ordered one of the larger storage huts to be cleared out and furnished specially to house her and her retinue. Her attendants staggered through the gates carrying a massive chest that was soon discovered to contain the Queen's clothes and jewellery. As soon as she was settled in, she sent two of her women out shopping in Ephesos, and they returned with armfuls of new robes, slippers, phials of perfume, and other luxuries from the east that made the older Melissae frown. They couldn't get rid of her, though. The Sanctuary Horn had been blown.

Lysippe spent the next few days with her nerves strung as tight as a bow. She shuddered every time she saw one of the Queen's women slip out of the Temple gates and exchange words with the soldiers waiting on the ship. At night she lay awake, sweating, expecting the Macedonians to storm the Temple, drag her and Tanais out, and murder them right there on the harbour steps beside the starlit bay of Ephesos. But the Queen and her retinue kept to themselves, and the days were a whirlwind of preparation for Artemis' Birthday. Lysippe didn't even have a chance to ask Hero what he'd been doing outside the Temple the night she'd spoken to the naiad. When she wasn't helping Annyla weave flowers into wreaths to decorate the Temple, she was in the Blood House clutching Tanais' hand and willing her to wake up. Then, when Annyla finally managed to escape her duties, they would hurry to the gallery beneath the roof of the Temple, where they spent their evenings searching through the piles of dusty scrolls in the goddess' library. They worked on far into the night by the glow of a small lamp, risking the Megabyxos' anger should they be discovered. But the preparations for the Festival meant many of the priests and priestesses were abroad long after they should have been asleep in their beds, and the Queen's presence had upset normal routine. The Megabyxos had more important things to concern him, and the door guards on the Sleeping Houses turned a blind eye to late-comers.

The eve of Artemis' Birthday arrived, but they were still no closer to finding a text that mentioned gryphons or magic stones, and Lysippe began to despair.

"Maybe I should go out and talk to the naiad again," she said, though it was the last thing she wanted to do. "I'm sure she was hiding something. Tanais isn't getting any better. If we don't find a clue soon, it'll be too late."

"I'm doing my best," Annyla muttered without looking up. The dark circles under her eyes showed how little sleep she had been getting, and Lysippe felt bad. To her, the scrolls were meaningless squiggles on papyrus, and she knew there were some written in languages Annyla couldn't read, either. What if one of those was the scroll they needed?

She sighed. "Maybe we'd be better just looking for the Stone itself?"

"Maybe you'd both better come out of there and explain what you're up to," said a stern voice from the gallery.

Annyla went white and dropped the scroll she was reading. Lysippe snatched up the only weapon within reach – the burning lamp – and swung round, her gaze raking the shadows.

The Megabyxos stepped out of the dark, robed as if for bed but carrying his bee-staff. "I hope you're not thinking of attacking me with that lamp," he said, looking from Lysippe to her companion. "Annyla, I'm surprised at you. As for you, girl—" His almond eyes returned to Lysippe. "Haven't I warned you before about breaking the rules?"

Lysippe lowered the lamp. How much had the Megabyxos heard? "It's my fault," she said, glancing at Annyla. "I asked her to come and read for me."

Annyla opened her mouth, but closed it when the Megabyxos said calmly, "And have you found what you're looking for?"

Lysippe glanced at Annyla again. "I was told – I mean, we heard there were some scrolls up here containing mysteries. We thought they might help heal my sister." She assumed what she hoped was an innocent expression. "We didn't want to bother you with it, sir, since everyone's so busy at the moment."

The Megabyxos smiled, but with his mouth only. "What a lot of interest we have all of a sudden in our mysteries! A merchant from over the sea, the Queen of Macedon, and now an escaped slave from Phrygia who can't even read. I'm afraid you'll have to wait your turn."

Annyla had gone paler still. "The Macedonian Queen? Is that why she's here?"

"Believe it or not, young priestess, our library used to be quite famous throughout the civilized world. A great number of scholars have come here over the years to consult our texts – and the secrets of the philosopher's scroll eluded them all."

"Then there *is* a scroll!" Lysippe said, so excited she

forgot she was talking to the chief priest of the Temple of Artemis.

The Megabyxos drew himself up and pointed his staff at her. "You, my girl, have more things to worry about than philosophers' riddles! You've claimed sanctuary in the Temple of Artemis, and that makes you my responsibility, whether I like it or not." His frown made it obvious that he didn't. "Queen Olympias is asking questions about slaves recently come from Phrygia. She wants to know what happened to them and if there were any tall girls among them. I told her the slaves sailed to Athens. But it's only a matter of time before she hears what happened at the river and realizes some of you are still here. I've no idea what you've done to draw the attention of the Macedonian Queen, but I'm warning you now – she's a powerful woman. King Philip is already expanding his borders south towards Athens. The very fact that his wife, carrying a child she believes to be his heir, dares sail openly to Ephesos to celebrate Artemis' Birthday proves how powerful Macedonia is becoming. I cannot afford to alienate Philip of Macedon. Understand?"

Lysippe understood only that her fears about the Macedonian Queen were justified. Olympias *was* looking for her and Tanais. She didn't like the way the Megabyxos was pointing his staff at her like a weapon.

It was Annyla who answered, a look of horror on her face. "No! You can't throw Lysippe and Tanais out! We've blown the Horn for them!"

The priest turned his head. "That's enough, young priestess," he said, his tone emotionless again. "I suggest both of you go to bed and forget all about the philosopher's scroll."

He moved his staff aside to let them pass, and stood watching until they'd hurried down the stairs and out past the flower-wreathed columns into the moonlight.

Annyla was still worried about the Megabyxos' veiled threat, but Lysippe took deep gulps of the night air, feeling better than she had since she'd woken in the Blood House after the escape. "At least we know where the scroll is now," she said. "All we have to do is sneak into the Queen's quarters and get a look at it."

Annyla looked at the shadowy storage hut the Queen had commandeered, and bit her lip. "We'll need more than a look! Didn't you hear what the Megabyxos said about riddles? And we can't risk taking the scroll away with us, or the Queen will create a fuss and the Megabyxos will guess we've got it. The celebrations are tomorrow. It'll be better to wait until she's gone home."

"What if she takes it with her?"

Annyla frowned. "The Megabyxos doesn't normally let people take texts out of the library, but I suppose he might make an exception for the Queen. We could make a copy, only..."

"It'll take too long?" Lysippe said, wondering how long the riddles would take to solve.

"Not necessarily. I know just the person to help us.

But we'll have to wait until the Queen and her attendants are out. Any ideas?"

"What happens during the celebrations tomorrow?"

"Well... there's the sacrifice, of course. The Megabyxos blesses everyone, the older priests and the Melissae and distinguished members of the public wash in the sea, and after the ceremony crowds come to share the sacrificial meat and we all get a holiday. But with the Queen here and the Ionian Satrap coming as well, I'm not sure it'll be a normal year."

"Will the Queen take part in the sea-washing, too?"

Annyla's lips twitched into a smile as she realized what Lysippe was thinking. "Most likely. She's supposed to have taken part in every cult mystery from here to Athens. I don't suppose she'll miss out on this one."

The plan that had seemed so simple in the middle of the night was considerably less simple the next morning. Melissa Aspasia strode into the Sleeping House before it was properly light and dragged off all the younger priestesses to help with last-moment preparations. Annyla hurried out last, struggling into her best tunic as she went, and mouthed back over her shoulder, "Meet you by the Amazon statues when the procession starts!"

But as Lysippe was working her way through the crowds towards the Temple, a priest grabbed her elbow. "You have to move your horse!" he shouted. "The Megabyxos will be sacrificing this afternoon, and he doesn't want it spoiling the ceremony by going wild with the smell of the blood."

With all the worry over the scroll and the Macedonian Queen, Lysippe had forgotten Northwind was still stabled in the altar stalls. She stopped, distracted. "Where do I put him?"

"How do I know?" the priest said. "Take him outside and graze him by the river or someplace till it's over."

Lysippe looked for Hero, hoping he would agree to take Northwind out for her. But as usual when she wanted to talk to him, the boy was nowhere to be seen. The Birthday procession was forming up at the gates of the Temple, where the glitter of bracelets and headdresses competed with the flash of incense burners fashioned to look like bees and swung by priests from golden chains. Laughter, chatter and music filled the scented air. There was no sign of the Queen and her retinue yet, nor of the Megabyxos.

She fought her way through the crowds into the altar court and slipped past the white rumps of the oxen that had been brought up from the city for the sacrifice. Her horse was snorting and pulling at his tether, agitated by all the noise and strange smells outside. "Shh, Northwind, it's me," she whispered in Scythian. "You're going to have to look after yourself for a while. I've got things to do. Stay near the river, and Smyrna will watch over you." She untied his halter rope and led him out of the stall, then stopped and looked back at the oxen. The altar had been prepared for the sacrifice with a long knife, an axe, a bowl to catch the blood and cakes of incense and scented oils to mask the smell. One of the beasts turned its head to watch Northwind pass, and its brown eyes gazed trustingly at Lysippe. With a grimace, she snatched up the knife and slipped from stall to stall, cutting all the tethers. She whistled softly to the oxen as she led Northwind around the back of the Temple away from the crowds, where the small gate gave access to the river bank. She opened the gate and pushed Northwind through. "Go!" she whispered, and stood aside as the oxen, their sacrifice garlands still tied around their necks, trotted quietly through after the little horse. She looked anxiously along the bank, but all seemed quiet. Nobody lurked in the bushes and no strange lights showed over the water. Everyone was down at the harbour, watching the ritual washing in the sea. She breathed a sigh of relief, shut the gate again, and hurried back to the Temple.

By the time she reached the Amazon statues on the pediment, two figures were there already, watching the distant ceremony. Annyla's white and orange robe fluttered in the morning breeze, catching the light. The other figure was taller and dressed scruffily despite the festival.

"Hero!" Lysippe said, with a rush of mixed emotions. "Where have you been?"

Hero had his back to the gallery and didn't hear her. But Annyla swung round, alerting him to her presence. He gave her an unreadable look. "What were you doin' down there, Amazon-girl?"

"Had to get my horse out of the altar stalls, didn't I?" Lysippe looked down into the courtyard and realized they must have had a bird's eye view of what she'd just done. She flushed. "The oxen must have got loose and followed me."

"Got loose, huh?" Hero pulled a face. "There's goin' to be trouble when the Megabyxos gets back from the harbour and finds his sacrifices have escaped, that's for sure! No doubt I'll get blamed for it."

"I couldn't just let them be killed!"

"Shh!" Annyla frowned at them both. "Let's go. We're wasting time."

Lysippe glanced doubtfully at Hero. "Why's he here?"

"I told you we needed someone to copy the scroll, didn't I?" Annyla said. "Hero's agreed to do it for us."

Lysippe looked at the grinning boy in surprise. He didn't seem to be carrying a stylus or any papyrus. But perhaps the Queen would have some in her quarters. "I didn't think you could even read!"

She didn't mean it to come out sounding quite so rude. But the boy's grin widened. "I told you before, Amazon-girl. Just because I'm deaf don't mean I'm stupid. But you're right – I can't. That's why we need Annyla."

"Then how—?"

"*Shh!*" Annyla hurried them down the stairs and across the courtyard, glancing nervously over her shoulder as they went. "Herostratus has got other talents. He doesn't need to read the scroll. You'll see."

Lysippe was still mystified. Yet despite Hero's uncanny ability to turn up whenever there was trouble, she was glad it was Hero creeping into the Queen's hut with them, and not a strange priest or priestess who might go running straight to the Megabyxos and betray them as soon as they'd finished copying the scroll. She wondered how Annyla had persuaded him to help.

It seemed the Queen's entire retinue had gone with her to the harbour, leaving the six-sided hut deserted. Lysippe breathed a little easier. The big black slave had scared her, but even the Queen's serving girls would have been a nuisance. Distant music and singing came from the harbour, where the crowds had gathered. The Macedonian soldiers were watching the ceremony from the deck of their ship – tiny, crimson-clad figures lined up along the rail. Lysippe hurried after the Annyla and Hero, glad when the harbour and the crowds were hidden by the courtyard wall. She looked for Northwind by the river, and was reassured to see his stubby tail swishing away flies among the white oxen rumps. She smiled to herself.

The door of the Queen's quarters stood open. As they slipped through, Lysippe's heart thumped and her palms grew sweaty. But no one was inside. The Queen's clothing chest was open, the bright robes overflowing on to the floor. There was a bed, piled with cushions, and mats on the floor where Lysippe supposed the servants must sleep. A three-legged table against one of the walls bore dishes of fruit, nuts, round white cheeses, several amphorae of wine and a large hydria of water.

Hero went straight to the food and popped a cheese into his mouth, washing it down with a swig of wine that made his eyes water. He glanced round, red-faced, to see if they had noticed. But Lysippe was too strung up to tease him, and Annyla was searching under the clothes, casting anxious glances over her shoulder.

"It's such a mess in here," she kept saying. "What if she's taken it with her? They'll be back soon. Someone should keep a lookout— ah!" She pulled aside a length of turquoise silk and brandished an old, yellowed scroll, carelessly rolled. She tipped it to the light coming through the building's only window, scanned it quickly, and hurried across to Hero. "I think this is it! Stop gorging yourself and get a good look!"

Hero's expression did not change. He obviously didn't understand a word of what he was looking at. Annyla frowned over Hero's shoulder, mouthing things. It seemed the scroll didn't make a lot of sense to her, either. Lysippe turned back to the door, wondering how long it would take Hero to make a copy. She intended to keep a lookout for the return of the procession – but stopped short as the door was suddenly pulled open in front of her.

The big black slave stood there, filling the entire doorway, silhouetted against the brightness outside. Lysippe turned with a shout of warning and saw Annyla push Hero towards the window. The big slave stepped inside. He had to duck to get through the door. Lysippe backed away from him and heard Hero grunt behind her. There was a scuffle as if someone had jumped out of the window, followed by a little scream from Annyla. Lysippe whirled, her heart thudding. Hero was still inside the hut, clutching the scroll and staring stiffly out of the window. Outside, a man wearing a helmet clasped Annyla against his chest. Blue eyes stared through the helmet slits as his sword glittered at the girl's throat. The Alchemist.

The door shut with a thud, and Lysippe jumped. With the appearance of the Alchemist, she'd almost forgotten they were not alone in the building. The big slave folded his arms and looked at Lysippe and Hero with emotionless eyes as his mistress stepped past him, pushing back a fold of her crimson himation. Lysippe cast another desperate look out of the window, but the Alchemist blocked their escape route that way, still holding his sword at Annyla's throat.

The Queen shook out her hair, and droplets of water landed on the rich robes lying around her feet. Close up, she was even younger than Lysippe had thought – barely older than Tanais. The Queen smiled and ran her hands luxuriously over her rounded stomach, her eyes shining. "That swim was so refreshing! I must attend Artemis' Birthday another year, when I've more time to enjoy the ceremonies. But this is proving most interesting. Set a trap with honey, and the wild bees will fly in." She laughed and walked round the hut to peer out at the Alchemist and the terrified Annyla. "Don't cut her yet,

Alchemist. Let's see how useful she can be to us."

She turned from the window and fixed her amber eyes on Hero and Lysippe, who had backed together to the centre of the six-sided building. Lysippe clutched Hero's hand, and he squeezed back.

"Don't worry," he whispered. "She ain't got no real power here."

The Queen's laugh was silvery and light. "An innocent young priestess, a scruffy slave boy with a bad accent, and a tall girl with yellow eyes who glares at me as if she'd like to cut out my heart. No prizes for guessing which of you is the Amazon I set my trap for – though apart from those eyes, you're quite disappointingly ordinary, I must say. Have you got your magic stone with you? I'm guessing not, otherwise you'd have tried to use it by now to save your friends and escape. Or maybe you wouldn't. Maybe you're a cleverer young Amazon than I thought."

The Queen had been pacing around the hut as she spoke, with Hero twisting round after her to keep his eyes on her lips. She stopped and gave him a curious look. "Your friend doesn't seem to trust me." She held out a hand. "The scroll, if you please?"

Hero clutched the scroll tighter.

"It's the property of the Temple of Artemis, and you have been caught stealing it. If you persist in defying me, I'll report you to the Megabyxos when he gets back from the harbour, and he'll punish you."

Hero scowled.

"Give it to her," Lysippe said. "We haven't time to copy it now, anyway."

The Queen smiled as Hero handed it over. "Better. Now, watch my lips carefully, boy. You are going to walk quietly over to my man at the door and let him blindfold you. You are not going to shout for help or try anything silly, because if you do, I'll tell the Alchemist out there he can do what he likes to your little friend. The priestess is so young. She has her whole career ahead of her. It would be very sad if you were the one responsible for ending it."

Hero's scowl deepened. But after another glance at the window, he went across to the big slave. As the blindfold dropped over his eyes, he stiffened. Lysippe tried to imagine what it would be like not to be able to see or hear what was happening around you, and felt a little sick. Did the Queen realize what she'd done to him? The slave took hold of the boy's wrists in one huge black fist and held them firmly so he could not undo the knot.

"Good, and now I think the Alchemist can get on with things more suited to his skills." The Queen waved her hand, and the Alchemist dragged Annyla across the deserted courtyard. Lysippe tried to see where they'd gone, but the Queen blocked her view. She smiled. "So, young Amazon, we meet at last. We should have a little time before the others get back from the harbour. Let's sit down, shall we? A woman in my condition must look after herself, particularly when she's carrying the son of a god."

Chapter 9

MACEDONIAN QUEEN
It makes more sense to throw out a corpse than manure.

The son of a god!

Lysippe's hastily-formed plan to deny she was an Amazon rushed out of her head as if someone had turned her upside down and pulled out a stopper. The Queen's amber eyes, so like her own, held her gaze, and the pretty lips curved into a knowing smile. There seemed little point trying to hide any more.

As if she sensed Lysippe's internal surrender, Olympias removed her tiara and relaxed into the cushions with a sigh. She pulled her damp curls over one shoulder, rested a hand on the swell of her belly, and said, "I was told there were two of you. Where's your sister?"

"Half-sister," Lysippe corrected. "The Alchemist killed her. Ask him!" She didn't have to pretend hatred as she spoke the lie that was the only thing she could think of to protect Tanais.

The Queen laughed. "Oh, I did ask him. He told me the same. But then he told me her body was taken into the Blood House of Artemis and hasn't come out again. From what the Megabyxos tells me about the mysteries of this Temple, that means she didn't die. I'm guessing she's in the grip of your fascinating Amazon healing-sleep. Such a useful gift, yet so inconvenient. You can't fight it, can you? No wonder so many Amazons are killed in battle. It's very sad, but I understand even trained healers sometimes can't tell the difference between the Amazon healing-sleep and death." She glanced towards the window with a smile. "Are you quite sure you know where your sister is, young Amazon?"

Lysippe, who had been working up the courage to ask the Queen about the god, looked out of the window. Her heart missed a beat.

Four of Queen Olympias' attendants were hurrying across the courtyard after the Alchemist, heading for the little gate at the back of the Temple. They carried a litter between them. On the litter lay a motionless body covered with a drab-coloured blanket. Lysippe didn't have to see the face hidden under the blanket to know who it was.

She rushed towards the door. "That's Tanais! Where are they taking her? Let me out!"

The Queen's slave held Hero like a shield, blocking her way. She tried to get round him, but he was as immovable as a massive, dark rock. She darted back to the window, but she was more muscular than Annyla, and her shoulders jammed in the small opening.

"If you try to leave that way, my slave will break the boy's neck," the Queen warned.

Lysippe whirled, fists clenched. "Let Hero go! He's got nothing to do with this." She cast another desperate glance out of the window.

"Sit down, young Amazon," the Queen said. "As far as the Melissae are concerned, your sister died in the night. A small suggestion was all they needed, along with a pinch or two of the Alchemist's powder that confuses the eye. A corpse isn't welcome in the Temple of Artemis, for reasons I'm sure have been explained to you – especially not on the goddess' Birthday. It's a bad omen. The young Melissae left in charge of the Blood House were more than happy to let my women deal with the funeral arrangements for her body." Seeing Lysippe's horrified expression, she smiled. "Oh, don't look at me like that! They're not really going to bury her. Once things have quietened down at the harbour, they'll take your sister to my ship. She'll be perfectly safe there – as long as you behave yourself."

"No!" Lysippe shouted, spinning round. "You can't just take her! Where's Melissa Aspasia? She'd never let this happen! What did the Alchemist do to Annyla? Where's the Megabyxos? He gave Tanais sanctuary."

"A debatable point, or so the Megabyxos tells me, since she was in no fit state to claim it for herself. However, he's too busy to concern himself with corpses just now."

"But Tanais isn't—"

"She'll be safe." The Queen's amber eyes hardened as she sat forward. "But not if you continue to be so childish. Sit down! Don't you want to know what happened to the rest of your grubby little tribe?" She bent, awkwardly because of her pregnant bump, and rummaged in the bottom of her clothing chest.

Lysippe's desperate plan to rush the slave at the door died half-formed when she saw what the Queen was sliding out from under the silks. The naiad's tale came back in a cold rush as Lysippe stared at the half-moon shield with its chipped gryphon design picked out in gold and black. The Queen turned it over, and there was the story of their tribe scratched into the underside beneath the leather arm-loop. It was unmistakably her mother's shield. There was the picture that told of Lysippe's birth by the god... the one showing Tanais' Scythian father... the ones of her and Tanais as little girls, taming Sunrise and Northwind... Olympias rested the shield on her knees and ran a finger over the scratched figures, watching Lysippe all the time.

"What did you do to them?" Lysippe whispered. "What did you do to my mother?"

"Sit down, and I'll tell you."

Lysippe forced her legs to carry her to the couch and perched on the very edge. She pushed her hands between her knees in an attempt to stop them trembling. *You're the last Amazon*, Smyrna had said. She hadn't believed the naiad, but why else would the Macedonian Queen have her mother's tribal shield that the Amazons would protect with their lives?

"That's better." The Queen regarded her shaking hands in amusement. "I must say, you're not really what I expected of an Amazon princess. I thought you'd fight more, and I'd have to hurt one or maybe both of your friends to convince you to behave. But it's easier like this. Despite what you might have heard, I don't enjoy hurting people if there's a better way to get what I want. It's just that some people are so stupidly stubborn. I'm glad you're turning out to be one of the sensible ones."

"What happened to my mother?" Lysippe insisted through clenched teeth.

"Ah yes, your Amazon queen. A fierce woman, wild and dirty like an animal. Wears skins – ugh! No way for a queen to behave, but what can you expect from a savage who has spent most of her life in a tent? Unfortunately, she was one of the stubborn sort who need some persuasion before they see sense."

Olympias' gaze flickered, almost as if she regretted this. But Lysippe barely noticed. Her head roared. She snatched the shield from Olympias' lap, leapt to her feet and raised the sharp corner of the half-moon over the Queen's swollen stomach. "If you've hurt her, I'll hurt *you*," she hissed. The words seemed to belong to someone else and everything in the hut blurred, though the gryphon on the shield gleamed gold and black as if someone had swiftly polished it without her noticing.

The Queen flinched. Her eyes widened a little as she

shifted backwards on the couch, both hands spread protectively over her unborn child. At the door, her slave transferred Hero's wrists into his other hand and took a step forward.

But the Queen looked past the shield into Lysippe's eyes and laughed softly. "She won't do it. She won't harm my son – will you, young Amazon?" She waved the big man back and gently cupped her hand under the shield. With her touch, the hut snapped back into focus. "Don't jump to conclusions," the Queen continued. "There are many ways to change the mind of a stubborn person without resorting to physical violence – which is, of course, precisely why I've separated you from your sister."

Lysippe's eyes filled with tears. "If you hurt Tanais..."

"I promise you I won't, provided you do what I ask. You have my word, the word of a Queen who shares your ancient blood. And actually, you'll be doing it for my son. You don't hate him, do you? The god visited me in the night, even as he visited your mother, so my son could be your little brother – half-brother, anyway. Think of it that way, if you like. Now, put the shield down and let's talk, shall we?" When Lysippe clutched it tighter, she sighed impatiently. "Oh, all right, keep it if it means that much to you – though why anyone would want to carry around a grubby old thing like that is beyond me."

Lysippe hugged the gryphon-shield to her chest. It made her feel stronger. She looked at Hero, still standing stiffly with the blindfold over his eyes in the grip of the big slave. "At least let Hero go," she said. "I won't do anything while you have Tanais."

The Queen's smile vanished. "Don't push your luck, young Amazon. We're wasting time. The others will be back from the harbour soon and I have a meeting with the Satrap, so let's get down to business, shall we?"

"Not until you tell me what you've done with my mother and the others. Someone —" She choked on the words. "Someone told me I was the last Amazon."

"Do you think I killed them?" The Queen looked at her curiously. "After inviting them to fight for my husband?"

Lysippe's heart leapt in hope. "Then they're still alive?"

"I wouldn't know," the Queen said with a little shrug. "They were so wild, they got away from my men – but not before I had them questioned. Amazons can't be interrogated in the traditional ways, you know. If they're hurt, they just fall asleep and won't wake up for anything until their bodies are healed. Most inconvenient. But fortunately the Alchemist offered his services to my men, and though I don't really hold with his unholy powders and potions, I admit they were effective in this case. He was able to confirm for me that the Amazons hadn't brought what I wanted with them. I was sure your Queen would have one, but no. And then I discovered two of you hadn't gone down to Themiscyra at all, but stayed up in a cave in the hills. So I sent my men all the way back to Phrygia to find you, and what happens? They send a message back with some tale that you'd been captured by slavers! I didn't believe it at first, Amazons being ready to fight to the death, and all that. But then I discovered you were youngsters, and that the Alchemist was with the slavers, and the whole thing started to make more sense. I ordered my men to track you, and when they told me you'd ended up in the Temple of Artemis Ephesia, I just couldn't resist coming to see you for myself."

"Your men followed us?" Lysippe's mind shied away from asking exactly what the Alchemist had done to her mother, though she knew now with chilling certainty what he must have been up to during his absences on the long march across Phrygia. But the important thing was, Oreithyia and the rest of her tribe were alive and free. Smyrna had lied. She took a deep breath and sat down again, the shield still clasped to her breast. "Why didn't they help us? We might have died in that slave chain!"

The Queen smiled. "You didn't die, though, did you? A period in chains never hurt anyone, except their pride – and you Amazons have enough of that to match the gods."

"But Tanais was wounded!"

"Your sister's still alive, and will be kept that way until you bring me what I want. The whole reason I bothered sending my messengers into the wilds of Scythia to invite your tribe to fight for my husband in the first place is because I was certain you would bring some of your magic Stones with you that ward off death."

Lysippe stiffened.

"Don't try telling me they don't exist. I know all about them, and I want one for my son. The Oracle I consulted after the god visited my bed told me I'd give birth to a boy who would conquer half the world but die before he'd finished his task. With one of your magic Amazon Stones, however, he needn't die. He'll be able to go on and conquer the rest. He'll be ruler of an empire far greater than Athens and her pathetic league of city-states, even greater than Persia! And I'll be there at his side to guide and advise him, his loving mother, immortal and beautiful like the legendary Amazons – only cleaner." She eyed Lysippe's dirty knees and the smudges on her tunic.

"We never had a Stone like that," Lysippe said, truthfully enough. "So you might as well let Tanais go."

The Queen stopped smiling and gave her a sharp look. "No, I can see that now. It's ironic, really. I invited you to come and fight for my husband, hoping you'd bring me your magic Stones. And you accepted the invitation in the hope that, as a reward for your services, he'd give you back your cities where your ancient Stones were buried – isn't that right? And the Alchemist, overhearing all this talk of magic Stones and assuming I was on the trail of the legendary Philosopher's Stone that can turn metal into gold, immediately spirited you away and offered me his services. Yet none of us has a single magic Stone between us! It's so tragically comic, somebody should write a play about it." She laughed.

"I don't think it's very funny," Lysippe said stiffly with another glance at the window.

The procession was on its way back from the harbour to the accompaniment of much laughter, music and dancing. The older Melissae, who were normally on duty at the Blood House, were acting like young girls again. Their wet hair, fresh from the ritual purification, steamed in the heat of the sun as they trailed chains of flowers through the incense clouds. Lysippe listened hopefully for the Sanctuary Horn. Surely, when the Melissae realized what had happened, they would send out the Temple guards to fetch Tanais back? But the commotion that arose in the courtyard when the procession returned was of an entirely different sort – outraged shouts, people running along the river bank, children yelling in excitement, frightened bellows and the thud of hooves. Lysippe's heart sank as she remembered the oxen she'd released earlier. And she'd thought the worst thing about today would be listening to the oxen die.

The Queen had heard as well. "They sound like they're having fun out there. You and your boyfriend can join them as soon as I've explained what I want you to do for me. Here in the Temple of Artemis, as I know your little priestess friend has told you, they have a legend about a magic Stone that protects people. The Alchemist, of course, thinks it is his Philosopher's Stone – but we know the truth, don't we? Ephesos was an ancient Amazon city, so naturally one of your magic Stones will have been buried here. Unfortunately, I don't know quite what I'm looking for, but I think you do. You're going to find it for me. When you do, you're going to send it to me in return for your sister. I have to go home after my meeting with the Satrap, because it's important my son is born where he can be properly protected. But I'll leave my trusty commander behind with some of his men. When you find the Stone, take it to Commander Cleitus. He'll be in Androklos' ruined shrine on the promontory above the main city harbour every night at midnight. The Alchemist will escort you there so you don't lose your way. When he has the Stone, Cleitus will return your sister to the Temple. You can go wherever you like after that – though I'd suggest you go back where you came from. My husband doesn't know anything about the invitation I sent to your tribe, and he's not going to be interested in a handful of grubby Amazons who have lost their weapons and horses when he's got highly-trained men with the latest equipment queuing up to fight for him."

"But we don't even know if the Stone's here!" Lysippe protested.

"Don't give me that. You're already looking for it. That's why you wanted a look at this scroll." She waved the philosopher's riddles.

"But—"

"Oh, I understand the problem. It's all hieroglyphs to me, too. But I'm sure your sister's safety will give you the incentive you need to work things out."

Lysippe's head was whirling. Outside, one of the recaptured oxen gave its death-bellow, accompanied by sweet singing from the Temple choir. The crowds were getting noisier. People were having a wonderful time, yet her world was falling apart. Even if they did find the Stone, how was she supposed to use it to heal Tanais, if she had to give it to Commander Cleitus before he'd release her sister? As for the Alchemist, he was hardly likely to let the Stone out of his sight if he thought it could turn metal to gold. And what about Smyrna? The naiad was sure to try to stop her if she found out the Stone was destined for Macedonia. She hadn't even asked about the god yet.

Before she could order her thoughts, Olympias stood up and retrieved her ruby tiara. She looked down at Lysippe. "I must get ready for my meeting with the Satrap now," she said abruptly. "I'm sure you're sensible enough not to tell anyone about our little bargain. I don't suppose the Megabyxos will be exactly thrilled to hear you're going to steal his magic Stone. It's our secret, all right?" She laid the scroll on the couch beside Lysippe and flicked a finger at her slave. "You can let the boy go now. Oh – and Lysippe?"

Lysippe had snatched up the scroll and was almost at the door, where Hero was ripping off his blindfold. But at the Queen's use of her name, she froze.

"Don't get any ideas about keeping the Stone for yourself and using it to rescue your sister or anything silly like that, will you? I have spies everywhere, and the Alchemist will be keeping an eye on you as well, remember? You'll find the little priestess in the Blood House."

She turned her back on them then, stepping out of her stained robe as if they did not exist. The big slave opened the door to let the Queen's giggling attendants, back from their treacherous errand to the harbour, slip inside.

Hero was staring around wildly, trying to reorientate himself. Lysippe grasped his hand and dragged him out of the hut. With her mother's shield a comforting weight on her arm and the philosopher's scroll clasped firmly between them, they fled.

Chapter 10

FORGER

They pray to statues as if one were to carry on a conversation with houses, not recognizing the true nature of gods and spirits.

Lysippe and Hero went straight to the Blood House, fearing the worst for their friend. But Annyla was still very much alive, screened by hastily-drawn curtains, screaming and sobbing. One of the Blood House guards was holding the girl, while an older Melissa tried to make her drink something out of a chipped orange and black bowl. Annyla pushed it away so violently, the bowl flew through the gap between the curtains and smashed at Lysippe's feet. She leapt over the fragments and dragged Hero through the curtain.

"You have to go after her!" Annyla cried. "She's not dead, I tell you! The Macedonians kidnapped her... you've got to stop the Queen leaving..." When she saw Lysippe and Hero, she sagged against the man who held her. "Thank Artemis! They think I'm hysterical. You've got to tell them to find Melissa Aspasia, and—"

"I'm here," said Aspasia, coming in behind them. "What in Artemis' Name is going on?" Her dark hair was damp and dishevelled from the sea-washing and there was a wine stain on her robe, but she appeared quite sober. She surveyed the scene with a little frown. "Annyla, get a grip on yourself. Lysippe, Herostratus... out!"

"But Tanais is in danger!" Lysippe protested. "We've got to go after her! Quick, while the Queen's still with the Satrap—"

"*Out*, and wait for me in the visitors' area. You're upsetting my patients."

There was no arguing with Melissa Aspasia. As they reluctantly left the curtained alcove, they heard Annyla explaining between breathless sobs what had happened. Aspasia interrupted now and then with quiet questions, and the girl gradually calmed down. The Temple guard was dismissed and returned to his position by the door. Lysippe wanted to rush down to the harbour and try to get Tanais back herself, but Hero refused to come with her.

"Don't be so stupid," he said, "the Alchemist is down there, to say nothing of all them Macedonian soldiers on the ship. Don't worry, if the Queen's got a meeting with the Satrap, she won't be leavin' just yet."

Lysippe supposed this was true, but she couldn't relax. She perched on the bench with the gryphon-shield on her knees, her gaze fixed on the curtain. Hero crossed one ankle over his knee and unrolled the scroll. It was a little crushed after their run from the Queen's quarters, and he flattened it out with much unnecessary rustling. While Hero ran his gaze over the writing, whistling tunelessly, Lysippe stared at the empty bed where Tanais had lain earlier that morning. The curtains had been tied back and the blanket neatly rolled, ready for a new patient. Why, oh why hadn't she stayed to guard her sister instead of chasing about after the stupid philosopher's scroll? Annyla had warned her most of the Blood House staff would be down at the harbour taking part in the Birthday celebrations. She should never have left Tanais in such inexperienced hands.

After what seemed an age, Melissa Aspasia slipped quietly out through the curtain and tugged it shut behind her.

Lysippe leapt to her feet. "How is she?"

"I've given her something to help her sleep," the priestess said. "She's been through a frightening ordeal, and you're not to disturb her. The girls here might see the results of violence in the outside world, but they're not accustomed to experiencing such things themselves. Don't be surprised if she needs a bit of time to get over it." She gave the shield a curious glance and regarded Lysippe levelly. "I don't know how this happened. The priestesses I left on duty while we were down at the harbour have been disciplined, but it's not entirely their fault. Annyla tells me the Alchemist was here. I believe he used some of his illusion powders on them. The guards at the door were deceived as well. The most important thing is, your sister doesn't appear to have been harmed. I've sent some of the Temple guards down to the harbour. Hopefully, they'll catch up with the people who took her before they reach the Macedonian ship." She looked at the door of the Blood House, where the sounds of revelry spilled through from the courtyard.

Lysippe frowned. "And if they don't?"

"Then I'm afraid we'll have to negotiate for her release. The Queen's ship is Macedonian territory. To board without permission would be seen as an invasion of Macedonia itself."

"That's stupid!" Hero said. "She's only got one ship and a few soldiers. The Temple guards can board it if they want! You can send to Ephesos for more men, and get the Persians to launch ships after her. The Satrap don't like her much – even I can tell that!"

Aspasia sighed. "It's not as simple as you think, Herostratus."

"Why not?"

"Because there's politics to consider. The Temple of Artemis is respected throughout the world, and Ephesos enjoys a certain independence as the main harbour on the trade route to the east. But we're caught between the Persians and the Greeks. Some of the islands in the League have broken off relationships with Athens, and the Greeks are getting nervous. That makes the Persians

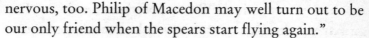

nervous, too. Philip of Macedon may well turn out to be our only friend when the spears start flying again."

Even though the Megabyxos had said the same thing, Lysippe could hardly believe what she was hearing. "But you can't just let her take Tanais! What about your sacred law of sanctuary? Doesn't that mean *anything*?"

Aspasia sighed again. "It's regrettable, but technically Tanais never claimed sanctuary. She hasn't regained consciousness since she arrived. The Megabyxos won't sacrifice the safety and reputation of his Temple to rescue one refugee slave who, as far as he knows, will be dead within the month. But if you want to go with your sister, Lysippe, no one will stop you. I know how close you two are. Knowing the Macedonian Queen's love of mysteries, your sister's abduction might have something to do with... what you are." She gave Hero a glance. "I doubt she'll harm you."

Lysippe thought of what the Queen had said about the Alchemist using his powders and potions on the Amazons, and shuddered. "I can't go with Tanais," she whispered. "I've got to stay here."

Misunderstanding her reasons, Melissa Aspasia gave her hand a little squeeze. "It's no shame to be scared, Lysippe. Many people stay with us well past the time they originally intended. Some even decide to become priests or Melissae and spend the rest of their lives here. Don't worry, we'll do everything in our power to get your sister back. I'll speak to the Megabyxos at once. It might help if he knew why Tanais is unlikely to die."

"No!" Lysippe said. "Please don't tell him!"

Aspasia frowned. "But it would encourage him to help your sister, Lysippe."

Hero gave her a puzzled look as well, and she realized how crazy it was to try to keep their identity from the chief priest after what had happened. She clutched the shield tighter. "Don't tell him," she whispered. "Please."

Melissa Aspasia's lips tightened, but she nodded. "All right, but he's going to be curious. A powerful Queen such as Olympias of Macedon doesn't just take a fancy to a sick girl and carry her off without good reason. Right now, though, I think it's best if you wait in here and let me deal with the Megabyxos. Someone let out all his sacrifices earlier, and he wasn't happy." Her gaze rested briefly on Hero.

Hero watched her leave, an amused twist to his lips. "She doesn't know I know you're Amazons, does she?"

"No," Lysippe said.

The boy chuckled and bent back over the scroll. "She doesn't know everything."

Lysippe eyed the top of his head, suspicious. So far, Hero hadn't asked what they'd been talking about in the Queen's hut while he'd been blindfolded. Yet she knew she'd have been burning with curiosity, had their positions been reversed.

"I never really thanked you for saving me from the Alchemist the other night," she said softly.

Hero didn't react. She quietly lifted the shield until it was poised behind Hero's head. Suddenly, she slammed her palm against the hardened leather with a loud bang.

The boy spun round and stared at her. "What was that for?"

"Did you hear what we were talking about in the Queen's hut?" she asked.

Hero's black eyes flashed. "Course not! I was blindfolded so I couldn't read your lips. The Alchemist must've told the Queen I was deaf. I'll bet she enjoyed every moment of it!"

"You turned round when I hit the shield just then," Lysippe said accusingly.

"What do you expect? You nearly took my hair off! I felt the air move and thought it was someone creepin' up behind me. I've had quite enough scares for one day, thank you very much!"

"You haven't asked me what we talked about yet."

"That's your business, ain't it? You'll tell when you're ready to."

They eyed each other. Lysippe was the first to lower her gaze. "I'm sorry," she said with a sigh. "It's just that I don't know who to trust any more. I appreciate you agreeing to help us copy the scroll, but you don't have to make a copy now the Queen's given it to us. We just need Annyla to wake up so we can read it." She frowned at the curtain. Another thought struck her. "If she can read, why can't *she* copy?"

Hero grinned. "She didn't tell you, did she?"

"Tell me what?"

Before Hero could answer, the doorway was

darkened by two Temple guards. He rolled up the scroll with a guilty expression. Lysippe leapt to her feet, fear clashing with hope. "Did you get my sister back?"

"You two are to come with us," said the tallest guard. "The Satrap wants to speak to you."

"The Satrap?" Lysippe glanced at Hero in confusion. "But isn't he in a meeting with the Queen?"

The other man chuckled. "He was until a few moments ago, and it's put him in a foul mood, so I'd advise you to be quick about it."

Hero looked uncomfortable. But Lysippe's heart leapt. "He's going to send the Persian navy after the Queen, isn't he?" she said. "I knew he would!"

The two men looked at each other. "Hurry up," was all they said.

They proved correct about the Satrap's mood. When they showed Lysippe and Hero into the inner room of the Temple that served as both the Treasury and the Megabyxos' private quarters, the Satrap was pacing up and down, shouting at the chief priest in Ionian-Greek seasoned with words of Persian that didn't sound very polite. He was dressed in a peculiar mixture of fashions. His beard glistened with oil in the Persian style, and over his plain linen tunic he wore a turquoise robe that glittered with tiny beads. Every time he strode past, a waft of sickly perfume made Lysippe's eyes water. She didn't understand everything he was saying, but she caught the gist of it. "Macedon scum... that tyrant Philip... dare send a woman here to deliver ultimatums to me... insult to the Emperor... crush Macedonia beneath the wheels of their chariots!"

Meanwhile, the Megabyxos was sweating beneath his heavy robes and looked uncomfortable. When the Temple guards brought Lysippe and Hero in, he grunted in relief. "Ah, here they are!"

The Satrap swung round with a scowl. "Who are these two?"

"The refugees you wanted to see. The ones who were in the Queen's quarters before your meeting with her."

The Satrap pressed a hand to his forehead, as if he didn't want to be reminded of the Macedonian Queen. "But they're just children." He looked Lysippe and Hero up and down without really seeing them. His gaze finished on the scroll, which was still in Hero's hand. "What did the Queen say to you, my dears?" he asked in a sickly tone that matched his perfume.

Hero looked at Lysippe and rolled his eyes. But Lysippe decided to play on the Satrap's attitude and said, "Please, sir, the Queen took my sister to her ship. She's very sick and she needs the Melissae to look after her. Can you send someone to get her back?"

The Satrap frowned at the Megabyxos. "What's all this nonsense about the girl's sister?"

"I don't know what she's talking about," the Megabyxos said, avoiding Lysippe's gaze.

"Ask Melissa Aspasia!" Lysippe said. "She—" She broke off as the Megabyxos' eyes flickered to her and away again. It was the briefest of glances, but in that moment she saw he knew about Tanais. She closed her mouth, remembering what he'd said about not alienating Philip of Macedon.

"Answer the Satrap!" snapped the Megabyxos, looking at Hero. "What did the Queen say to you?"

Hero scowled. "Nothin' I could hear. Deaf, ain't I?"

A wild giggle rose in Lysippe's throat and threatened to emerge as a sob. She clenched her fists and eyed the two Temple guards standing by the door.

The Satrap shook his head. "Never mind. Did she give you that scroll? Let me see it."

When Hero didn't move, one of the guards snatched the scroll from his hand and carried it across to the Satrap, who unrolled it and frowned at the neat Greek lettering. It obviously made no sense to him, either. "I'll have to confiscate this," he said.

Lysippe opened her mouth to protest, but the Megabyxos got there first. "It's nothing," he said. "Just some old philosopher's mysteries. The Queen wanted to broaden her education."

"Mysteries, eh?" The Satrap re-rolled the scroll and tucked it under his arm. He smiled for the first time. "Don't worry, priest, it'll be returned to you in good condition when I've finished with it. In the meantime, I'd like to remind you that the Temple of Artemis Ephesia has much Persian gold in its coffers, and Ephesos is still part of the Persian Empire. You enjoy a comfortable existence here, Megabyxos. But I wonder how long your goddess would remain popular if her gold ran out?" His gaze strayed to the big chests at the back of the room.

The Megabyxos looked as if he'd eaten too much. He gave a stiff nod. "Keep the scroll as long as you like. And if you want to interview these two again, I'll make sure they're brought to you in a better frame of mind." He frowned at Hero and Lysippe.

"That won't be necessary," the Satrap said, gathering his beaded robe about him. "I've more important things to do than talk to rude children – such as making sure our proud Queen Olympias sails back to Macedonia with all her men and doesn't accidentally leave anyone behind on our shores." He strode from the Temple, glaring at anyone who didn't get out of his way quickly enough.

The Satrap's perfume lingered, making Lysippe feel sick. She watched him leave in despair. The Megabyxos was lecturing her and Hero on manners, but she didn't hear a word. All she could think was: *The Satrap's not with the Queen any more.* There was nothing to stop the Macedonians leaving Ephesos.

As soon as the Megabyxos dismissed them, she raced out of the Temple and stared round wildly. The Satrap was nowhere to be seen, and the door to the Queen's hut swung open. She ran for the Temple gates. The sun was sinking into the sea, and the sky had turned deep purple. Torches flared in the warm evening air, lighting up the great marble columns of the Temple and making the whole building glow until it must have been visible clear across the plain. The celebrations were getting wilder, as if no one cared what the Macedonian Queen had done. Lysippe wondered if they even knew. A breeze sprang up from nowhere, ruffling her hair and bringing the smell of roasting meat from the altar.

"Where are you going?" Hero hurried after her.

"Down to the harbour to help Tanais!"

Hero pointed silently at the bay.

"Oh no... *no!*"

Just visible on the horizon, a ship under full sail was heading out to open sea. The Royal Star of Macedon, emblazoned across the crimson cloth, glittered unmistakably in the setting sun.

Despair washed over Lysippe like a dark wave. She collapsed against the wall and dropped her head in her hands. "The Queen's taking Tanais to Macedonia! We should have gone after her straightaway! Now we haven't even got the scroll... Oh, Hero, what am I going to *do*?"

Hero gazed after the ship, frowning. "Why would she take Tanais all the way to Macedonia? More likely, she'll drop her off someplace on route where she can be hidden. Any rate, I can still copy the scroll, if you want."

Lysippe took deep breaths as her brain began to work again. "How can you copy the scroll if we haven't got it any more? Are you going to break into the Satrap's mansion and steal it back?" She looked at the white buildings of the city and the twin peaks that rose above them against the sky. She didn't know where the Satrap stayed while he was in Ephesos, but maybe it wasn't such a bad idea. It would certainly be easier than chasing the Queen's ship across the sea.

Hero grinned as he jumped off the wall. "Easier than that. I'll show you. C'mon!"

He set off through the partying crowds towards the honeycomb complex where the priests lived and studied. Not knowing what else to do, Lysippe followed.

Unwashed robes and damp sandals were scattered everywhere, and the whole place smelled of male sweat. Lysippe wrinkled her nose, uncomfortable. But the priests themselves were all out celebrating the goddess' Birthday. Hero rummaged around, collecting a blank tablet and a stylus. He cleared a space on one of the tables, righted a stool and lit a lamp. He flexed his fingers and picked up the stylus with a little smile. "Watch carefully, Amazon-girl," he said, and closed his eyes.

Lysippe couldn't concentrate. She was aware of Hero making marks in the wax, but her whole attention was on the door and the distant sea. The laughter and music outside seemed part of another world. *Tanais!* she screamed silently. *Tanais, come back!*

Then she realized what Hero was doing.

Keeping his eyes closed, he moved his hand quickly over the beeswax surface, leaving behind neat strings of Greek letters. At some point he opened his eyes to check what he'd written, though Lysippe was certain he could have carried on happily writing with them shut. Amazement replaced her despair as she watched him work.

When he'd filled one side of the tablet, he showed it to her with a grin. "You'll still need Annyla to read it, but it's genuine, I promise. If you find me some more tablets, I'll do the rest for you. I'll need some of that roast ox too, and somethin' to drink. Copyin's hard work, and there was a lot of stuff on that scroll. Probably take me all night."

In spite of her worry over Tanais, Lysippe stared at the tablet. "How do you do it?"

Hero shrugged. "Got that sort of memory, ain't I? My master always used to say it made up for me not bein' able to hear. Wish I had good ears instead – it's got me in all sorts of trouble."

Lysippe watched him turn the tablet to start on the other side, and had a sudden insight. "That's what happened last time you were here, isn't it?" she said. "You copied something you shouldn't have."

Hero grunted. "And the rest! My master used to send me to places like this and get me to examine rare stuff. Then he'd make me copy it for him, and sell the copies as the original." He shrugged. "It was quite fun at first. Only thing was, if people found out they'd been sold a copy, he'd blame me an' beat me so they'd think it was my fault and go away. Then, when things quietened down, he'd have somethin' else he wanted copied." The boy pulled a face. "He sent me to the Temple of Artemis lots of times – told me to say I'd run away and needed sanctuary. They've got valuable originals in here from all over the world, you know – not only scrolls, but paintings, statues, lyres that belonged to famous musicians, all sorts. And they're all dedicated to Artemis, so they never leave the Temple. My master used to give the Megabyxos a share of the profits for keepin' his mouth shut. Should've been perfect. Only they fell out over somethin' to do with the goddess' necklaces. That's when I knew I had to run away. But here I am, back again, pullin' off the same old trick! The Megabyxos'll probably kill me if he finds out – if my master don't kill me first, that is." He grimaced at the door.

Lysippe touched Hero's hand, distracted for the moment from her own worries. "I won't let either of them touch you, I promise. When I find the Stone, I'll use it to help you, somehow. Where's your master now? He sounds horrid." Something niggled at the back of her mind, but she had too many other things to worry about, and the thought escaped.

"He is horrid." Hero avoided her gaze. His lips tightened as he bent back over his work. "When we find it, you use that Stone to save your sister, Amazon-girl," he muttered. "I'm a lost cause."

Chapter 11

ANDROKLOS' SHRINE
A dry soul is wisest and best.

It was dark by the time Lysippe had fought her way through the celebrating crowds and taken Hero his food. The great Temple was lit by flaring torches that made the shadows dance, leaving her light-headed and dizzy. On her way back out, someone tried to give her one of Artemis' special birthday cakes baked in the shape of a stag and soaked in honey. She thrust it back at them, sickened by the thought of eating.

She stopped in the courtyard and took deep breaths of the night air. The moon was rising, huge and round in the smoke, and stars sprinkled the sky above the bay. The party was getting wilder by the moment. The crowds had spilled out of the Temple gates on to the river bank and along the Sacred Way into the streets of the city, where they danced and sang praises to Artemis. She saw Melissa Aspasia hurrying back to the Blood

House with a groaning celebrant who appeared to have hit his head. In the shadows round the back of the Novices' Sleeping House, someone was throwing up.

Lysippe turned away in disgust. Hero was copying the philosopher's scroll. Annyla was still asleep in the Blood House. The Melissae were busy, and the Megabyxos was off on some business of his own. No one seemed to care about Tanais. People didn't even seem to notice Lysippe as they jostled past. Tears in her eyes, she clung to her mother's shield and ran her fingers over the gryphon design. As she did so, she thought of Hero's story and a daring idea began to form.

Queen Olympias didn't know what the Gryphon Stone looked like, and she wasn't here to test it. No one else dared touch it. Who would know if Lysippe brought a fake Stone out of the Temple? With luck, the substitute wouldn't be discovered until the Queen's Commander got back to Macedonia, and by that time, if Hero was right about the island hideout, she and Tanais would be safely away. She could hide her sister in the mountains until she found the real Stone to heal her. All she had to do was get past the Alchemist...

She looked at the stars. Midnight, the Queen had said. Commander Cleitus would be at Androklos' Shrine every night at midnight. There was still time.

Heart thudding, she reversed the shield and slipped her arm through the leather loop. The crowds and torches blurred around her as, raising the shield to hide her face, she ducked into the Temple. It was quieter inside, the silence broken only by muffled giggles from the shadows. On her way through the columns, she glimpsed figures embracing in dark corners, but they ignored her as she made her way to the inner sanctuary of the goddess. She paused at the door, her palms sweaty, listening for the strange whispers she'd heard the first time she'd come here. But the inner room was filled with its usual, incense-scented hush. Someone had lit fresh candles, which burned around Artemis' feet like a starlit sea, and the gryphons were frozen in place, their amber eyes glowing in the candlelight.

Slightly relieved, Lysippe propped her shield against the wall and slid an arrow out of one of the quivers at the goddess' feet. Standing on tip-toe, she used the arrowhead to prise a large amber bead out of its setting in one of the goddess' necklaces. Its swirling golden depths glowed in the light of the candles, as magical as any stone she'd ever seen.

"Sorry, Artemis," she whispered. "But I need it for my sister."

She wrapped the bead in a square of embroidered linen someone had dedicated to the goddess, and knotted the bundle securely to her girdle. Trembling a little, she slipped the shield back on her arm. She was about to leave the sanctuary when her eye fell on a bow in the shadows round the back of the statue. The weapon had obviously been dedicated with the arrows. It was a little longer than she was used to, and beautifully made. Before she could think too much about what she might need it for, Lysippe strapped the quiver about her waist, slung the bow over her shoulder, and hurried out of the Temple.

She kept her head low as she ran for the gate in the back wall. But if anyone noticed she was carrying a weapon, no one raised the alarm. Maybe they thought she was in fancy dress for the procession. A separate party was happening on the river bank. Some people were in the water at the ford, splashing and singing, fully-clothed. Lysippe looked nervously for a helmet with a blue crest or any suspicious sparkling lights, but to her relief there was no sign of the Alchemist or the naiad. She supposed the crowds must be keeping them both away.

She slipped out of the gate and whistled softly. She was worried someone might have caught Northwind again, but he came trotting obediently along the bank. He nuzzled the shield, flaring his nostrils. She pushed his nose away and vaulted on his back without bothering with a halter. He turned his head and gave her a surprised look, then snorted and broke into a trot.

She guided him with her knees along the bank between the groups of celebrants, past the ford, and into the barley that grew beside the Sacred Way. It was close to harvest, so the ripe heads reached almost as high as her own, pale and ghostly in the moonlight. Keeping the Sacred Way and the city to her right, she turned Northwind away from the river and urged him into a canter, crouching low over his neck as he broke a path through the stalks. The horse tossed his head when he got seeds in his eyes, and Lysippe gripped her borrowed bow more firmly. But the coil of fear and tension, that had been tightening inside her ever since the Alchemist's sword had struck Tanais, unwound a little as she rode. She used the shield to ward off the stalks as they whipped past, and grinned as the speed and action after so long confined by walls raised her spirits.

The barley was interrupted by a road that branched off the Sacred Way and cut across her path, leading to a pass through the mountains to the south. She halted Northwind and waited under cover of the stalks, breathing heavily, while she checked for pursuit. To her right, the marble buildings of Ephesos shone white in the moonlight. The noise and flaming torches in the streets indicated that the celebration was far from over. But the road was deserted, and the planting continued beyond it. As Northwind trotted over the ruts left by cartwheels and plunged back into the cover of the barley, she couldn't resist a shout of triumph.

"Come and catch me, Alchemist!" she called. "Wherever you are!"

She successfully skirted the city in this way, but the barley thinned out when the plain narrowed, and she was forced to rejoin the Sacred Way where it led through the less populated Smyrna District between the hills to the coast. There were several houses scattered across the slopes, but the inhabitants all seemed to be at the party. Sheep scuttled out of her way as she trotted Northwind through the pass, raking the shadows with her gaze, every nerve alight. Her skin prickled as she rode beneath a row of cave entrances, but no slavers ran out of the hills to ambush her. The main city harbour lay ahead, glittering in the moonlight with several ships at anchor. Above the harbour, on the promontory just as the Queen had described, a circle of crumbling columns rose dark against the sky.

Androklos' Shrine.

Northwind slowed as Lysippe's knees unconsciously tightened. She felt very exposed. She fitted an arrow to her bow and turned the little horse up the track that led to the strange, octagonal ruin. The wind blew up the hill, teasing a song from the reeds that moaned around the broken columns. She lowered the shield to rest her arm and looked round for the Commander. What if the Satrap had found the Queen's men and sent them away, or – worse – had them killed?

A soft chuckle came from the bushes to her left. "It's all right, it's our girl – she must have given her escort the slip."

Shadowy, cloaked shapes rose from both sides of the path and stepped towards Northwind's head. They paused, confused when they saw the horse wore no bridle. Lysippe spun the horse in a circle, bringing the bow round to aim her arrow at the heart of the man who had spoken. The shield got in the way, but she kept her aim.

"Stay back! Or I'll shoot! I'm not bluffing."

The man pushed back the hood of his cloak and regarded her with a level gaze. "There are five of my men hidden behind you who would take immediate revenge for that. But I don't think you came here to kill me, did you, young Amazon?"

Again, Lysippe's heart jumped in her chest. The man wore only a peasant's rags under his dark cloak, but he carried a good sword with his hand resting on the hilt. His skin was as black as the big slave the Queen had brought into the Temple, though it was obvious this man was no slave, nor ever had been. He spoke accented Greek.

"I could kill you if I wanted to!" she said. "My arrow's faster than their swords."

He acknowledged this with a short nod. "You could certainly put that arrow in me. I'm not so sure about the killing. You're younger than I thought you'd be, though you've got the Queen's eyes, all right – like a lion's. They tell me a lion was killed here by the man who built this shrine. Have you ever killed a lion, young Amazon? Have you ever killed a man?"

"Are you Commander Cleitus?" she demanded, her fist tightening on the bow.

The man smiled slightly. "Seems I'll have to get a better disguise. Not so loud – let's have this conversation inside the shrine, shall we? No one comes up here, not even the Satrap's men. They think it's haunted." He regarded her speculatively. "It's a spooky place, with the way the wind sings round the columns. I can see you're not afraid of ghosts, but I think you'd better leave your horse out here."

"No," Lysippe said. "Northwind comes with me."

Again, the Commander smiled. "You prefer to stay mounted so you can make a quick retreat, is that it? Can't say I blame you, though I'd prefer not to have to look up so much – after sitting about up here in this wind, my neck's gone terribly stiff."

Lysippe frowned as she walked Northwind up the track after Cleitus. She'd expected to hate the Macedonian Commander on sight. She hadn't really cared that he'd be in trouble when he took his Queen a fake Stone. She hadn't counted on him being so... human.

They stopped in the grassy centre of the shrine, surrounded by the old, crumbling columns. A small fire burned behind a pile of stones, where it would not be visible from below, and two more men in drab clothing got to their feet as they entered. They stared at Lysippe curiously. Her back prickled. Five on the hill, two here, Cleitus himself... how many men had the Queen left behind? She couldn't see Tanais with them, but at least the Alchemist didn't seem to be here. She relaxed slightly, but kept her arrow aimed at the Commander's heart.

"Were you there when the Alchemist used his powders on my mother?" she demanded.

The black man's eyes narrowed slightly. "I do not get involved with such matters. I wasn't with the Queen when she questioned the Amazons."

"But you must have seen them! You're supposed to be her Commander, aren't you? What happened to them? The Queen said they escaped."

At this, Cleitus smiled. "I heard the same."

Lysippe frowned again. "How? Where did they go?"

"I didn't have time to ask. They were in a hurry to leave and unwilling to trust me – understandable, given the circumstances."

Again, the Commander wasn't reacting the way she'd expected him to. She frowned. "Did you *help* them escape?" she whispered, lowering her bow slightly.

Cleitus' expression hardened. "Understand this, young Amazon. I'm loyal to Macedonia above all else. My sister has been chosen to help nurse the royal child after the Queen gives birth. It's a great honour, and I will do nothing to endanger her position." He paused. "But I don't kill unarmed women, be they Greek, Persian, or Amazon. As to where your tribe went, I'd say that's obvious. Or are Amazon mothers so different from other women?"

Lysippe lowered her bow still further. "They don't know we were taken as slaves, do they? They'll have gone back to the cave!" She had another sudden suspicion. "Did the Queen send the Alchemist with those slavers to capture us?"

The Commander shook his head. "I expect she would have, if she'd thought it would help her get her hands on your magic Stone. But they hardly helped our cause, bringing you here to Ephesos – that was the Alchemist's doing, so I understand. No, she thought she'd caught you all down in Themiscyra. Took time to discover you two existed, let alone where you'd been taken so we could track you." He raised an eyebrow. "Was that all you came here for?"

"I have the Stone."

Cleitus' gaze flew to her face. Lysippe kept her expression as straight as she could. After studying her for a long moment, the Commander stretched out a hand.

"Good. Give it to me."

Lysippe untied the bundle from her waist and tossed it down to him. His men sucked in their breath and took a collective step backwards. Cleitus made no move to pick up the stone. Slowly, he raised his eyes. "I've heard these magic Stones can turn those who are not pure-bred Amazons into dust. Is this true?"

Lysippe was backing Northwind in an attempt to keep all the Macedonians in sight. But they moved as well, making sure she remained surrounded. "Ash," she said. "It'll turn you to ash. That's why I wrapped it up for you. You mustn't unwrap it until you get it to your Queen, or it'll kill you. Where's my sister? I want to see her now."

Cleitus still made no move to touch the linen-wrapped offering. "Your sister will be returned to you when you bring me the true Stone," he said.

Lysippe's heart sank.

Cleitus took a step forward and rested a dark hand on Northwind's mane. He looked up into her face. "Good try, young Amazon. But if you really had brought me your magic Stone, you'd not surrender it so easily, not without first seeing your sister was safe. The Queen said you might try something like this." He stooped and unknotted the cloth, exposing the amber to the moonlight. "Pretty – but not, I think, capable of warding off death."

He kicked the bead to one of his men, who caught it by reflex then dropped it again as if it were a hot coal. When nothing happened to him, the man laughed in relief and retrieved the amber so he could show it to the others, who chuckled too.

Lysippe tensed. She raised her bow again. "Where's Tanais? If your Queen thinks I'm going to send the Stone across the sea to her when I need it to heal my sister, she's crazy!"

Cleitus acknowledged this with another nod. "I know your dilemma, young Amazon, and I sympathize. The truth is, we need to test the Stone first. The Queen left orders as to how this should be done, and I hope you'll believe me when I say I'll do everything I can to make sure you get a chance to help your sister. She's perfectly safe, no more than half a day's sail from here. When you bring the Stone to me, I'll take you to her and make sure you get some time alone together to do what you need to before I return to Macedonia."

Lysippe lowered the bow again and leant forward in renewed hope. "Where is she? Which island did you take her to?"

Cleitus shook his head. "I can't tell you that, I'm afraid. And it won't do you any good to look for her. There are hundreds of uninhabited rocks along this coastline, every one of them riddled with caves where a person can be hidden indefinitely. Go back to the Temple, young Amazon, and find that magic Stone of yours. I, or one of my men, will keep watch here every night. But don't go telling the Satrap, will you? Because if soldiers start sniffing around up here, you'll not know where to find us when the time comes, and your sister will suffer for it."

As Lysippe listened with a mixture of hope and frustration, a pebble rattled on the hillside behind them. The Commander's men stopped chuckling and whipped out their swords. A ragged group of men armed with new spears raced, puffing, into the ruin. Their leader glared at Lysippe with his cold, blue eyes. He was not wearing his helmet, and his silver hair was stuck to his head with sweat. She suppressed a shudder. She wasn't really surprised to see the Alchemist, only surprised he'd taken so long to find her.

"She rode her horse through the barley!" the Alchemist said. "Got past us somehow. It won't happen again."

Cleitus held up a hand, and his men sheathed their weapons. "I wondered what you were up to, Alchemist." He sniffed the newcomers' breath and his look turned cold. "Your men found some unwatered wine, did they? I thought you were supposed to be keeping watch on the

Temple so you could escort the girl here when she emerged with the Stone? My Queen didn't give you good Macedonian gold to fund the drinking habits of your private army."

The Alchemist transferred his glare to the Commander. "What I do with your Queen's gold is my own affair. It's a Festival. The wine's free. People have been going in and out all night. How are we supposed to notice one scruffy slave sneak out?"

Cleitus looked at Lysippe in amusement. "Hardly sneaked, I think. Fortunately, the girl isn't the sort to run from her problems. But in future, keep a better watch. I'm sure I don't have to remind you this 'scruffy slave' is the only one who can safely touch the Stone we're both looking for. It would be most inconvenient if she were suddenly to decide to run off into the mountains before she found the real Stone. The one she brought me tonight is no good to my Queen, but it might hire you a man who can keep his eyes open." He jerked his head, and the Macedonian soldier who had retrieved Lysippe's bead presented it to the Alchemist with a little leer.

The Alchemist's fist clenched around the amber, and his fingers twitched towards the pouch at his belt, but he contented himself with another glower at Lysippe. Though she was insulted by the suggestion that she might abandon her sister, the Macedonian Commander went up several notches in her eyes.

Cleitus looked up at her and said softly, "I'm afraid you'll have to go back with the Alchemist. I can't risk being recognized in Ephesos. But I look forward to our next meeting, young Amazon." His gaze held hers a moment, before he cast another disgusted look at the Alchemist and beckoned to his men. The Macedonians scuffed out their fire and melted into the night like ghosts.

Lysippe swung Northwind round and aimed her arrow at the Alchemist. "Stay away from me! If you touch me, I'll put this in your eye."

The Alchemist took a surprised step backwards. Then he laughed. "No, you won't. I know you can't bring yourself to hurt living things." He flicked a finger, and his men closed in.

Lysippe's hands trembled. *He tried to kill Tanais*, she told herself. *He used his foul powders on my mother.* But still she could not make herself do it. Her eyes filled in frustration.

While she hesitated, the Alchemist stepped forward and, with a movement so swift Lysippe barely saw it coming, snatched the bow and arrow from her hand. She tried to hold on to the weapon, but the shield hampered her. With a cold smile, the Alchemist snapped the beautiful bow across his knee and tossed the broken pieces into the ashes of the Macedonians' fire.

Lysippe whipped out another arrow and pointed it at him. "Stay away! I mean it!"

The Alchemist shook his head. "You Amazons are so predictable. But don't worry, I'm not going to hurt you, at least not tonight. You haven't completed your task yet."

"You hurt Tanais! And my mother!"

The blue eyes glittered. "So, the Commander told you about that, did he? Did he tell you what I did to her?"

"She escaped! She's coming to get her revenge!"

The Alchemist laughed. "Oh, I don't think so. She taunted me about not being able to go out in the sun without my helmet, so I made sure she'd never see the sun again."

"That's a lie!"

Lysippe threw the arrow in a fit of fury, but the Alchemist stepped out of range and laughed again. "Did you really think the Commander would fall for your little trick? At least you could have done some research first and chosen a stone that looked the part! This old bit of amber wouldn't fool anyone." He tossed the bead Cleitus had given him into the fire on top of the broken bow.

Lysippe was looking for a gap between the spears so she could make her escape, but his words made her pause. "It was you," she whispered, her hatred for the man increasing. "You're Hero's old master, aren't you? The one who made him copy things?"

The lashless eyes glittered. "Why do you think I went chasing all the way out into the wilds after him? He's far too valuable to lose as a runaway."

"I'll tell the Megabyxos."

"You do that, and I'll tell him you're planning on stealing his Sanctuary Stone. Then he'll throw you out of the Temple, and you'll never see your sister or your mother again. Now then, let's be sensible, shall we? Hand over that shield and get down off your horse, and I might let you walk back to the Temple rather than have you dragged back like a slave." He glanced at one of his men, and there was a clank behind her.

With a chill of horror, Lysippe realized they'd brought manacles for her. Her head whirled. She raised the shield and dug her heels into Northwind's sides with a choked cry. The shrine blurred. She expected the Alchemist to throw his illusion-powder and order his men to stop her. But as she rode through them, they looked round in confusion, their spears wavering. The Alchemist himself was staring at the spot where she and Northwind had been a moment before. He looked as if he were trying to see someone dressed in dark clothing lurking in a shadow.

Lysippe didn't stop to think about it. Shivering with reaction, she galloped Northwind back along the Sacred Way and didn't stop until she was safely inside the Temple gates.

Smyrna speaks...

Another surprise! The child has managed to use the gryphon-shield of her tribe to turn the gaze of mortals. What is more, she seems to have stumbled upon this skill by accident with no instruction from her mother in the usual way. I suspect, however, that her mother had no idea how to use the shield for such a purpose. Had she possessed the ancient knowledge, she and her tribe would not have been so easily captured.

So, a lost skill of the Amazons has been restored! I don't know whether to rejoice or weep. Certainly, I must be on my guard. For if the child should discover the truth about the gryphons in the same way she discovered how to use the shield, I anticipate difficulty persuading her to do as I ask.

It is said that great need can sometimes awaken dormant powers in those who have the pure blood, and the abduction of her sister seems to have been the catalyst for this. An unfortunate development, yet one which I might be able to use to my advantage. I must ask my sisters in the ocean where the girl is being kept. That knowledge may be a useful bargaining tool the next time the young one and I meet.

Chapter 12

SHIELD
I searched my nature.

There were many sore heads the morning after Artemis' Birthday. The Megabyxos remained in his rooms; reluctant priests and priestesses went about their dawn chores, groaning softly; even Hero was allowed to sleep, exhausted after the night he'd spent copying the entire philosopher's scroll from memory. Annyla was still resting in the Blood House, and the guard at the door refused to let Lysippe in at such an early hour, saying Melissa Aspasia had left orders that the novices and younger refugees were to spend the morning in their beds. Too tired to argue, Lysippe re-installed Northwind in the altar court, rubbed him down with a handful of straw, and crept back into the Novices' Sleeping House. She hid the gryphon-shield under her blanket and lay staring at the ceiling, replaying the encounter with Commander Cleitus and the Alchemist over in her head.

She planned to creep out again as soon as the guard changed. But, worried as she was about Tanais, the strain of the previous day and night caught up with her. Before the sun touched the beehives on the Sacred Hill, she was asleep.

When she woke that afternoon, the Temple had returned to its normal routine. She went straight to the Blood House, but Annyla wasn't there and the Melissae shooed her out again. She eventually tracked down her friend in the Temple with the other young priestesses, helping to remove the dead flowers and tidy up after the party.

As soon as she saw Lysippe, Annyla dropped the garland she'd been unwinding from a column and rushed across with a choked cry. "Lysippe! Are you all right? They told me you were sleeping and I wasn't to disturb you. I know about your sister – we all think it's terrible, the way the Megabyxos let the Macedonians sail away with her like that!"

Two of the other girls ventured across and gave Lysippe hesitant smiles. "We're sorry," mumbled the eldest. "But we really thought she was dead and we didn't know what to do... we'd never have let them take her, otherwise."

The other girl's eyes filled with tears. With her golden ringlets, she reminded Lysippe of an older version of Timareta. "Your poor sister! She was so badly hurt, and now she hasn't even got Melissa Aspasia to look after her. Those barbarians will never keep her alive."

"Shh!" said the older girl, giving her a dig in the ribs. These two had been on duty in the Blood House yesterday, Lysippe realized. A true Amazon would have killed them before they got as far as apologizing. "It wasn't your fault," she said firmly. "It was the Alchemist's doing. Tanais isn't going to die. I'm going to find her before then."

She watched Annyla. But apart from touching her throat at the mention of the Alchemist, she seemed recovered from her scare. Lysippe pulled her away from the others and told her in whispers about her midnight meeting with Commander Cleitus in the shrine and how she'd escaped the Alchemist afterwards.

Annyla's eyes widened. "You went to Androklos' Shrine? Alone at night?"

"Not alone. I had Northwind – and Mother's gryphon-shield."

"But he's only a horse!" Annyla was not impressed by her mention of the shield. "That place is evil, Lysippe. It's haunted by the ghost of a flying lion, and bad things happen to people who see it – the last time the ghost appeared, a ship was wrecked on the rocks beyond the headland and everyone on board drowned. The Alchemist might have killed you... or worse." She touched her throat again and shuddered.

Lysippe forced a smile. "The Alchemist won't try anything until we find the Stone. He's supposed to be keeping watch on the Temple to make sure I don't run away before then, that's all. Commander Cleitus was

furious he'd let me get past him. Besides, lions don't fly."
But even as she spoke, she thought of the gryphon
design on her mother's shield, wings spread either side of
its lion's body. "There's something I want to show you,"
she went on quickly. "And we need to look at those
tablets Hero copied. When can you get away?"

She thought her friend might refuse to help once she
heard the Stone would have to be sent across the sea in
exchange for Tanais' life. But Annyla said of course they
must continue looking for it. They didn't have any
choice now that Tanais was in danger. So they agreed to
meet in the altar court at dusk.

While she was waiting for Annyla to finish her duties,
Lysippe collected the shield from its hiding place and
went to check on Northwind. She'd been hoping for
some time alone to think. But Hero was mucking out the
stalls the oxen had dirtied before the sacrifice.

She paused to collect her thoughts, marched into the
court and caught the boy's arm. "Why didn't you tell me
the Alchemist was your old master?"

Hero swung round, his pitchfork raised like a
weapon. Reflexively, Lysippe ducked behind the shield,
and the boy peered past her in much the same way as the
Alchemist had done. Lysippe lowered the shield again,
her skin prickling.

"Don't creep up on me like that!" Hero gave her a
defensive, black-eyed stare. "Who told you?"

"He told me himself!" She explained where she'd
been last night. "That's why you were with him on the

river bank when I went to look for Northwind, isn't it? You're copying stuff for him again."

The boy shrugged. "So what? Don't make no difference to you."

"Yes, it does. He's supposed to be working for the Macedonians now, but I'm sure he's planning to cheat them somehow. I think Queen Olympias has Amazon blood, and that's why she wants to get her hands on the Stone. Be careful, Hero. You'll only get caught in the middle again, and you're bound to come off worst."

"Wouldn't count on it," Hero muttered, forking straw viciously at the wall.

There was a short silence. Lysippe frowned, unable to work out why the boy was so hostile. "What did you do with the tablets you wrote?" she asked, changing the subject. "I hope you didn't leave them in the priests' quarters. If the Megabyxos recognizes the philosopher's work, he might use it as an excuse to throw you out of the Temple."

"I'm not that stupid!" Hero's scowl deepened. He wiped the hair from his eyes and pointed to Northwind's stall. "I hid them in your horse's bed, in the corner where it's mucky. The priests of Artemis like to keep their hands clean, and the Melissae are far too busy to come in here. No one'll find 'em, don't worry."

They eyed each other warily.

"Thank you," Lysippe said.

"For what?"

"Copying the riddles."

Hero shrugged and forked another heap of dirty straw out of the stall. "You still need someone to read 'em. Don't make no sense to me."

"Annyla's coming down here tonight."

The boy didn't comment, but kept an eye on her lips as he worked.

"I'd like you to be there. I want to show you something."

Hero gave her a level stare across his fork. "Thought you didn't trust me?"

"You'd only spy on us, anyway, and three heads are better than two. Will you help us, Hero? Please?"

The boy muttered something about having quite enough to do without bending his brains over some stupid philosopher's riddles. But she saw him grin as he bent back to his task.

When she raised her mother's gryphon-shield in the shadows of the altar court that evening, Lysippe had an audience of three – Annyla, Hero and her horse. She watched their eyes unfocus, blink, and focus on her again with puzzled expressions. Northwind snorted and flared his nostrils at the shield as he'd done last night. Annyla frowned as she looked round the court, then at Lysippe. Hero was the first to accept what she'd done.

He whistled, impressed. "So *that's* how you got past the Alchemist! The shield makes you vanish, just like an alchemy trick! How d'you do it? Is there some sort of special powder worked into the design?" He ran his fingernail over the dirty black and gold paint.

Lysippe hugged the shield protectively. "I don't know how it happens. I didn't even realize what I was doing at first – I just needed it to hide me, and somehow it did. But this is our tribal shield, passed down from mother to daughter for generations. It's supposed to have ancient powers. Mother used it to summon an oread back in the cave at Themiscyra..." She faltered, then rushed on. "So maybe I can use it to summon Smyrna again. At least I know I can use the shield to get out of the Sleeping House and hide from the Alchemist and his men. I'm going to go to the river and ask Smyrna to find out where Tanais has been taken."

"I'm not sure that's such a good idea, Lysippe." Annyla was still frowning at the shield. "It's like you blur round the edges, and you did sort of vanish for a moment. But once I knew where to look, I could see you again. Maybe it's like the trick the Megabyxos does with the goddess' statue and the angle of the sun, only in reverse? If you move too far, you become visible again."

Hero nodded. "If the shield's as old as you say, there's probably not much powder, or whatever, left on it. I wouldn't count on it hidin' you from the Alchemist – he knows about such tricks, remember?"

Lysippe shook her head. "It's not alchemy. I think it's the power of the gryphon."

Hero and Annyla exchanged a glance. But they couldn't deny that Lysippe had somehow managed to make herself invisible, at least for a moment. And the vanishing trick didn't work when Hero or Annyla tried holding the shield, so it did seem to be an Amazon skill like the healing-sleep. Now she was certain the shield worked, Lysippe wanted to go to the river at once. But the other two counselled caution.

"We haven't looked at the philosopher's riddles yet," Annyla said. "Even if the naiad tells you where Tanais has been taken, we still need to find the Stone so we can heal her. Didn't you say Smyrna wanted the Stone for herself? She might not *want* to help."

Hero nodded. "And it sounds like the Alchemist used the Macedonian gold to hire mercenaries and buy weapons. He's bound to have 'em posted out there, watchin' the river bank, 'specially after you sneaked past him before."

"They won't see me. I've got the shield, remember?"

"They'll see the naiad's lights," Hero said darkly. "We all saw them last time. Then they'll see you, and the Alchemist don't like people who make fools of him. I know. Want another look at my back?"

Lysippe gripped the shield tighter. She was worried enough about summoning the naiad again, without her friends trying to talk her out of it. "I'm going, all right?" she said firmly. "Tonight, after we've discovered where the Stone's hidden. Then I'll have something to bargain with, and Smyrna will have to help us."

But solving the philosopher's riddles proved more complicated than they'd thought. The three friends spent evening after evening in Northwind's stall, using the dusk-hour between supper and bedtime to examine the writings Hero had copied. The tablets had a soft, beeswax surface designed so students could easily correct their mistakes. Hero used the flat end of his stylus to erase any text they decided was no help, leaving only the parts that seemed to refer to the Temple or to magic. Annyla said they shouldn't rub out any of it, but Hero was firm. "You got to get rid of the unimportant bits so you can see the whole thing," he said. "An' you got to trust your head to fill in the detail afterwards. That's how I remember stuff. If I tried to memorize the whole lot right down to the last tiny squiggle, I'd forget where I'd started long before I got to the end." Lysippe and Annyla were still doubtful. But Hero said he could just as easily replace the bits they'd rubbed out if they decided they needed them later on, so they let him do what he wanted. It made them feel like they were getting somewhere as the long, warm days of Thargelion gave way to the sticky summer month of Skeroforion.

After their meetings Lysippe lay awake, sweating in the heat, thinking of all the places where the Stone might be hidden. Each morning, she'd leap out of bed with a new theory – only to have her hopes dashed when she hurried to that part of the Temple and found nothing. She crept into the inner sanctuary time after time, remembering what had happened when Annyla had first taken her to see Artemis' statue and its guardian gryphons. But although she sometimes experienced the same dizziness in the inner room when she approached the statue, the whispers didn't return. The amber bead she'd prised out of its setting had been replaced, its theft put down to high spirits during the festival, as were presumably the missing bow and the arrows out of the quiver.

She grew more and more worried about Tanais. The Queen would give birth soon, and then Commander Cleitus would get impatient. She knew she couldn't put off her visit to the naiad much longer, but Hero proved correct about the Alchemist's men. They patrolled the river bank openly, wearing cast-off Greek helmets like the Alchemist's, fitted with blue crests as if they were soldiers in a real army. Every time the Megabyxos sent out the Temple guards to chase them away, they returned in greater numbers and lined up along the wall, hands on their sword hilts, staring in a threatening manner. The Satrap grew nervous and requested military support from Persia. But the Emperor was in far-off Babylon. Messengers took a month to reach him and another month to return, and no soldiers arrived. Hero said darkly that messengers could disappear just as easily as other people, but Lysippe had too many other things on her mind to care. All she knew was that the Satrap had confiscated their scroll when they'd needed it most, and the interview he'd insisted upon that terrible day had prevented them from stopping the Macedonian Queen setting sail with Tanais.

Every day, Lysippe felt sure they must be closer to discovering the secret of where the Stone was hidden.

Yet even when Hero had rubbed out most of what he had written, the riddles became no clearer. Most of the fragments that remained mentioned alchemy and the properties of fire, and she began to suspect Hero wasn't trying to find the Stone at all, but instead working on something else his master had told him to investigate.

Finally, unable to bear the terrible uncertainty any longer, Lysippe waited for a cloudy night and feigned sleep until Annyla's breathing slowed and deepened. She slipped off her pallet, held the shield behind her back, and gave the guard on the door the usual excuse. He was suspicious this time and watched her closely. But as soon as she was outside, she raised the shield and darted past him.

She ran straight for the courtyard wall and scrambled over. One of the Alchemist's men sat on a rock nearby, spitting out the pips of an orange. His spear lay on the ground beside him and his blue-crested helmet was balanced on top. Keeping the shield high, Lysippe crept past him and made for the ford.

She waded into the water, wincing at the cold around her thighs, and whistled as she would for her horse. "Smyrna!" she called softly. "I have to talk to you."

She waited, shivering as she watched the man on the bank. The shield might hide her from his eyes, but he'd hear if she splashed or called too loudly. The clouds parted, and the moon turned the water pale silver and picked out the hives on the Sacred Hill. The Alchemist's man got up and stretched. Another helmeted man came along the bank and exchanged a few words with his comrade. They both laughed.

Lysippe took advantage of the distraction to call again. "Smyrna! I have the gryphon-shield! I command you to come!" Her teeth chattered. The water rippled past her. A large fish with a golden crescent on its head slipped between her ankles, making her skin twitch. But no naiad sparkled into sight.

"Please, Smyrna... The Macedonians took my sister to an island somewhere near here! Please ask the oceanids where she is."

She waited until the sky paled over the eastern mountains and her arm grew so tired she could hardly keep the shield high enough to hide her from the man who'd taken over the watch. But the only sign that the river was haunted was the briefest of glitters at the corner of her eye as she gave up and waded back to the bank.

She froze, staring at the spot. But the glitter had already gone. Annyla was right. Smyrna obviously wasn't going to help.

She barely had the strength to crawl back over the wall. Still shivering, she crept back into the Sleeping House and pulled her blanket over her head. It took her a long time to get warm.

The dark shadows under Lysippe's eyes the next morning did not go unnoticed, and she'd developed a chill that made her sneeze. Melissa Aspasia whisked her off to the Blood House. She assured her that a Temple messenger had been sent to Pella to negotiate the release of her sister and said she must be patient and try not to worry so.

Lysippe thought of what Hero had said about messengers going missing. Then she thought of Tanais, dying alone on some island before they could find the Stone, and started shivering again. She wanted to ask Melissa Aspasia so many things. How someone could have a god as a father, why Amazons transformed into nymphs when other people simply died, whether Tanais was enough Amazon to transform, and what would happen to her if she did... But when she tried to speak, the questions came out in a muddle, all mixed up in her head with the Macedonian Queen and her unborn son who was also supposed to have a god as a father. "She's an Amazon too, isn't she?" Lysippe rambled. "She's got yellow eyes like me, and she lay with a god like Mother, but she didn't know about the shield! I have to summon the naiad..."

Aspasia shook her head and summoned another Melissa. Between them, they made Lysippe swallow a potion that smelled suspiciously like the one they'd given Annyla. Then Melissa Aspasia put Lysippe to bed in the Blood House and stroked her damp hair until she stopped sneezing and fell into an exhausted sleep.

After that episode, Lysippe found her days filled with light duties about the Temple and its grounds. She topped up the oil in the Temple lamps, garlanded statues in fresh flowers, fetched water from the fountain, gutted the fish the priests brought back from the rivers and the sea, melted beeswax to make candles, and completed a thousand other small tasks that kept her nearly as busy as the Melissae themselves. She was glad of the work, because it stopped her dwelling on her failure to summon the naiad or thinking too much about what might be happening to Tanais.

She managed some more rational conversations with Melissa Aspasia about Amazons, but the priestess seemed far more interested in the healing-sleep and how it might help her other patients, than in the truth about Lysippe's father. She took samples of Lysippe's hair, nails, saliva and blood, and went off thoughtfully to test them. Meanwhile, Lysippe, Annyla and Hero continued to meet every evening to discuss the riddles, and Lysippe consoled herself with thoughts of how, once they found the Stone, she'd use it to *make* Smyrna tell her where Tanais was.

The barley was harvested by the sickle-wielding citizens of Ephesos, and fresh straw cut from the stalks and left to turn gold in the sun. But still the answer to the riddles evaded them. Then, one hot, airless afternoon, Lysippe was in the priests' complex helping pour hot wax into moulds to make candles. On her way out of the workroom, she accidentally knocked over an unset mould. The wax dripped into the brazier and fizzled into flame on the hot coals. As the priests jumped up to put the fire out, Lysippe's head blazed. She rushed out of the complex, ignoring the priests who laughingly called after her that she'd burn the place down if she wasn't careful, and raced to the altar court.

"What's wrong?" Hero said, looking up from his work. "Is there news of your sister...?"

"Fire!" Lysippe gasped. "You were right, Hero! The philosopher's scroll had it right, all that stuff about fire and transformation. That's what must have made them whisper!"

"What are you talkin' about?" Hero frowned at her. "You're not coming down with another fever, are you? Your eyes have gone strange..."

Lysippe shook her head wildly. "No! I'm fine. The statues I heard in the sanctuary! The gryphons!"

She turned excitedly to Annyla, who had run into the altar court after her, alerted by the shouting. "That's what happened the first time you took me to see the goddess, don't you remember? I knocked over the candles, and her robe caught alight! That's when I thought I heard the gryphons whispering to me. I kept going back to listen, but it's usually so cool inside the Temple even on hot days like this, and the whispers never came back. I thought I'd imagined them, but what if I didn't? I want to try lighting another fire in there."

Hero laughed. "Whisperin' statues? And I thought there was somethin' wrong with *my* ears!"

But Annyla's expression was serious. "You can't light a fire inside the Temple of Artemis, Lysippe! Even if you did hear the gryphon statues whispering, how's that going to help us find the Stone?"

"Don't you see? I'm sure they were trying to tell me something last time – and Smyrna told me not to let the Stone get hot! What if she only said that to make sure I wouldn't learn how to use it before I gave it to her? The gryphon statues and the Stone must be connected somehow. What if they were giving me instructions? The whispers were soft last time, but we only had a tiny fire. Maybe if we make the statue hot enough, I'll be able to hear what they're saying." She eyed the other two, suddenly aware what a big thing she was asking of them. "It's worth a try, isn't it? We could take off the goddess' robes and jewels, replace them with some old sacking... and we can have some water ready to put the fire out afterwards. If we do it at night, there'll be no one in the Temple except the Megabyxos, and he'll be asleep in his room. I can use my shield to hide us."

"Even if no one notices the fire, it'll stink of smoke afterwards," Annyla protested.

"The Temple's always full of smoke! We'll just have to light lots of incense the next the morning to mask the smell, and pretend we lit too much by mistake. Please Annyla, I'm sure it'll work."

Hero broke into a slow grin. "With any luck, the Megabyxos will choke. Serve him right for lettin' the Macedonians take Tanais! We'll have to wrap our faces, though, so we don't pass out ourselves while we're in there."

Annyla frowned at him. "You're not coming with us, Hero."

"Just try an' stop me."

"But you're bound to get blamed for the fire, if someone sees you in the Temple!"

Hero gave her an amused look. "I do believe you care about me, my sweet Melissa."

Annyla blushed.

Before Lysippe could wonder at her reaction, Hero chuckled and went on, "You can't get a proper fire goin' with just the heat off your face, you know! You'll need oil and alchemist's powders to make it really hot. And if you don't know what you're doin', you'll burn the whole place down. I know how to do it so it'll be safe, and I know how to put it out again, after. It'll take me a day or two to get the stuff, though." He thought for a moment and lowered his voice. "How about we wait till the dark of the moon? I've a feeling Lysippe's magic shield's goin' to need a bit of help to hide what we're up to this time!"

Chapter 13

FIRE

All things equally exchange for fire,
as does fire for all things.

The inner sanctuary of the Temple was spooky at night. Shadows moved when Annyla swung her lantern around, making Lysippe jump. The panes of glass in the roof high above Artemis' statue were dark, and not a glimmer of starlight shone through the clouds to touch her crown. The three friends moved swiftly, stripping off the goddess' fine robes and jewels, replacing them with the sacks they had brought from the storerooms – first a wet layer, then a dry one. This gave Lysippe her first clear view of the animals carved into the statue itself. On the goddess' legs and breast and all around her shoulders, tiny marble bees, gryphons, lions and stags fought for space. The two large gryphons that flanked her watched the process with their amber eyes, making Lysippe's hands sweat.

With the shield to hide them, it had been easy to slip out of the Sleeping House and creep past the guards into the Temple. Hero had met them inside, and they'd swiftly collected the things they needed from the hiding place in the roof where Hero had stored them earlier. But now they were actually standing before the goddess, the fire no longer seemed such a good idea. What if she'd imagined the whispers? That would be bad enough. What really worried Lysippe, though, was the possibility Smyrna's warning might be genuine. What if the Stone lost its power when it got hot?

As she stared at the gryphons in an agony of indecision, Annyla carefully folded Artemis' robes and took them outside the door. "Lysippe!" she hissed, coming back in to find her still standing there. "We've got to get a move on!"

Lysippe pushed her doubts to the back of her mind and helped the girl soak strips of linen from the large hydria they'd filled at the fountain that morning and smuggled into the sanctuary. Her hands shook, and she kept wasting water. Hero whistled softly to himself as he moved around the statue, pouring his mixture of oil and secret alchemist powders over the outer sacking. He seemed to be the only one enjoying himself. They moved the goddess' offerings to a safe distance, and finally everything was ready.

They stood in the middle of the cleared marble floor, holding their strips of wet linen and staring at each other.

"Wind's getting up," Hero whispered. "We ought to

shut the doors. Otherwise there'll be a draught, and the fire might get out of hand."

Annyla closed them softly, looked at Lysippe and bit her lip. "Well... this is it. Good luck."

Lysippe eyed the stone gryphons. "I don't need luck. Either they'll speak to me, or they won't."

"Just remember to ask 'em where the Stone is," Hero said. "Or all this will be a waste of time." Grimly, he tied the wet linen over his mouth and nose and touched the lantern flame to a corner of the sacking. There was a bright green fizzle, and then fire leapt up the goddess' legs so swiftly and violently that Lysippe and Annyla staggered backwards to escape the sudden heat.

Hero took Annyla's hand and pulled her to the back of the sanctuary. Smoke was pooling under the glass roof. Legs trembling, Lysippe swiftly wound her own strip of wet linen over her face and perched on the bench before the statue. The fire was hot against her cheeks and lit the goddess' serene face with a flickering orange glow. But Hero actually did seem to know what he was doing, and the flames showed no sign of spreading. She stared at the gryphons expectantly.

"Talk to me," she willed. "Tell me where Smyrna's Stone is hidden! Tell me how to heal Tanais!"

There was a noise outside the doors. Annyla and Hero looked round nervously. But Lysippe forgot everything else as the whispers came again.

She leant forward, shivering with excitement. The whispers were louder than last time, yet she still couldn't quite make out any words. Still staring at the gryphons, she rose from the bench and crept forwards into the smoke and the heat.

"Careful, Lysippe—!" Annyla called.

Her warning turned into a scream as the doors to the inner sanctuary burst open with a great crash. Wind whirled through the room, catching the flames and sending them up to the roof in a roaring, flaring column. The glass shattered, and Lysippe staggered backwards as glittering fragments rained down through the smoke. She was vaguely aware of other bodies in the sanctuary, but dared not take her eyes off the statue.

"No, you idiots!" Hero shouted behind her, his voice muffled behind his linen bandage. "Shut the doors! Get more water!" There was a scuffle at the back of the room and the sound of a jar shattering. Water splashed over the feet of the goddess, sizzling on the hot marble.

Another glass panel shattered. The wind, with a clear passage through the sanctuary, fanned the flames even higher, and one of the gallery rails overhead started to smoulder. Lysippe's head spun. She felt faint with the heat, the smoke, and the whispers that filled her head but still made no sense.

Annyla screamed again. Lysippe turned in time to see more Temple guards burst through the doors. Two of them held a struggling Hero. Another guard was trying to drag Annyla out of the sanctuary, while she fought to reach the hydria.

"We have to put the fire out!" Annyla sobbed. "Let

Herostratus go – he knows how!"

"Don't be silly!" the guard prised her fingers off the handles. "Come out of the way, and let the priests deal with it."

Outside, someone was blowing the bronze horns, over and over again, into the night. Bleary-eyed priests and priestesses, still in their sleeping clothes, were running through the columns, shouting. Through the open doors of the sanctuary, Lysippe saw them snatch up Temple treasures and stagger outside again. A few of them tried to get up to the roof, but the beams had caught and most of the wooden gallery was on fire. The old cedar staircase in the middle of the Temple was acting like a vast chimney. Others raced into the sanctuary and beat at the goddess' flaming robes with curtains they'd hastily torn down in an attempt to stop the fire spreading. They pushed Lysippe aside and yelled at her to get out before she got hurt. The men who'd caught Hero dragged the boy away and pushed him roughly against the wall at the back of the room.

"You're in real trouble now, Herostratus!" one of them shouted, coughing with the smoke. He pulled off the boy's linen mask and brandished it before his eyes. "Did you think this would save you? It's evidence this fire was no accident! You started it on purpose, didn't you? *Didn't you?*"

Hero didn't waste time protesting his innocence. "Shut the door!" he yelled hoarsely. "You're making it worse—"

"Shut your mouth!" the Temple guard yelled back, and thumped him to reinforce his order. Hero grunted and spat out a bloody tooth.

Dizzy, Lysippe crouched in the midst of the running, yelling people. The whispers were growing louder all the time, but she still couldn't hear what they were saying.

"Where's the Gryphon Stone?" she shouted. "You have to tell me where the Stone is hidden!" With an effort, she ignored the confusion around her and seized her shield from its safe place by the wall. "I'm the last Amazon! I hold the gryphon-shield! I command you!"

There was laughter in her head, like wings beating. Then a small, sly hiss: *Here.*

Lysippe froze. The word hadn't seemed to come from either of the gryphon statues, but from the goddess' legs which were now completely wreathed in flame. She pulled her mask higher, raised the shield to protect herself from the heat, and edged closer to the fire.

A priest almost knocked her over. "Everyone out!" He yelled. "We're going to lose the statue – LOOK OUT!"

People scattered as Artemis' statue split from toe to crown with a *CRACK* that shook the very Temple foundations. A splinter flew out of the heart of the fire and struck Lysippe above her right eye in an explosion of light and pain. She staggered backwards, tripped over the bench and sprawled amidst fragments of glass and burning stone. The shield was knocked from her arm and skittered across the floor. People were screaming all around her. The paint on the gryphons' wings peeled off in flaming flakes, and their eyes burned as if they were alive. The goddess' golden hands were melting. Very slowly, the flaming statue, her arms still outstretched, toppled towards her.

"Run, Lysippe!" Hero yelled from the door, where the guards were dragging him out.

Dazed, Lysippe blinked up at the falling goddess. As the statue toppled, a perfectly-round, black and gold stone, the size of a baby's head, rolled out through the crack from a hollow place inside the goddess' legs and bounced on the marble floor in front of her.

Move. The whisper came from the stone.

Suddenly, Lysippe realized the danger she was in. Her heart pounded in terror, and she rolled aside. The statue crashed in a great spray of sparks and debris where she'd been lying only moments before.

She staggered up, coughing, half blinded by smoke, and ripped the linen from her face. It was almost dry, but she wrapped it around her hands and plunged them into the flames where she'd seen the Stone roll – only to stagger backwards again when something darted between them, so fast it was a blur, and disappeared up the column of flame. Whatever it was – a bee? some kind of bird? – emerged from the top in a fountain of sparks and flew wildly around the roof, trailing fierce flames that caused beams to explode and collapse behind it. Then it found the broken glass in the roof and escaped into the darkness. As Lysippe stared after the burning creature, trying to make her smoke-blind eyes focus properly, something dark and heavy was thrown over her from behind and strong arms dragged her backwards.

"No!" she protested, struggling to reach the Stone she'd glimpsed in the heart of the fire. "Let me go! The Stone, my shield—" It was no good. Her strength had left her. The heavy thing over her head was a wet curtain. As she staggered under its weight, the arms gathered her up in a bundle. She was vaguely aware of being thrown over someone's shoulder and carried at a run through the terrible heat and smoke, out into the night.

Her rescuer dropped her, none too gently, in the courtyard and rolled her a few times to put out the last of the flames. Then he pulled back the curtain to let her breathe. Lysippe lay on her back, gasping. She realized the horrible smell of burnt hair was coming from her own head. Previously unnoticed scalds all over her body began to sting as the cool air touched them. Clouds raced across the sky, lit from below by the flickering orange glow. The wind had torn them into rags, but the stars were dimmed by the light of the fire. The entire Temple of Artemis was ablaze. It seemed impossible anyone could have got out alive. The Novices' Sleeping House was burning as well, also one side of the priests' complex. Priestesses with soot-smudged faces were throwing water at the Blood House walls, while others staggered out of the door with patients on litters, which they placed in rows in the open at a safer distance from the flames.

Lysippe's limbs were already heavy with the onset of the healing-sleep. She saw Hero being supported towards the gates by two of the guards. The boy's hands had been tied behind him, though he looked overcome by smoke and wasn't fighting them. She hoped Annyla had got out safely. Then a wild, panicked neigh sounded between the horn blasts, and she fought off her lethargy in sudden fear for her horse.

Over the altar court hovered the flaming, bird-like creature that had flown out of the Temple. It left a trail of flame and destruction everywhere it went. It dropped behind the altar walls, and a coil of smoke rose from within. Northwind gave another wild neigh of fright. Lysippe remembered all the fresh straw she and Hero had shaken up for the horse earlier that evening, and made a valiant effort to stand.

"Stay there!" snapped her rescuer, and something sharp pushed her back down.

Lysippe looked to see what it was. To her surprise, a spear was pointed at her breast. "But my horse... Northwind's still in the altar court! He'll burn!"

"You should have thought of that before you and your friends set fire to the Temple, shouldn't you?" The guard's voice was cold. She blinked at him and recognized the man who stood outside the Sleeping House at night. The one she'd tricked so many times.

"Please!" she cried, coughing up more black ash.

"There's something in there that sets things on fire! It came out of the goddess' statue. Where are they taking Hero? Tell him he's got to get my horse out... We never meant it to burn like that, it was that creature... I think it's evil!"

"The only evil thing in there is whoever started that fire," the guard said. But his tone softened slightly as she coughed again. "Smoke makes people see strange things. Lie down. You're badly burned. The Melissae will attend to you in due course."

"You've got to help Northwind!" Again, Lysippe fought the healing-sleep and tried to stand. Again, the guard pushed her back. She wet her cracked lips and attempted a whistle. Everything was spinning now.

There was another neigh, followed by the rattle of hooves on stone, and suddenly her horse was there. She had a glimpse of Northwind's legs and his belly, dark with sweat, as he reared over her. The guard ducked with a surprised shout. She thought at first the horse was attacking him. Then she saw the flames in the sky above Northwind's snapping teeth and had her first clear view of the creature that had escaped from the statue.

Its wings were covered in fluffy blue and red feathers. It had the head of an eagle and the body of a miniature lion-cub, and its black fur shone gold at the ends as if it had been dipped in paint. A tiny lion's tail lashed the air, leaving a trail of flames that were fanned by its frantic wing beats. Scarlet claws protruded from oversized paws, and its eyes were yellow like Lysippe's own. It emitted high shrieks as it swooped and dived. It seemed bigger than it had inside the Temple, but it was still only about the size of a large crow.

Some of her fear dissipated. "Gryphon!" Lysippe whispered, watching the creature make an enthusiastic but ineffectual swipe at Northwind's ears. The horse reared again and struck out with his forehooves. The little gryphon beat its wings wildly and circled higher, shrieking again. Small as the creature was, her horse was clearly terrified. The guard, however, seemed unable to see the gryphon, and thought the horse was simply afraid of the fire. "Get out of here, you stupid animal!" he shouted, giving Northwind a whack across the quarters with his spear shaft. A few of the people running past paused to wave their arms at the horse, but most of them were too busy fighting the fire and rescuing the Temple treasures to notice the trouble in the corner of the courtyard.

Lysippe raised her head. She was too weary to marvel at the creature from the legends. "Stop it," she croaked. "Leave Northwind alone, and stop setting things on fire!"

To her surprise, the gryphon back-winged and fixed her with one of its yellow eyes. *What do now?* it whispered.

"I don't know... go dip your tail in the sea."

The gryphon gave Northwind a final sly swipe with its scarlet claws, and flew off obediently towards the harbour.

"Then go and find my sister!" Lysippe called after it, but her voice was hoarse with smoke, and she didn't know if it had heard.

Northwind came back to earth, trembling. The guard lowered his spear in relief and tried to soothe the horse. Lysippe roused herself a final time. She tried to see if the Alchemist's men were still watching the river bank, but it was impossible to tell with all the panicking crowds trying to stop the fire spreading to the city. "Go," she whispered. "Go to the river." Her horse snorted and trotted off.

Lysippe lay back with a sigh. Had she really spoken to a gryphon? The healing-sleep was creeping up her limbs, taking away the pain of her burns. She realized another man had joined her rescuer. The two spoke in low voices, glancing at her, and the newcomer pointed to the sky over the bay.

The Temple guard grimaced. "You saw Androklos' lion? I think I did, too. Maybe that's why the horse went so crazy. It's an evil night, that's no mistake. We've lost the Temple. This is no childish prank, despite what it looks like. Heads are going to roll for this, you mark my words."

Smyrna speaks...

I warned her! Didn't I warn her not to let the Stone get hot? So what does she do? She sets the Temple on fire! It is my fault. Not only did I underestimate the child, I failed to see her desperate need.

Maybe I should have told her the truth about her sister, that night she came to my river begging me to help her. But I honestly thought it would be best if she didn't know. I was a mother once, and so I sought to protect her from the trials of death and all that follows.

There is no hiding the truth now, though. The gryphon has flown, and it is only a matter of time before the child realizes what has happened. The question is, what will she do next? The power of the gryphon is hers to command. It is a great responsibility for one so young, and she is more alone now than ever before.

Chapter 14

DAMAGE
Good and bad are the same.

Lysippe woke with a terrible sense that something was wrong. She was lying on a reed mat on the floor of a small, empty room, and her hands and arms were swathed in linen bandages. Her head felt strangely light, reminding her of when she'd fallen in a thorn bush back on the steppe as a child, and her mother had cut her hair to free her. She lifted a clumsy fist and struggled to peel off the bandages so she could feel her head, but her fingers were imprisoned under the linen and she could not manage the knots.

She sat up, confused by the aftermath of the healing-sleep, and wrinkled her nose. She was alone and the door was closed, but a bitter smell invaded the room. The sunlight outside the window-hole was dull bronze. Women were talking in subdued voices nearby.

"Don't know how we're expected to work in these

conditions." ... "The goddess only knows what'll happen to us now." ... "Never understand why anyone would want to do such a terrible thing!" ... "Have they questioned the youngsters yet?"

Lysippe's heart gave two violent thumps. She scrambled to her feet and stumbled to the window. The smoking ruins visible in the distance at the foot of the Sacred Hill brought back everything that had happened in a sickening rush. She stared at them in horror.

The room where she'd woken was on the second storey of one of the big city houses close to the agora. But instead of the bustling market she remembered, the citizens of Ephesos and their slaves hung about in little groups under the ash-blackened colonnades, muttering and casting glances at the smoking wasteland near the river where their Temple had stood. Women clustered around the fountain with their hydria, exchanging whispers and tearful hugs instead of their usual gossip. Even the small children playing in the streets seemed subdued. When one of them threw a ball near the ruins, they ran home without trying to get it back. Lysippe could see why. Men wearing helmets with blue crests patrolled the perimeter.

She closed her eyes so she wouldn't have to see any more.

"I hope you're satisfied," said a cold voice behind her. "The Temple burnt to the ground, and took part of Ephesos with it. The barley stubble caught alight and the wind fanned the flames. We were lucky not to lose the whole city. It's a miracle no one was killed. Why did you do it? Was it some kind of twisted revenge for your sister's abduction? Or did you just not approve of our sacrifices?"

Lysippe whirled. Melissa Aspasia stood in the doorway, frowning at her. Soot had turned the priestess's robes grey, and dark circles ringed her eyes. She'd coiled her singed hair up in a scarf.

"I..." Lysippe's throat was sore and dry. "We never meant for it to burn down," she said in a small voice that ended in a coughing fit. She staggered back to the mat and reached for the hydria of water beside it. But the bandages defeated her and she could not grip the handles.

Melissa Aspasia pressed her lips together, took the hydria from her and poured some water into a bowl so she could drink. As Lysippe swallowed gratefully, she saw the terrible betrayal in the priestess's eyes and felt awful.

"I'm sorry," she whispered.

"You're *sorry*? Is that supposed to bring back our Temple and the priceless treasures we lost in the fire? We rescued as many as we could, but the rest are gone for ever. Gone, Lysippe. All those things people dedicated their whole lives to creating and left in the care of their goddess, because they believed she would keep them safe. You've betrayed their trust. Even the bees swarmed from their hives on the hill. They hate smoke. The priests are out on the plain even as we speak, trying to recapture the queens. They wanted to smear you in honey and peg you out there as bait. Their fury's worn off a bit, but at the start it was all I could do to keep them from dragging you out of here while you slept."

Lysippe closed her eyes. "How long have I been asleep?"

"Five days."

"Five days!" She looked out of the window again in despair. "But—"

"It's still smouldering, yes. What did you expect? Fires are a lot easier to start than they are to put out. I thought better of you, Lysippe. We took you and your friends in and gave you sanctuary. I concealed your true nature from the Megabyxos so he wouldn't sell you to the highest bidder. And *this* is how you repay us!" Melissa Aspasia shook her head as she replaced the hydria. She kept hold of the handles with white knuckles, taking deep breaths as if afraid to speak in case the words choked her. Lysippe struggled to think of something else to say, except nothing seemed right.

Finally, Aspasia straightened. "Sit down," she said coldly. "Let's see if your Amazon powers have healed your burns. I dare say they have, from the way you're leaping around – though if there was any justice in the world, you'd suffer as badly as the other poor souls we've been treating in here, screaming from the pain of their burns day and night. None of us have had a wink of sleep. I'd take you to see the results of your handiwork, if I hadn't been instructed to keep you isolated for your own good."

Lysippe hardly heard. Five days ... still smouldering... There was still a chance no one would have found the Stone.

She sat meekly on the mat while Melissa Aspasia unwound her bandages and examined the new, pink skin beneath. There was no pain now, but she remembered how much it had hurt when she'd plunged her hands into the fire.

"Where's Hero and Annyla?" she asked. "Can I see them?"

Melissa Aspasia's lips pressed tight. "No, you can't. You're to stay in this room, and be thankful the Megabyxos left you in my care and didn't hand you over to those idiots out there, fighting over Ephesos as if they had nothing better to do!"

Lysippe's mouth dried as she remembered the soldiers. "Annyla..."

"I'm talking about the boy. As a priestess, Annyla has been dealt with according to Temple Law, though I doubt this business was her idea."

"It wasn't Hero's fault!"

"No? He started the fire, or so he told the Satrap before the fighting broke out – and though I normally wouldn't believe a word that boy says, in this case I think I do."

"No, it was my idea! I..." She hung her head. "I wanted to try something."

Melissa Aspasia stood up and went to the door. "When you've decided to tell the truth, Lysippe, I'll be back to hear it. Until then, don't get any ideas about leaving this room. There are guards outside the door and the window's too small for you to escape through – I checked. I apologize for the lack of a proper bed, but there are more needy cases."

Lysippe's eyes filled. "At least tell me what happened to my horse. And did anyone see a gryphon? Its tail was on fire! That must be why so much of the city burned. I'm sorry, I think I must have summoned it somehow. I didn't mean to, but I was trying to find Smyrna's Stone..." With a great sense of relief, she told Melissa Aspasia everything. How she'd spoken to the naiad in the river, how they'd hoped the fire would make the gryphon statues in the sanctuary speak, and how Queen Olympias wanted the Gryphon Stone in exchange for Tanais' life. "So you see, you have to let me out," she finished. "Otherwise my sister will die."

Melissa Aspasia listened in silence, one hand on the door. When Lysippe had finished, her eyes were still cold. "There are people in here close to death," she said quietly. "The sacred sanctuary of Artemis is destroyed. All Ephesos is in mourning. The Alchemist has taken advantage of the confusion to abduct the Satrap and take over the city. I'd have thought even you would have more sensitivity than to make up stories at a time like this."

"But it's not a story!" Lysippe protested. "You know

we Amazons are different from other people. There really was a gryphon, and I have to—"

The door closed with a bang. With sinking heart, she heard the locking-bar fall into place on the other side.

The first thing she did was try the window. But she couldn't even get her head through. She banged on the door. Apart from an unseen guard who told her to shut up, no one came. Frightened now, she returned to the window and whistled for Northwind. But wherever her horse was, he couldn't hear her. She scanned the sky. If the gryphon had been real and not a smoke-induced hallucination, it was nowhere in sight. She wasn't sure she wanted it to come back, anyway. It would only set something else on fire, and enough things had burned already.

She slid to her knees and watched the smoking ruin of the Temple turn angry red as the sun set. "I never meant for it to burn down," she whispered. "Really, I didn't."

There was a soft snort of sympathy below. Her heart lifted, and she pressed her cheek against the wall so she could see her horse. His eye gleamed in the shadows as he raised his head. "Hide, Northwind!" she whispered. "Wait for me."

She watched until he'd trotted down a nearby alley, then left the window and drank the rest of the water. She curled up on the mat and tried not to think of what the Alchemist might be doing to her friends.

Sometime during the night, there was a soft scrape at the door. Lysippe was instantly alert, remembering what

Melissa Aspasia had said about the priests wanting revenge. But the small figure who slipped inside was Annyla, looking pale and drawn.

The girl flung her arms around Lysippe's neck. "Oh, Lysippe, I've been so worried!" she cried. "They wouldn't tell me where you were. I've had the worst jobs to do as punishment for helping to start the fire, and I'm supposed to pray to Artemis for forgiveness a whole hour every day, so I've hardly had any time to look for you. I thought you'd been taken to the Satrap's mansion and interrogated like Hero was! Then I was sure the Alchemist must have got you – he's set himself up as a tyrant king, and his men are dragging citizens off the streets if they dare protest."

Lysippe winced and fended the girl off.

"Sorry... did you get terribly burnt? They wouldn't let me go back into the fire, but I managed to rescue your—" She slammed a hand to her mouth. "Lysippe, your beautiful *hair*!"

Lysippe raised a hand to her head. She'd forgotten the light feeling. Frazzled ends close to her scalp were all that remained of her long, thick locks. "Doesn't matter," she said, remembering how silly she'd been about having it braided back before the slavers had captured her and Tanais. "Listen, Annyla, we have to go back to the Temple! I saw the Stone in the fire, but they snatched me out of there before I had a chance to get hold of it."

"The Temple's gone," Annyla said, tears in her eyes. "All gone."

"I know."

"We should never have trusted Herostratus!" Annyla paced the little room, her fists clenched. "Serves him right if he's back in the Alchemist's chains! I hope he gets whipped every single day!" She stopped at the window, where the dull glow coming from the ruin lit the lower slopes of the Sacred Hill and its empty beehives. She thumped the wall and let out a furious sob. "Oh, Artemis, I don't mean that!"

Lysippe turned cold. "The Alchemist has put Hero in chains? Are you sure?"

"I don't know where else he can be. Hero used to be his slave, so by rights the Alchemist still owns him, I suppose – not that anyone'll stop the Alchemist doing exactly what he wants, now. Poor Herostratus! Why did he burn down the whole Temple like that? He must be stupid, destroying his only sanctuary."

"It was the gryphon, not Hero." Lysippe stared at the door. "We have to find that Stone, Annyla, or everything will be for nothing. How did you get in here? Are the guards still outside?"

"They're asleep," the girl said with a sly smile. "I slipped some sleeping powder into their wine. And the Melissae are exhausted – there's only one or two on duty tonight. Melissa Aspasia's gone to see the Megabyxos about you. That's how I found out you were here. Oh, and I brought you this – it's a bit singed, but I found it in the salvage pile. Someone must have rescued it, thinking it was a Temple treasure. I thought you might need it."

She reached into the corridor and dragged a blackened, half-moon shield through the door. She held the shield at arm's length, as if she were afraid of it. "I hope it still works."

Lysippe's heart lifted. She ran a hand across the singed gryphon-design, tried it on her arm, and smiled as the room blurred and Annyla's eyes lost their focus. She seized the girl's hand, making her gasp. "Well done! Stay close to me, and I'll hide us both."

As they crept past the snoring guards and through the house, Lysippe's guilt increased. Everywhere she looked, people lay swathed in bandages, moaning in their sleep. These must have been the less needy cases, since they had mats on the floor similar to hers. She hated to think what the patients in the beds looked like.

They emerged on to a balcony overlooking a central courtyard, where they crouched behind the shield while Lysippe whistled softly for Northwind. Hoof beats and an answering snort came from the street. The guards patrolling below stiffened in surprise as the little horse sailed over the gate and trotted across the courtyard. "Isn't that one of the girls who burnt down the Temple?" one said, peering at Annyla. His expression darkened as Lysippe lowered the shield. "It's both the girls! Stop them!"

Quickly, Lysippe legged Annyla up on the horse's back, vaulted on behind her and urged Northwind towards the gate. Annyla gave a little scream as the horse's muscles bunched, and Lysippe lifted her feet so they would not catch on the wood. Then they were over the gate and galloping up the moonlit street towards the remains of the Temple of Artemis.

The shield deflected the watchful gazes of the mercenaries patrolling the perimeter, and the horse saved them the problem of how to negotiate the hot ash without getting burnt feet. But they were forced to slow down when they neared the site of the Temple. As Northwind's hooves crunched the rubble, Lysippe's palms turned sweaty. Annyla made small noises of distress as she recognized the smoking remains of the Sleeping House and the Blood House. All that remained of the great Temple of Artemis itself was a cracked step and the twisted wreckage of fallen columns. Northwind snorted, reluctant to go further in.

"Stay here," Lysippe whispered, and jumped down into the still-warm debris.

"Be careful!" Annyla called, clinging on to Northwind's mane.

Lysippe clambered over the fallen columns and around unrecognizable, soot-covered lumps until she reached the eerily glowing inner sanctuary. She used the shield to dig through the rubble, coughing as the ash rose in clouds.

"Quick, Lysippe!" Annyla called behind her. "The soldiers have seen us!"

Lysippe rummaged faster, her breath coming in gasps. What if the salvage squads had found the Stone already? What if it had burnt with the rest?

Her heart leapt as she glimpsed a gleam of black and gold under the ash. She abandoned the shield and fell to her knees so she could dig with her bare hands. She hardly felt the heat as she scraped the ash aside.

The Gryphon Stone.

It lay before her, its colour undiminished by the fire, rising from the ash like a bubble about to burst with unknown powers. There was no time to be afraid. She took a deep breath, plunged her hands into the rubble to free the Stone, and gasped in dismay as her fingers encountered only crumbling debris.

"What's wrong?" Annyla called. "Lysippe! Are you all right?"

"Fine... I'm fine." Frowning, Lysippe lifted the Stone and turned it over. Its outer surface – the part she'd seen – was rounded and beautiful, but this was only part of the original Stone. Its underside was rough and charred, the edges jagged as if they'd cracked under great force. She dug desperately around it and uncovered two similar, smaller pieces. She stared at them, numb. They didn't even fit together properly. It was as if the centre of the Stone had been burnt out.

"*Lysippe!*" Annyla screamed. "Hurry!"

There was no time to dig for the missing centre. She scooped up the three pieces and raced back through the rubble to where she'd left her friend, the shield dragging at one elbow, the broken Stone clasped in her cupped hands. Annyla was staring in terror at the soldiers running through the ash towards them. But when she saw what Lysippe was holding, her face lit up with relief. "You found it!"

"Give me your headscarf," Lysippe ordered. She bound the pieces of the Stone in the linen, tied the bundle to her girdle so her hands would be free, leapt on Northwind's back behind Annyla and urged the horse towards the river.

"Did anything happen when you touched it?" Annyla asked breathlessly. "Does it work?"

The soldiers were running diagonally to cut them off. Although they were surrounded and escape was hopeless, Lysippe raised the shield and brought her other hand down on Northwind's rump, urging the horse to greater speed. "No!" she shouted back. "It doesn't work. Why do you think we're running away? It's broken. The Gryphon Stone's broken!"

Annyla moaned and whispered something about their sacred sanctuary. All Lysippe could think of was Smyrna's warning, and how she'd so stupidly ignored it. The heat had obviously been too much for the Stone. Now she couldn't heal Tanais, couldn't even get her back from the Macedonians.

They'd destroyed the Temple of Artemis for nothing.

Chapter 15

GRYPHON
They rise up and become conscious guardians of the living and the dead.

Northwind shied as he neared the river, reminding Lysippe they had more immediate problems. The Alchemist's men formed a line in front of them, spears braced against the rubble that separated the Temple grounds from the bank. The points made a wicked, glittering line in the moonlight. "Stop!" one called, his hand raised imperiously.

Lysippe dug her heels into Northwind's ribs and rode straight at him. Annyla gasped as they bore down on the spear points. It seemed the little horse would leap over them, as he'd cleared the gate back in the city. But at the last moment, the Alchemist rose from behind the rubble and threw some of his treacherous powder into the horse's eyes. The air filled with glittering green stars. Northwind swerved and slid to a stop in a snorting cloud of ash.

Lysippe was thrown against Annyla, who clutched at the horse's neck. The bundle containing the broken Stone swung up and struck Lysippe on the side of the head. Momentarily stunned, she didn't notice the shield slipping from her arm. The Alchemist strode out of the fading stars and caught it.

"Careless," he said, swinging the shield to knock Annyla, who was already off balance, over Northwind's shoulder. In the same movement, he grasped Lysippe's ankle and pulled her off the horse as well.

She landed flat on her back at the Alchemist's feet, the broken Stone digging into her hip and her ankle still imprisoned in his big hand. It was the one that had been broken on the march through Phrygia. He smiled down at her and squeezed harder. She kicked desperately. But a bristling array of spears held her still and more men ran up with flaring torches to surround them. While two of the mercenaries picked up the terrified Annyla and held her between them, the Alchemist removed his helmet, crouched, and stared into Lysippe's face. The scar above his left eye pulsed with excitement.

"I knew you'd come back for the Stone, slave," he said. "How nice of you to wrap it up for me."

Lysippe glared back at him, fear making her reckless. "You'd better watch out! Or I'll use it on you."

The Alchemist grinned. "Go on, then. Blast me to a cinder."

Lysippe fumbled for the bundle beneath her. The men's hands tensed on their spears. But the Alchemist laughed. "Relax! She can't do anything. How do you think we caught her so easily? The magic has gone from this place, I told you so."

"I'll summon the gryphon again!" Lysippe threatened. "The Stone lets me do that!" She whistled without much hope. "*Gryphon!*" she called. "I have your Stone. Come to me!"

The Alchemist shook his head. Carefully, he untied the bundle from her waist and passed it to one of his men. "Give it up, slave. You know as well as I do that the Stone's broken – which puts you in a rather awkward position, doesn't it? The Queen of Macedonia is hardly going to want broken magic for her son. The Oracle was right about that part, you know. She gave birth to a boy five nights ago – the very same night our beloved Temple caught fire. A strange coincidence, don't you think? Must be a sign."

The sky over the sea remained dark. There was no sign of a flame-tailed creature. She must have imagined the gryphon, after all. Lysippe's strength left her as she realized what the Alchemist must have been up to while she'd been lying helpless in the healing-sleep. "You broke the Stone on purpose... you never intended to let the Queen have it, did you? Wait till I tell Commander Cleitus!"

The Alchemist bared his teeth. "I wouldn't tell the Macedonians the Stone is broken, if I were you. Once Olympias hears, your sister's life won't be worth a handful of that ash you're lying in. Do you really think I wanted it broken? That was an unfortunate accident, like the one that put an end to my lucrative little counterfeiting business here. Or did you burn the Temple down on purpose? Is that how you Amazons fight these days? By destroying innocent lives because you haven't the courage to kill your enemy face to face?"

His words struck deep. "No one died in the fire," Lysippe whispered. She closed her eyes and hoped he'd let Annyla go, now he had what he wanted.

"But you're right about one thing," the Alchemist continued. "The Philosopher's Stone is much too valuable to give to the Queen of Macedonia, broken or not. I believe it still has power, and I think you know very well how to mend it – otherwise why were you sneaking off with it in the middle of the night? So you're going to mend the Stone for me. Then, when it's whole again, you're going to teach me how to use it to make gold and transform myself into an immortal. Then, if you're a good slave, maybe we'll work on getting your sister back."

Lysippe stared at him in fresh despair. "But I can't mend it!"

"Sure you can." The Alchemist stroked her ankle with the edge of the shield. "You can mend broken bones well enough, and use this shield to make yourself invisible, and spread fire – Herostratus told me how you put your hands in the flames and threw them over half of Ephesos. And if you don't know how to mend it yourself, then you can always ask your friend the naiad to do it for you. In fact, why don't you ask her right now? We'll wait. And in case you get any ideas about crossing me, remember I'm the only one who can get your sister back and keep the Stone here in Ephesos. Otherwise, you'll lose one or the other of them – which isn't what you want, is it?"

"You're crazy if you think I'm going to work with you! Anyway, Smyrna won't come with you here."

The Alchemist smiled. "Not work with me – *for* me. And I think the naiad will come, given the right encouragement. She did before." While he was speaking, he'd been pulling off Lysippe's sandals. He beckoned one of his men forward. Lysippe's blood chilled when she saw the manacles he carried. The Alchemist knelt and locked them about her ankles himself. They were of thick iron and a short, heavy chain joined them so that she couldn't kick properly. "This should stop you slipping through the net," he said. "It's difficult to swim with iron on your legs, but no doubt your naiad friend will stop you drowning. While you're talking with the nymph, my men will keep their net across the river. Oh yes, and I almost forgot—" He turned to stroke Annyla's cheek. "I'll keep your little priestess friend with me as extra insurance." He tested the chain, making sure Lysippe couldn't pull her feet through the manacles. "All right, throw her in."

"No!" Annyla gasped, realizing what they intended. "You can't! She'll drown!"

The mercenaries put down their spears and lifted Lysippe between them. The stars and the ruins spun sickeningly as they carried her to the river where it deepened below the ford, and swung her by the wrists and ankles. They let go with a collective grunt. Black water and shadowy rocks blurred beneath her. She flailed her arms desperately and only just avoided a large rock as she hit the water with a loud splash, scraping her leg on the submerged part of the rock as she sank. She kicked in panic. But she was out of her depth, and the chain around her ankles dragged her down. There was no time to take a decent breath. As the water closed over her head, the Alchemist laughed.

She fought the instinct to breathe. But her lungs screamed with pain, and her struggles ceased as the last of her air bubbled between her lips. Why fight any more? Why not stay here, under the water where it was cool and peaceful, for ever?

"Don't give in, little sister."

The voice was faint and far-off like a voice in a dream, but it brought her to her senses. Tanais! If she drowned, there would be no one to rescue her sister. She kicked frantically towards the torchlight that rippled orange overhead, and broke the surface with a great, gasping breath. The men's laughter struck her like a physical blow. Annyla was screaming at them to pull her out. She had a glimpse of helmeted faces leaning close to watch the fun.

"Smyrna!" she cried with even less hope than she'd called for the gryphon.

But as she was sinking again, blue and silver reflected

in the metal and she knew the naiad had come.

"Smyrna! Watch out, there's a net—"

The chain dragged her down before she could finish the warning. But the naiad joined her at the bottom of the river in a blaze of silver light, her hair floating around her and her scales glittering. She didn't seem to have trouble breathing underwater. Her luminous eyes watched with cool pity as Lysippe thrashed her chained legs and fought to reach the surface again.

"A fine mess you're in, aren't you? I warned you not to let it get hot."

"Help me—" Lysippe gasped, getting her mouth above the surface long enough to voice the plea before she sank again.

"Let the current take you. Follow me."

As the naiad spoke, a sudden surge of water came from upstream, bearing down upon them in a dark wave. Lysippe was swept downriver after Smyrna, straight towards the net the men had strung between the banks. She expected to find Smyrna entangled in the cords, but the naiad's ghostly form elongated until it was no thicker than an eel, and she flickered through one of the holes to emerge safely on the other side. The net ballooned with the sudden current, and the men on the bank shouted in surprise as Lysippe was washed against it with a thump. While they struggled to hold her weight as well as the force of the water, she grasped the cords and hauled herself to the surface. She got in several good breaths before the men on the far bank lost their grip, and she was once more swept helplessly downriver in a tangle of net and chain and foaming silver water.

An eternity of bubbles later, the current slackened and Lysippe felt something smooth under her knees. She clung desperately to the underwater shelf and found herself in the middle of the Temple harbour kneeling on a slab of marble fitted with posts and rings for tying up boats, though none was in use tonight.

"*This is as far as I can go,*" said Smyrna. "*It is the sacred place where fresh water mixes with salt. We can protect you here for a while.*"

Lysippe coughed the last of the water from her lungs and blinked warily at the glittering silver lights that danced around the harbour. Smyrna hadn't come when she'd wanted her to find Tanais. But she'd saved her life – twice. She decided on truth.

"The Alchemist's got the Stone!" she gasped. "It's broken, but he thinks I can mend it. *Can* it be mended?"

Something very like laughter formed in her head. The silver lights dispersed, and she saw that the nymph in front of her was not Smyrna – the face was different, her colouring green and turquoise, rather than blue and silver. And she wasn't alone. Several voices spoke at once.

"*She's young for this, Smyrna.*"

"*You say she's never killed?*"

"*However did she manage to hatch the gryphon?*"

Lysippe blinked again. She was surrounded by nymphs with swirling hair and shining faces. Through their ghostly bodies, the torches of the Alchemist's private army could be seen making their way slowly downriver. The men were searching for something in the water. With a start, Lysippe realized they must be looking for her body.

Shivering, she pulled her chained feet on to the slab and wrapped her arms around her knees. She studied the nymphs more carefully. They had webbed hands and feet like Smyrna, but their hair was seaweed-coloured and they were plumper. "You're oceanids, aren't you?" she said. "Did you see where the Macedonians took my sister? She's supposed to be on an island—"

"*We haven't much time,*" interrupted Smyrna. "*You hatched the gryphon, so you command it, and I must explain what happens next. Though what use a gryphon who can't kill will be to you, I don't know!*"

There it was again. Hatched.

Lysippe's brain finally began to work. The cracked Stone... the missing, burnt-out centre... the creature she'd seen after the fire, that had been so much smaller than she'd imagined...

"It was an egg," she whispered, wondering why she hadn't seen it before. "That's what the legends mean! The Gryphon Stones are gryphon's *eggs!*"

"*Slow, isn't she?*"

"*You should have told her the truth in the first place, Smyrna. Then she'd have been more careful.*"

"*She wouldn't. She'd have tried to hatch it for a pet.*"

"*We should have waited for the others of her tribe to get here. At least we know they can fight.*"

"They're still in the mountains. How was I to know they would escape the Macedonians? It's too late now, anyway. The gryphon's hatched and my reign on this earth is over."

"Wait!" Forgetting the chain, Lysippe almost overbalanced into the harbour. She slithered back to safety and stared at the sparkling, swirling nymphs. "Are you saying you've seen my mother and the others? Where are they? Are they all right?"

"You'd better hurry up and tell her about the gryphon, Smyrna, and hope she's old enough to understand."

"She's old enough. The gryphon doesn't hatch for just anyone."

Lysippe couldn't tell which nymph had stood up for her. The torches were coming closer to the harbour, and the men's shouts could be heard clearly across the water. Any moment now, they'd see her.

"Stop talking about me as if I'm not here!" She clenched her fists and glared at the oceanids and their naiad queen. "I'm not a child any more – at least, I don't feel like one any more. I appreciate you saving me from drowning, and I'll do my best to help you. I just don't understand everything yet. I know you're the ghosts of Amazons who have fallen in battle, and I know you can talk to each other in places like this. You say I command the gryphon now. That makes me your leader, doesn't it? So I order you to tell me the truth! Where have the Macedonians taken my sister? Where's my mother and the rest of my tribe? Why do Amazons transform into nymphs? Will that happen to me? Can the gryphon heal my sister? Why do the legends call the eggs Stones? Is my father really a god? I want to know everything!"

The oceanids swirled in agitation. Smyrna sighed and slid on to the marble beside Lysippe, sparkling gently.

"We really don't have time for this. But you hatched the gryphon, so I must answer." She gave another bubbling sigh. *"The truth about gryphons is this. They live in the land beyond the sky, along with many other creatures men normally dismiss as fantasy. It is necessary for a gryphon's egg to spend many years hardening on earth before it can hatch. Some eggs never hatch, and that is why men call them Stones. Amazons used to know the truth, but so much has been lost, and what remains is corrupted by superstition. Without Amazons, gryphons would die out as a species, and without gryphons, we are condemned to live like mortal women. We look after the eggs when they drop to earth, until the young gryphons are ready to fly back to their home beyond the sky. In return, the unhatched gryphon bestows upon us strength and healing abilities, and does its best to make sure we do not die before it is ready to hatch. That's why we take these spirit forms following violent death, so we remain bound to the earth until our task is done. It is an ancient partnership, and strong Amazons make strong gryphons, for always the young gryphon takes on the characteristics of the one who hatches it. That's why yours can't kill."*

Smyrna paused to stare at the twin peaks of Mount

Lepre Akte that rose black against the stars above the city.

"My daughter should have been the one who hatched that egg! She'd been trained from an early age to lead the tribe. If the men we fought hadn't stolen the egg, she'd have hatched the gryphon so it could carry me and my sisters to the land beyond the sky. But the men of Ephesos not only took the egg. They dragged my daughter into their caves and murdered her where I could not reach her. Until the gryphon flies, we are condemned to our separate prisons – I to my river, she to her cave. That is why I wanted you to bring me the egg so I could hatch it and free us both. Never before, in all our long history, has a gryphon been hatched by an untrained child like you."

"So... a gryphon's a sort of guardian of the dead?" Lysippe said, willing to forgive the 'untrained child' because she was so fascinated by Smyrna's story. "It takes your souls to... Hades?" She used the Greek word she'd learnt in the Temple, which referred to a shadowy place under the earth where Annyla had told her souls went after death.

Smyrna laughed. *"The Greeks know little about the lands beyond the sky! They've invented their own gods and goddesses to hide their ignorance. The Persians still remember, and it is said dragons were seen in Babylon when the city surrendered to them back when I was a girl. But even their knowledge is fading as creatures like dragons and gryphons become less common in the lands of men. The gryphon will obey you until it has grown to its full size, so you can use it to help you sort out your problems before it flies with our souls. I only hope for your sake that it's up to the task. Usually, gryphons can be relied upon to be fierce. They peck out men's eyes, eat their horses, and burn their cities. Yet I understand that the one you hatched didn't even consume your horse when it emerged! We must thank the First Mother that it at least has a proper fiery tail."*

"Where's my mother and sister?" Lysippe insisted, still trying to get everything Smyrna had told her straight in her head. The various legends about the Stone were starting to make sense – only instead of being immortal, Amazons transformed. She wondered quite what the Macedonian Queen's son would have done with the Stone, if she'd obtained it for him. Or was he a sort of Amazon, too?

"Don't worry," Smyrna said. *"Your mother and her tribe are on their way. They've got horses and replacement weapons, and the oreads and dryads up in the mountains say they're riding hard. They'll get here soon enough."*

Lysippe's heart fluttered. She hardly dared ask. "And my sister?"

There was a pause before the naiad answered. *"Your sister was taken to a small island further up the coast. The Macedonians have established a garrison there. It's supposed to be secret, but they've trireme warships moored in the inlet. Mortals are so stupid sometimes."* She sparkled a little. *"They don't have medical facilities on the island. Your sister is... changed. Be prepared."*

Lysippe stared out to sea in fresh hope. But the harbour was deserted. Every vessel, down to the last canoe, had been removed from the vicinity of the Temple because of the danger of it catching fire. She twisted round on the slab, saw Androklos' Shrine on the promontory and remembered the main harbour beyond. "I have to get to the other harbour! If I find a boat, can you lead me to the island?"

The oceanids swirled in amusement. Smyrna laughed again. *"A boat? That's mortal thinking. Why sail all that way against the wind, when you can ride your gryphon?"*

Lysippe's heart missed a beat. The naiad was pointing to the sky above the bay where an orange star burned fierce and low on the horizon. As she watched, the star grew until she could see the gryphon's shadowy wings, its curved beak, and its tail trailing flames through the night. It shrieked as it swooped towards the slab where Lysippe crouched. Smyrna slipped back into the water and joined her sisters, their scales rippling with reflected fire as they gazed up at the creature in awe.

"Beautiful," the oceanids whispered. *"Seems the child hasn't done too badly, after all."*

The Alchemist's men had reached the shore and were squinting at the harbour. They obviously couldn't see Lysippe in the middle of the glittering, sparkling nymphs. But one of them pointed to the gryphon. "It's Androklos' lion!" he cried. "It's bad luck!"

"Don't be so stupid!" the Alchemist shouted. "That's no ghost. Can't you see the slave? She's sitting right there on the mooring stone! Go in and fetch her back, you half-blind fools."

Lysippe stared uncertainly at the gryphon. It had grown since she'd last seen it on the night of the fire, but she didn't know how she was supposed to ride it with her legs chained together.

"Tell it to take you to your sister," Smyrna advised. *"That's what you want, isn't it? Then my daughter and I can leave this place and be together again in the land beyond the sky."*

The naiad stared at the gryphon with such longing in her luminous eyes, it tore Lysippe's heart. The oceanids stared in the same manner.

"We're glad you hatched the egg," they whispered. *"We've been too long in this mortal sea. We're so tired, so cold."*

"I'll be as quick as I can," Lysippe promised them. She scrambled to her feet, faced the gryphon and took a deep breath. "Gryphon, I command you to take me to my sister!"

The creature landed with cat-like grace on the mooring slab, picking up its paws in distaste as they touched the water. It folded its glowing blue and red wings, and cocked its head to regard Lysippe from one fiery eye. It was growing a mane like an adult lion's, curly and black with golden highlights. Lysippe grasped a handful of the soft fur and hauled herself up the gryphon's shoulder until she knelt in the warm hollow of its neck where the mane changed to feathers.

She shut her eyes and clung on tightly as the creature sprang into the air. Powerful wing beats whistled past her ears and her head filled with something fierce and bright. She risked a peep and was alarmed to see how high they were already. Far below, the Alchemist's men had been persuaded into the harbour with their nets. But the nymphs evaded them easily. The oceanids streamed out to sea in glimmers of turquoise and green, while Smyrna flickered, eel-formed, past the men's legs and returned to her river. Lysippe looked for Annyla and Northwind among the torches on the shore, but couldn't see them. She hoped they'd be all right until she got back. The Alchemist stood on the edge of the harbour steps with his helmet dangling from one hand, cursing his men and staring after the gryphon with a puzzled expression, as if he'd seen something but couldn't decide what it was.

The gryphon quickly left behind the smouldering ruins. As they rose above the smoke that hung over the Ephesian plain, Lysippe breathed deeply, her scorched lungs welcoming the cool night air. They flew past the shrine where she'd met Commander Cleitus, past the hills that enclosed the bay, and headed out to open sea. With the chain on her ankles, Lysippe dared not let go of the gryphon's mane. But she hardly felt the ache in her arms, or spared a thought for the jagged rocks below. "Tanais," she whispered fiercely. "Tanais, wait for me. I'm coming!"

Chapter 16

TRANSFORMATION
Immortal mortals, mortal immortals,
living their death and dying their life.

The sky was paling by the time the gryphon started to lose height. Lysippe peered over its shoulder and saw they were heading towards a small island with a natural harbour in which several long, narrow warships were anchored. As they descended, the sun rose and illuminated a pennant flapping from the mast of the largest vessel. Lysippe's breath tightened as she recognized the Royal Star of Macedon on its crimson background.

"That's the Queen's ship!" she hissed.

Sensing her hatred, the gryphon swooped low over the deck, its red and blue wings whispering through the air like those of an eagle hunting its prey. As it flew over the mast, it lashed its tail and the pennant caught fire. The men lounging on the deck leapt to their feet and shouted in alarm as the flames ate the cloth and burning fragments floated into the sea.

Lysippe clutched the gryphon's mane tighter. "Stop that and take me to my sister!" she commanded, hoping Tanais wasn't down on the ship.

You make fire, the gryphon reminded her. *I am only like you.*

But the creature wheeled away from the ships and flew to the cliffs, its head cocked to one side, searching. Suddenly, it dived and landed on a ledge high up the sheer rock face. It folded its wings and shook itself in a satisfied manner, while Lysippe slid off its back and stood on trembling legs. At first, she thought the gryphon had disobeyed her. Then she saw the crack in the cliff.

"Where's Tanais?" she asked, eyeing the crack with trepidation.

They put her inside rocks.

"In there?" The crack didn't look large enough to squeeze her hand through. She imagined being walled up inside and shuddered.

Beneath here. But entrance to sea-cave guarded by many men and we cannot kill. I enlarge hole. You go down shaft. Find sister at bottom.

While Lysippe crouched at the side of the ledge, the gryphon scraped furiously at the cliff face with its claws and beak. Excavated rocks tumbled off the ledge behind them and splashed into the sea. When it seemed to have finished, she hobbled closer to the crevice. She peered in despair down the dark shaft.

"I'll never be able to climb down there with this chain on my feet! How am I going to get Tanais back up, if she's still in the healing-sleep?"

You say only take you to sister, not get sister out. This best way. I not fit inside rocks.

Lysippe closed her eyes and rested her forehead against the cliff. She thought of commanding the gryphon to take her to the cave it had mentioned. But even if the Macedonians couldn't see the gryphon, they'd see her as soon as she dismounted. Why had she been so stupid as to drop the shield at the Alchemist's feet? She realized she hadn't even asked Smyrna how she intended to heal Tanais, now the gryphon had hatched.

She took a deep breath. So she'd have to do this the hard way. "Can you at least get this chain off?" she asked the creature.

I try. It lowered its head and fastened its black beak around the chain linking Lysippe's ankles. The gryphon's eyes narrowed with effort as it bit. There was a snap and a rattle, and the gryphon scrabbled backwards, its wings beating frantically as it fought to stay on the ledge.

In spite of everything, Lysippe laughed. The manacles were still locked on her ankles with the heavy links swinging from them, but at least she had full use of her legs again. "Thank you, gryphon!" she said. "Wait here."

Before she could think about it too much, she swung her legs into the shaft, braced her back and feet against the rock, and lowered herself into the dark.

The chain scraped against the sides of the shaft and

her breathing sounded loud in the enclosed space. The crevice twisted back on itself and the daylight above faded, leaving her to feel her way down an ever-narrowing space. She started to sweat at the thought of getting stuck. Then she heard voices below. She found foot and hand holds and paused as torchlight flickered orange beneath her.

"I'm telling you, Cleitus, we say nothing about this until we get our hands on the Amazons' Stone!" That was the Queen, her whisper fierce.

"But your Majesty!" Commander Cleitus answered. "We can still save her. We can get healers from the Temple of Artemis. They're busy after the fire, but I think they'd come."

"And have them tell everyone what we're doing here? The Megabyxos might be willing to take Macedonian gold in exchange for an injured refugee, but I don't suppose he'll be pleased to know we've established a garrison so close to his shores. He's bound to inform the Satrap, and if the Persians get wind of it we'll have to give up the whole idea. It'll put our invasion plans back years. Be sensible, Cleitus! It doesn't matter if the girl dies. She'll serve her purpose, dead or alive. In fact, I can't believe her sister hasn't brought you the Stone yet. I realize the increased security after the fire made it difficult for you to investigate further, but we need to know what's going on in Ephesos. I would have come earlier, only I was rather busy giving birth to my son."

Lysippe held her breath. Tanais! was all she could think. They're talking about Tanais.

The conversation did not sound promising. It seemed Tanais had developed some kind of rash. Cleitus was trying to show the Queen, but the Queen was obviously more worried about the fire and what had happened to the Stone. Shortly afterwards, the torchlight faded. Lysippe listened to the silence while she counted a hundred beats of her heart. She slithered down the rest of the shaft so rapidly that the sudden drop through space into wet sand made her cry out.

She crouched in the gloom while her eyes adjusted. Grey light filtered into the cave, along with the echoes of waves washing against rock. A dim shape curled between two boulders, covered by the same rough blanket that had covered her sister when she'd been taken from the Blood House.

"Tanais..?" Lysippe whispered, scrambling across and pulling off the blanket. She felt for her sister's hands. They were cold – so very cold – and slimy like fish. A rope bound her wrists, winding down to join another rope around her ankles. Her tunic was torn and wet around the hem, and the bandages the Melissae had applied in the Temple were filthy and frayed. It was too dim in the cave to see if Tanais' wounds were still bleeding, and Lysippe dared not probe too much in case she hurt her sister more. "Tanais!" she tugged frantically at the knots. "Oh, Tanais, what have they done to you?"

The hands flopped free at last. Lysippe rubbed them

fiercely to get some warmth back into the flesh, but froze when she felt the strange flap of skin between the thumb and first finger.

Violent death, Smyrna had said. Lysippe's stomach twisted as the naiad's warning and Cleitus' mention of a rash merged to make chilling sense.

"No... no, Tanais, no! Don't transform, you can't! I'm here now. Wake up!" She shook her sister frantically.

"Lysippe..? Are you a dream?"

The voice was weak and faint, but her sister reached up to touch Lysippe's face. The cold hand with its frightening webs paused at her frazzled hair and moved on to trace the tears on her cheeks.

"You're crying, little sister. Don't cry. My wounds don't hurt at all now. You were right all along about the oread and the other spirits – they're so beautiful, Lysippe! I'm glad I can see them at last. The oceanids come in here sometimes and sing to me. They told me you were coming. I've been waiting for you. I wanted to tell you I'm sorry I said all those things about your father. There was no man in the camp the night Mother got pregnant with you, only a star that flamed across the sky. I was young and scared, and I didn't understand. I do now. The oceanids told me the star was a gryphon's egg falling to earth, and that it gave Mother the power to dream of the god. They also say that after I've transformed I'll be able to help you. We'll find Mother, and we'll take our revenge on the Alchemist. Little sister, don't cry. Please don't cry. I didn't want you to see me like this... I'll be beautiful soon, very soon..."

"No, Tanais!" Lysippe grabbed her sister's wrists in anguish. "No, don't die! I've found the Stone. You're right, it was an egg, but it broke and hatched a gryphon! Smyrna says Mother's on her way to Ephesos. We'll fight off the Alchemist and the Macedonians, and the Persians too, if we have to! We'll get you safe and we'll find a way to heal you, I promise. You can't die now. *You can't.*"

There was a faint glimmer under her hands – scales glinting. She stared at them in horror. "Tanais! Don't! I burnt down the Temple of Artemis for you. I can't lead the tribe after Mother's gone. You have to do it. You're much stronger than me, you always were. You're a proper Amazon. You can hunt and kill like Amazons are supposed to. It doesn't matter that your father was a Scythian. Tanais, *please* don't transform..." She threw herself over her sister's body, holding it tightly as if she could stop what was happening by the force of her love alone.

Commander Cleitus, alerted by her anguished sobs, raced into the cave with his men close behind. The torchlight half-blinded Lysippe. Tanais whimpered and slithered behind one of the boulders with her arms wrapped over her head. A curl of green hair trailed over the top of the rock like weed.

The Macedonians took one look at Tanais, threw down their torches and ran out again, screaming about plague. Cleitus bellowed after them, but they did not return. He stared at Lysippe, who was still on her knees in the damp sand, and frowned at Tanais. He looked cautiously round the cave, one hand resting on the hilt of his sword.

"How did you get in here, young Amazon? Have you brought your magic Stone? I'm guessing you must have, or you'd never have got past my men – and I see you've managed to rouse your sister." He considered the whimpering Tanais, glanced at the entrance to the cave, and seemed to come to a decision. "Give the Stone to me and get out of here. There's a boat tied up outside. Get your sister away from this place, and I'll see the Queen doesn't—"

"You'll see the Queen doesn't what?" said an imperious voice behind them. "What's all this nonsense your men are shouting about plague? I thought you said it was just a rash?" Olympias' amber eyes picked out Lysippe in the shadows, and she started. "What's that girl doing in here? I said to make sure she stayed in Ephesos! Have you gone crazy, Cleitus? How long has she been here?"

Lysippe glared at the young woman who stood haloed by light in the entrance of the cave. She was so upset, she couldn't think straight. She scrambled to her feet and sprang towards the Queen, fists clenched. "You killed my sister! If you hadn't taken her from the Temple, she wouldn't have died!" Olympias took a surprised step backwards, and Commander Cleitus drew his sword and stepped between them.

"Now then, young Amazon, you know that's not true. The Alchemist was the one who wounded her, and she's not dead yet. If you hand over the Stone, I'll make sure she gets proper treatment."

Lysippe raised her chin and faced them both, her heart hammering. "I haven't brought the Stone," she said through gritted teeth. "Because the Alchemist took it from me. He plans to keep it for himself and use its powers to set himself up as a King and an Emperor. If you want it, you'd better go and get it off him. You'd better watch out, though, because his men have captured the Satrap and are in charge of Ephesos. You shouldn't have given him so much gold."

The Queen glanced at Cleitus. "Is this true?"

Cleitus lowered his sword slightly. "By all reports, Ephesos has been in chaos since the Temple burnt down. It's quite possible the Alchemist has taken advantage of the confusion to seize power, though I understand the Megabyxos is still in charge of Temple affairs."

Olympias narrowed her eyes at Lysippe. "I expected the Alchemist to try something like this, though I have to say I didn't realize the extent of his ambitions. He's more stupid than I thought. The Persians will crush his little army like a mosquito! And you say he's got the Stone?"

Lysippe nodded, watching the Queen carefully. But it seemed she knew as little about gryphon eggs as Lysippe had done before she'd learnt the truth from Smyrna.

"If you haven't got the Stone, and Cleitus didn't bring

you to the island, how did you get in here?" Olympias demanded.

Lysippe pointed up at the shaft. "I flew across the sea on a gryphon and climbed down."

There was a brief silence. For an instant, the Queen looked unsure. Then she began to laugh. "Flew on a gryphon! Have you ever heard anything like it?" She jerked her head at Cleitus and said, "Search the girl. If she really hasn't got the Stone, we'll pay a visit to our would-be Emperor and show him what happens to people who think they can defy Macedonia. I expect he sent the girl. You must have been followed back here one night."

The Commander hesitated. He glanced again at Tanais, who still huddled behind her rock. "And her sister?"

The Queen made a dismissive gesture. "She's no use to us now, is she? Secure them both in here. After we've dealt with the Alchemist, the girl can take her sister's body and bury it, or whatever Amazons do with their dead."

Lysippe's heart twisted. But the Queen's words confirmed how little she knew about Amazons, despite her yellow eyes.

"You didn't really lie with a god at all, did you?" she shouted after her. "You made it up so I'd get the Stone for you!"

Olympias whirled with an expression between surprise and fury. Commander Cleitus stiffened. But the

Queen merely shook her head at Lysippe and laughed again. "My son will be the proof of that," she said quietly. Then she turned on her heel and strode from the cave.

Lysippe clenched her fists again, angrier than if the Queen had struck her. Cleitus sheathed his sword and picked up the discarded rope. He stepped towards Lysippe, a look of regret on his dark face. "I'm sorry about this, young Amazon, but—"

"Gryphon!" Lysippe called, the echoes ringing up the shaft. "Come down to the beach!" She looked in anguish at her sister. But there was no way she'd be able to carry her out of the cave past Commander Cleitus, evade the Macedonians and lift her on to the gryphon's back. "Oceanids!" she cried. "Come and help Tanais!"

A look of alarm crossed Cleitus' face as a roaring sounded in the tunnel that led from the beach. The roar grew louder, and a wall of foaming water rushed into the cave, knocking Lysippe off her feet and sweeping up Tanais. Cleitus staggered and clutched at a rock as silver-green arms and swirling hair surrounded the dying girl, sucking her out through the tunnel to the open sea. *Welcome, sister, welcome!* The oceanids' song faded with the receding wave. It was over very quickly.

Before the Commander could recover, Lysippe staggered to her feet and ran for the beach. She found the Macedonian soldiers in confusion, rescuing their wet belongings from the rocks where they'd been carried by the freak wave. They obviously couldn't see the gryphon. But Queen Olympias stood apart, staring at the sky as the creature spiralled down out of the sun, a look of total disbelief on her face.

Commander Cleitus appeared at the cave mouth and shouted orders. His men abandoned their packs and rushed towards Lysippe. The gryphon landed at the edge of the waves, sending up great gouts of steam as it lashed its fiery tail. Arms trembling, Lysippe hauled herself up its mane and into the hollow of its neck. It had grown again, so even now her legs were free she couldn't sit comfortably astride. She settled for kneeling as before. "See?" she shouted down at the Queen. "You can see the gryphon, can't you? I'm telling the truth! The Alchemist has the Stone!"

Before the soldiers could get close enough to drag her off the creature, she twisted her hands into the gryphon's mane and gave it the order to fly back to Ephesos. Only when she was safely in the air with the sun and wind on her face did she surrender to the tears that choked her.

Smyrna speaks...

My sisters in the ocean tell me the elder girl is transforming nicely. I am glad for her. Death is not painful for us, once transformation begins. The only pain we feel is that of losing the battle to remain alive, and while this should not be underestimated – it is, after all, an Amazon's first real taste of defeat and inevitably removes some of the warrior from us – there are other rewards.

The young one does not understand this. She sees only her loss, and her misery makes her weak. I wish I could help her, but I cannot. I had my chance and she does not trust me. Now it is up to her tribe to give her the strength she needs. I only hope the sight of her mother will not be too much of a shock... why, oh why, do we fight so among ourselves?

Chapter 17

ALCHEMY
Eyes and ears are bad witnesses.

The smoke that hung over Ephesos was visible far out to sea as an ominous haze against the mountains. Lysippe peered at it through her tears and wondered why she was continuing to fight.

She looked down. Somewhere under the turquoise water, Smyrna and the oceanids were waiting patiently for Lysippe to finish her task so the gryphon could carry them from the world. All she had to do was slide off its neck, slip beneath the glittering waves and join Tanais in the place that held no pain.

When I fly, new egg falls to strongest Amazon.

The gryphon's words snatched her back. She clung tighter to its mane, trembling as she realized how close she'd come to following her thoughts.

"Wh – what did you say?"

You live. Rejoin tribe. Protect egg.

A new egg? Lysippe wiped her tears and looked ahead more hopefully. Smyrna had told her the eggs fell from the sky – she just hadn't said where or when.

Already, they were losing height over the bay. The crumbling columns of Androklos' Shrine shimmered into view on the promontory. Seven horses stamped nervously in the octagonal enclosure, while their riders crouched behind the fallen stones, bows raised and arrows nocked to the strings. Lysippe's heart gave a peculiar little jump. "Mother..." she whispered. "It's Mother!"

Her joy and relief was replaced by anger as she saw the blue crests of the Alchemist's troops surrounding the shrine. Most of the men were on foot. The Alchemist, however, rode a little horse covered in foam which snorted and reared as the big man wrenched its head round and brought his whip down across its quarters. Lysippe felt the pain as if the lash had struck her own back. "He's riding Northwind!" she cried, torn between rescuing her horse and rushing to see if her mother was all right.

The Amazons had recognized the horse too. As Lysippe hesitated, one of the figures on the hill stood with a terrible cry and released an arrow that curved towards the Alchemist. But although her aim was deadly, the distance was too great. The Alchemist wrenched Northwind back on his haunches and the arrow fell short.

The Alchemist laughed. "Amazons! You are

surrounded and outnumbered! Surrender, and I'll let you live as my slaves. Resist, and you'll die slow and horrible deaths at the hands of my men. They know how to treat women who get above their station." The mercenaries whistled in agreement and beat their axes and swords against their shields to show their enthusiasm.

None of them had noticed the gryphon flying out of the sun. Lysippe's arms turned weak when she saw the true state of the Amazons trapped in the shrine. They had lost their war-axes and half-moon shields. Some of them were barefoot. Their tunics and breeches were torn, and fading bruises showed through the holes. Their horses were bony and rheumy-eyed – the only animal Lysippe recognized was Tanais' mare Sunrise, and she was lame. Even the bows were not the beautifully-crafted weapons she remembered, but old ones that had been fitted with new strings. The Amazon who had shot the arrow was Melanippe, her mother's closest friend.

Sensing her confusion, the gryphon circled, and one of the men finally looked up. "It's Androklos' lion!" he cried.

The Alchemist dragged Northwind round, squinted into the sun through the eye slits of his helmet, and drew his sword. "Of course it is!" he roared. "It's come to prophesy the end of the Amazon race! There are only seven of them. Seven of you will die under Amazon arrows. The rest of you will kill Amazons seven times over in revenge for your comrades' deaths." He abandoned his whip and used the flat of his sword to beat Northwind into submission. The horse carried the Alchemist at a reluctant, crabwise trot through his troops as he picked out seven unfortunate mercenaries. "You men go first," he ordered. "Everyone else, form up behind. When I give the word... CHARGE!"

"Stop them!" Lysippe screamed to the gryphon.

I cannot kill.

"I don't care. Set something on fire! Keep them away from that shrine!"

The gryphon let out an ear-splitting shriek and dragged its tail through the dry grass of the hillside, leaving a trail of flames and a burning tree between the shrine and the army below. Northwind snorted in fear and whipped round. He bolted back along the Sacred Way towards the city, the Alchemist cursing and sawing at his mouth to no avail. The men, finding themselves leaderless, fell back before the flames. Six of them lay dead on the hillside, Amazon arrows protruding from their necks. The gryphon landed carefully in the shrine, sending the horses penned there into a frenzy. Lysippe flung herself off its back and stumbled across to her mother, the loose links of the chain bruising her legs.

The Amazons stared at the gryphon with wide eyes, but they remained at their posts. They sent another volley of arrows down on the Alchemist's men to keep them at bay, while Melanippe rushed across the shrine to intercept Lysippe.

"Oreithyia!" she shouted, the Scythian language

strange to Lysippe's ears after her time in the Temple. "It's your daughter. Don't shoot!"

Queen Oreithyia swung round, her bow raised and an arrow on the string. Lysippe skidded to a halt, her stomach churning in confusion. The crackling grass and smoke, the singing of the Amazons' bows, the frightened neighs of the horses and the shouts of the men... all these receded to a great distance as she stared at that arrow aimed at her heart.

"Mother?" she whispered, realizing she couldn't have recognized her. "It's me... my hair got burnt, that's all."

Very slowly, Oreithyia lowered the bow. Her face twisted, creasing some strange blisters around her eyes. She threw down the weapon and opened her arms. "Lysippe! Oh thank you, First Mother, thank you!"

Lysippe flung herself into her mother's open arms and fought back her tears. "I'm sorry, Mother," she choked out, her face pressed to the ragged tunic with its familiar smell of horse and sweat. "I found the Stone and hatched the gryphon, but it was too late to save Tanais, and she— oh, Mother, I think Tanais transformed into an oceanid! It was the Alchemist's fault. He wounded her when we escaped, and..." Everything that had happened since they'd parted in the cave above Themiscyra came out in an incoherent rush.

Oreithyia stiffened at the mention of the Alchemist, but she didn't say anything. While Lysippe was speaking, her mother's hands explored every part of her, from her frazzled hair to the manacles on her ankles, eventually returning to Lysippe's face. Even as Tanais had done, she wiped the tears from her cheeks. Gently, she said, "Lysippe, did you say you hatched a gryphon?"

"Yes, I— it's here, can't you see it? I thought all Amazons could. Even Queen Olympias can!"

She looked round, afraid the gryphon had already flown away with the nymphs to the land beyond the sky. But it crouched in the centre of the ruin, its wings folded and its fiery tail coiled carefully over its back. The horses had calmed down a bit, but every time the creature moved they snorted in terror. Between loosing arrows at the Alchemist's men, the Amazons were giving the gryphon looks of wonder and awe. But Oreithyia's eyes remained unfocused. A horrible chill crept over Lysippe and she looked more closely at the blisters on her mother's face.

Melanippe dropped a hand on her shoulder. "Your mother's blind, Lysippe," she said softly. "The Macedonians were convinced she'd hidden the Gryphon Stone, and tried to make her tell where."

"No..." Lysippe stared at her mother's eyes in horror.

Oreithyia's hand groped for her cheek and rested against it. Her palm was callused from riding and fighting, yet her touch was as gentle as a foal's whisker. "Of course, I had nothing to tell them. The Macedonians realized that in the end. It was the man you call the Alchemist who took my sight. He did it with his powders in a way that stopped me falling into the healing-sleep, so it didn't hurt much – at least, not physically." She paused, as if in memory. "Melanippe tells me there was a Commander with black skin who stopped the Alchemist before he could use his techniques on the rest of us, and one day we found the door of our prison had not been locked. We went straight back to the cave above Themiscyra, but you were long gone. We lost your tracks in the mountains – they were too stale even for an Amazon to follow. But when we heard about the gryphon – or rather, Androklos' famous flying lion that had been sighted in Ephesos – we came as quickly as we could. The legends say only Amazons can summon gryphons, and you were the only one I could think of who might have the power. So the Stone was an egg? I should have guessed!"

She broke off and straightened her shoulders, proud and strong, the way Lysippe remembered her. Her nostrils flared as she listened to the sounds of the fighting. "My eyes are healing, but I fear it's going to take time before I see the world again. And now you tell me this Alchemist who blinded me is the same man who killed Tanais. Would that I had my sight back so I could see him die! Is he still working for the Macedonians? Are they here, too?"

Lysippe grimaced. "No, he's working for himself – he always was. But Queen Olympias is coming! The Macedonians have a garrison on an island up the coast. When they get here, there'll be trouble." She quickly explained how she'd told the Macedonian Queen that the Alchemist had the Stone, but had omitted to tell her it was broken. "She doesn't know about the gryphon eggs. When she sees the Stone's broken, she'll think the Alchemist did it. I hope she blinds him with his own powders! I hope she kills him! Then you can kill her for betraying us." Her voice emerged fierce and hard.

Oreithyia sighed. "You've done well, daughter. But the Queen didn't hurt me, not really. The Alchemist did that."

"She gave the orders! That makes her responsible."

"Maybe. But she was angry when she arrived and saw what he'd done."

"She betrayed us. She's part Amazon. She told me her son's father was a god like mine! I don't know whether to believe her, but the gryphon said the new egg is supposed to come to the strongest Amazon... what if it comes to *her*?"

There was a short silence. "The strongest isn't necessarily the person who has the most power," said her mother. "What do you think, Melanippe?"

But Melanippe was looking down the hill. She dropped a hand on Oreithyia's arm. "I'm afraid we'll have to discuss this later. Right now, we've the problem of the Alchemist's army. Lysippe, can you persuade your gryphon to drive them back again? We're almost out of arrows."

Lysippe followed her gaze. The Alchemist was back in command. But he was on foot, covered in dust, and cursing "that stupid, good-for-nothing horse". Northwind must have thrown him. She smiled tightly, gave her mother a final hug, and accepted Melanippe's leg up on to the gryphon's neck. The fire the creature had started on the hill had fizzled out for lack of things to burn. The men would soon gather their courage to cross the blackened area. She looked hopefully out to sea, but the Macedonian ships were still specks on the horizon.

"We need more time," she whispered. She looked inland towards the city, wondering if the Megabyxos would be any help. Then she saw the younger priests out on the plain rounding up their stray bees, and had an idea. "Take me to the Sacred Hill!" she commanded.

She'd never tried to summon insects before, but the bees streamed obediently out of their hives in response to her whistle and formed a dark, buzzing cloud that followed the gryphon as if it were a huge queen. As they returned over the plain, more bees joined them and the priests threw themselves face-down into the flowers with yells of alarm.

The massive swarm buzzed so loudly, Lysippe could hear little else as the gryphon approached Androklos' Shrine. The Amazons were still holding their ground, though they were out of arrows and had salvaged swords and axes from the dead to engage their attackers in fierce hand-to-hand fighting. Melanippe stayed close to Oreithyia who, with the shouted guidance of her friend, cut down her opponents with uncanny accuracy. Meanwhile, the Alchemist and half his forces were running down the hill towards the harbour, leaving the rest of his men to finish off the Amazons. Lysippe directed the gryphon at them with a cry of fury.

The mercenaries scattered, yelling in terror as the swarm found unprotected flesh between the gaps of the men's armour and began to sting. The only one who didn't run was the Alchemist. He stood as still as a statue and covered his eyes as the bees flew inside the eye slits of his men's helmets, driving them to greater panic. Some of them fled blindly over the edge of the cliff and fell to their deaths on the rocks below. Others led the swarm back towards their comrades, who swung their shields like weapons, driving the bees to greater fury.

"Don't hit them, you fools!" the Alchemist shouted. "Stand still until they've gone!"

But the mercenaries were fleeing the hill. "Artemis is angry!" they yelled. "She's sent her creatures to punish us!" ... "We didn't get paid for this!"

The Amazons took advantage of the panic to vault on their horses and ride down the survivors, their stolen axes whirling and war cries on their lips. The few men who had stood their ground turned and fled after the others.

In all the confusion, Lysippe lost sight of the Alchemist. Then she realized where he must have gone. A strong onshore wind had blown up from nowhere, and the Queen's ship was racing into the bay with its crimson sail stretched tight and the Royal Star of Macedon glittering in the sunlight. It led three triremes with their oars flashing at full speed. Around their bows glimmered the turquoise and green scales of the oceanids, calling up the wind and the waves to speed the Macedonian fleet ever faster towards Ephesos.

"The beach!" Lysippe shouted down to the Amazons. "The Alchemist's gone to the beach to meet the Macedonians!"

Melanippe looked up and waved to show she'd understood, then swung her axe and cut down another fleeing mercenary.

As Lysippe urged the gryphon after the Alchemist, she saw two men break away from the group and hurry back along the side of the valley towards the caves she'd spotted during her midnight ride to the Shrine. She stared after them with a bad feeling. But there was no time to see what they were up to, because the Macedonian ships had arrived at the harbour and were disgorging troops to form an escort of bristling spears for their young Queen. Lysippe directed the gryphon to a vantage point on the cliff where she would be able to see and hear everything that was going on, slipped off its back and crept closer to the edge.

Directly below, the Alchemist awaited the Macedonian Queen on the white sand. The remnants of his army were drawn up behind him in ragged ranks, the blue crests on their helmets blowing in the breeze as they nervously fingered their weapons. The courage of the Amazons had unnerved them, and it was obvious they had not expected the Macedonians to arrive in such numbers.

Queen Olympias walked along the beach with the menacing grace of a hunting cat, her golden hair flying about her and the rubies in her tiara glowing in the sunlight like drops of blood. She looked even younger now she'd lost her pregnant bump, but her amber eyes were fixed upon the Alchemist as if he were an errant child. Commander Cleitus walked at her side, his hand resting on the hilt of his sword and his dark face wary.

Lysippe wasn't the only one watching to see what would happen. The swarm of bees and the arrival of the Macedonian ships had not gone unnoticed. The citizens of Ephesos were hurrying up the Sacred Way to block the quay in muttering groups – though, this time, they'd left their women safe in the city with their slaves. The Megabyxos pushed through the crowd, jumped down on the beach and marched up to the tense soldiers. The priest was puffing, and his face was scarlet with the heat. "What is the meaning of this?" he demanded. "What do you think you're doing, Alchemist? Inviting the Macedonians to our shores with *warships*!" He gestured to the triremes. "We'll have the Persian army down on us before we can blink, and Ephesos will become a battlefield!"

The Alchemist laughed. "This is no time to get nervous, Megabyxos. Or would you feel safer if you were to join the Satrap in my caves? The Queen and I have an understanding." He smiled at Olympias, who had halted several paces away. "Isn't that right, your Majesty?

Olympias glared at the Alchemist. "I do not work with traitors," she said, and raised a slender hand. The Macedonians lowered their long spears, several of them pointing at the Alchemist's breast.

He laughed again, though it had a nervous catch to it. "My gracious Queen! What have I done? I wasn't expecting you to come in person, but I'm delighted to be able to deliver my congratulations on the birth of your son. You'll be pleased to hear I've secured the Philosopher's Stone for you, and it is even now on its way to us."

The Queen's eyes narrowed. Commander Cleitus glanced to where the Alchemist was pointing, and Lysippe clutched at the wiry grass, scarcely able to breathe, as the men who had gone back to the caves hurried along the beach escorting a familiar, scruffy figure. It was Hero, and he carried a beautifully-fashioned box. On the lid, the sixteen-pointed star of Macedon glittered in gold leaf. The box was exactly the right size and shape to hold a gryphon's egg.

The bad feeling Lysippe had experienced earlier returned. "The new egg!" she whispered. "The Alchemist can't have found it, he *can't* have!"

She watched in disbelief as Hero carefully set down the box in the sand at his master's feet.

The Alchemist ruffled the boy's hair to make him look up. "Open it," he ordered.

Slowly, with great ceremony, Hero lifted the lid.

Everyone craned forward to look, including the

Megabyxos and Queen Olympias. The Alchemist folded his arms and smiled in a self-satisfied manner. The crowd muttered uncomfortably. "What's in the box?" ... "Is that our Sanctuary Stone?" ... "He can't just give it to the Macedonians! Stop him!" A few of the braver citizens ran down on to the sand, only to be brought up short by the mercenaries' swords.

There were so many people around the chest, Lysippe couldn't see what it contained. But the Megabyxos' reaction was enough to confirm her fears.

"You have betrayed Artemis!" he cried in a terrible voice, throwing his arms to the sky as if he were conducting a sacrifice. "She'll strike you down for this! Your bones will be scattered to the four winds, and your spirit will not rest as long as the Goddess is worshipped in the world!"

The Alchemist laughed. "But Artemis doesn't have an altar any more, does she, Megabyxos? Ephesos no longer has a Temple. What need does your goddess have of a magic Stone? The Macedonians will make better use of it than you, I'm sure." He motioned to his men, and they seized the chief priest's arms and dragged him back.

The Queen instructed her men to pick up the box. But Commander Cleitus laid a hand on her arm. "The Alchemist is tricky, Majesty," he said. "It might be a good idea to test the Stone before we take it back to Pella."

The Queen looked hard at the Alchemist and considered the still-furious Megabyxos. "Yes," she said, her eyes narrowing again. "Yes, of course. The priest puts on a good act, but we all know what experienced actors priests are. You thought you could trick me into taking some substitute bauble, did you?"

"I swear it's genuine, my gracious Queen!" the Alchemist said, but Lysippe saw his hand move behind his back in a secret signal to his men.

"Good, then you won't mind if I test it, will you? Touch it."

"Me, your Majesty?" The Alchemist blanched.

"Who better to test its powers than a traitor?" the Queen snapped. At a nod from her, four Macedonian soldiers seized the Alchemist, pushed him to his knees and forced his hand towards the box. The Alchemist resisted, then suddenly lurched forwards, taking them by surprise.

"No!" Lysippe cried, leaping to her feet. "Don't let him—"

There was an almighty BANG and a blinding flash. Stars fountained out of the box to fill the air above the beach with thick, green smoke. People screamed and ran in all directions. Commander Cleitus put an arm around his Queen and hurried her back towards the ships, shouting orders. The gryphon took off as rocks avalanched down the cliff, leaving Lysippe clinging to the edge, her ears ringing and her eyes watering. When the smoke cleared, she saw the mercenaries had lost their hold on the Megabyxos and were fighting the Macedonians. The Alchemist's men were outnumbered and outarmed, and tried to retreat. But with furious battle-cries, the Amazons galloped down the hill and fell on them from behind. The Alchemist himself had vanished without trace, and the crowds at the harbour were jumping up and down and shouting in excitement. "Did you see?" ... "Our Stone blasted the Alchemist!" ... "Turned him to ash!" ... "It was the goddess!" ... "Artemis!" ... "Great is Artemis Ephesia!"

Lysippe scrambled down the cliff path and raced into the smoke that hung over the open box. There, nestled in sheep's wool, was a perfectly round, black and gold egg exactly like the one she'd seen in the heart of the fire before the gryphon had hatched. It was singed slightly at one side, but otherwise smooth and whole.

She caught her breath and reached into the box. But the lid thudded shut on her fingers and Commander Cleitus faced her over the Star of Macedon, his expression forbidding. "Sorry, young Amazon, this isn't for you. The Alchemist is finished, so you'll be all right. We have to go before the Persians find us here." While Lysippe sucked her bruised fingers, he snatched up the box and ran with it back towards the harbour, where Olympias was directing her troops in a tactical withdrawal.

"Come back!" Lysippe shouted after him. "Please don't take it! I need it for my sister!"

Men were dying all around her in a confusion of flashing swords, spears and axes. She plunged into the mêlée, heedless of the danger. Something caught the end of the chain attached to her ankle and tugged her off balance. As she fell face down in the sand, a pair of arms fastened about her legs. She kicked frantically, certain her attacker was an enemy, but found herself staring into Hero's black eyes.

"Get off me!" she yelled, still kicking. "You were working for the Alchemist all along, weren't you? You tricked me into helping you start the fire, then you made sure I'd fly off to that island after Tanais, while you stayed here with your precious master and waited for the new egg so you could give it to the Macedonians! I hate you!"

"Lysippe..." Hero spat out sand. "Lysippe, calm down, you don't understand..."

She scrambled away from him and staggered down to the water. The fighting was over. All along the beach, the Alchemist's men lay groaning and bleeding into the white sand. The survivors threw down their weapons and surrendered to the Amazons, whose small tribe had been reinforced by the angry citizens of Ephesos, brandishing swords salvaged from the dead in an untrained but frightening manner at the mercenaries who had tried to take over their city.

Lysippe splashed into the sea and called for the oceanids. "You've got to stop those ships!" she cried. "They're stealing the new egg!" Desperately, she searched the sky above the cliffs. "Gryphon! Stop them! Set the ships on fire!"

But there was no answering glitter from the calm

waters of the bay, and the gryphon didn't come. Lysippe stared after the ships, numb inside.

When Hero joined her, she didn't even have the strength to splash him. "Go away," she said in a dull tone. "The gryphon's flown and my sister's transformed. We haven't even got the new egg – Queen Olympias is going to give it to her son. He's only a baby. What's he going to do with it?"

"Play with it, I expect," Hero said. "Made it pretty enough, didn't I?"

Lysippe blinked at him, hope stirring for the first time since she'd seen him carry the box to the beach. Hero's lip twisted up at one corner.

"You... made it?" she whispered.

Hero grinned. He'd lost another tooth – rather guiltily, Lysippe recalled how it had been knocked out on the night of the fire. That violence had been real.

"Course! Did you really think the Alchemist would give the Philosopher's Stone to the Macedonians? That's why he was so keen on me helpin' you find it. You weren't meant to break it. But he always planned on me makin' a copy to give the Queen while he kept the original, and I got a good enough look at it fallin' out of that burning statue when it was still whole, despite them Temple guards dragging me out the door. Must've been good, to fool a real live Amazon like you!"

Chapter 18

DIVINE JUDGEMENT
For human beings, character is the divine force.

For a moment, Lysippe could not move. Then her legs unlocked. If the egg the Macedonians had taken was a copy, then maybe the gryphon hadn't flown yet. She might still have a chance of finding the new egg and helping Tanais! Pushing Hero aside, she splashed out of the water and raced back along the beach, scanning the sky.

"Hey, wait!" Hero came after her. "Where are you goin'?"

"To find the gryphon!"

"Gryphons aren't real."

"Yes they are! The Stones are their eggs! But I think only Amazons can see them properly, like we see nymphs when most people only see strange lights. Instead of the gryphons, you see some kind of flying ghost, only you have to look really carefully or you don't even see that... oh, I haven't time to explain! I've got to find the new egg and get it to Tanais. Maybe it isn't too late to save her."

Hero grabbed her arm. "First we have to go after the Alchemist, and quick. That green smoke was a trick so he could sneak off the beach. He knew the Queen would make him test the Stone, so he rigged the box with his alchemist's powders to make it look as if it had blasted him to ash. He's still got your broken Stone – or egg, or whatever – in his caves. I think he's goin' to try to mend it himself."

"He can't, so it doesn't matter. My sister's more important."

"He's goin' to use blood—"

"I don't care! Tanais is *dying*!"

"—from his captives."

Lysippe stopped.

"Finally!" Hero planted himself in front of her, breathing hard. "I'm sorry to hear about your sister, Lysippe, really I am. I liked her a lot. She was so brave, the way she cut that chain so we could all escape. But I've been tryin' to tell you – the Alchemist's got Annyla in his caves. She don't deserve to die as well."

Lysippe's heart, that she'd thought was dead and cold after losing Tanais to the sea, stirred in sudden fear for her friend. She looked at the dark openings in the hillside and closed her eyes. At least Tanais would be an oceanid. Annyla's soul would fly straight out of the world and be lost for ever.

She sighed and headed for the harbour end of the beach, where the Amazons had dismounted and were talking to the Megabyxos. "Why did you do it, Hero?" she said as they hurried to join them. "Why did you help the Alchemist, after what he did to you?"

The boy avoided her gaze. "What choice did I have? He'd caught me, good and proper. But when he found out you were Amazons and goin' after the Philosopher's Stone, he promised if I made one last copy for him, he'd free me."

"And you *believed* him?"

Hero shrugged. "Saved me a beatin'." When she grimaced, he rushed on. "I wouldn't have hurt you or your sister, Lysippe. I never thought makin' a copy of the Stone would hurt anyone, and you wanted to find it, anyway. I wasn't goin' to give it to the Alchemist. I made two copies, one for him and one for the Queen. I meant to swap 'em somehow, so you could keep the real one. But then you went and broke it... How was I to know the Philosopher's Stone was a gryphon's egg? You could've told me!"

"I didn't know, either!"

Hero scowled, as if he didn't believe her. For that matter, she didn't know whether to believe him. Had he really made an extra copy? But there wasn't time for further explanations. They needed all their breath to fight their way through the excited priests who, curious to see the famous warriors of legend, had surrounded the Megabyxos and the Amazons. Redundant Temple guards were helping the citizens of Ephesos herd their prisoners back along the Sacred Way to the city, where they would be held awaiting trial. Meanwhile, Melissae in their sun-glaring white and orange moved through the bodies on the beach, looking for wounded and piling up the dead for burial.

"Mother!" Lysippe called, elbowing aside the priests. "The Alchemist is still alive! You can't trust the Megabyxos."

The Megabyxos frowned at the interruption. He was still red in the face from his exertions on the beach, but obviously back in control of the situation. He shook his head at them. "Ah, so the young refugees who burnt down my Temple have come out of hiding at last. I wondered when you two were going to show up." He held up a hand to silence the angry muttering of the crowd. His gaze passed over Hero and came to rest on Lysippe. "If you'd told me who you were in the first place, young Amazon, I'd have helped you, and things need never have gone this far. But what's done is done. We must release the Satrap and smoke out that tyrant Alchemist – not literally," he added with another stern look at Lysippe.

"Mother!" Lysippe insisted. "The Megabyxos sold Tanais to the Macedonians! You can't trust him!"

Oreithyia groped for her shoulder and squeezed hard. "Steady, Lysippe. I know what happened – it seems there have been some tragic misunderstandings around here, but the Megabyxos is right. We have to put them behind us and work together now."

Lysippe still didn't trust the Megabyxos. But as the priests and Amazons resumed their plans for storming the Alchemist's hillside fortress, Melanippe drew her aside and spoke softly in Scythian. "The Megabyxos' first duty is to his Temple," she explained. "With the Alchemist's army defeated and the Macedonians gone home, his best bet is to free the Satrap and reinstate himself with Persia. He's going to need a lot of gold to rebuild the Temple of Artemis to its former glory and re-establish himself here in Ephesos. Right now, your mother thinks he'll do just about anything to make sure the Alchemist is finished. Trust her, Lysippe. She might have lost her sight, but she hasn't lost her wits." She smiled grimly and used her thumb to test the blade of an axe she'd picked up from the battlefield.

It was a steep climb to the caves that formed the entrance to the Alchemist's underground laboratory, and no one spoke much as they scrambled up through the rocks. The narrow tunnels winding down into the darkness reminded Lysippe uncomfortably of the sea-cave on the island where Tanais had transformed. She was glad of Hero's company almost as much as she was of her mother's. The Megabyxos had been reluctant to bring the boy, but agreed it would be useful to have a guide who knew the layout inside, and not even Melanippe could stop Oreithyia from coming. Besides, as the Amazon queen pointed out, she could see as well as any of them in the dark.

The Amazons lit torches, which flared in unexpected draughts as they ventured further into the hill. The tunnel they were following branched several times, but Hero seemed to know exactly where he was going. Finally, they descended a flight of rough steps and came to a junction. Hero pointed. "The captives are kept down there. The alchemy chamber is that way."

The Megabyxos immediately led the priests and Temple guards towards the alchemy chamber. Melanippe started to wave the Amazons after him, but Lysippe pointed the other way. "We've got to rescue Annyla and the others," she reminded them.

Melanippe looked to Oreithyia for a decision, but the Amazon Queen was standing motionless at the bottom of the steps, her blind eyes staring at the rock and her mouth forming soundless words.

"Oreithyia...?" Melanippe frowned.

Suddenly, Oreithyia darted towards an alcove no one had noticed in the shadows and began throwing things across the floor. The rattling echoed down the tunnels. With a cry of triumph, she emerged with the half-moon shield of their tribe. She ran her hand across the gryphon design, then – more tenderly – around its inside curve. The Amazons cheered.

Finding the shield heartened the whole tribe. Oreithyia sent three of the Amazons after the Megabyxos, while she and Melanippe accompanied Lysippe, Hero, and the remaining two Amazons down the second tunnel.

They hadn't gone far when the odour of unwashed

bodies and human excrement seeped out of the darkness ahead, making Lysippe feel faint. Even Hero, who must have been used to it, covered his nose. Lysippe's steps slowed. Suddenly, they encountered bars across the tunnel. Out of the darkness beyond came small moans and rustles, as if animals were penned there.

Hero searched along the rock. "He's taken the key!" He flung himself at the bars. "Annyla? Are you in there? We've come to get you out!"

Melanippe examined the barred gate. There was a complicated metal locking bar with several bolts, all firmly in place. She tried forcing the lock with the point of an arrow, then gave it a great blow with her axe, but the bars and bolts were well-made and sturdy. The captives beyond scrambled to their feet and crowded round the gate, blinking in the torchlight. Lysippe winced at the sight of their drawn, pale faces, bruises and open sores. Arms thrust through the bars, trying to reach her. She took a step back, sickened as she remembered the rumours in the slave chain, that the Alchemist used human blood in his experiments.

Hero pushed through the grasping hands. "Where *is* she?" he cried. "What's he done to her?"

"Please..." A small girl with tangled, dirty hair matched his progress along the other side of the gate. "You got to listen..." But Hero kept shrugging her off, still calling for Annyla.

Lysippe watched the boy with mixed feelings. She wanted Annyla to be safe as much as he did. But after what had happened to Tanais, the fate of these poor captives seemed unimportant. Then she looked closer at the small girl. Underneath the dirt, her hair still showed a glimmer of gold.

"Timareta!" She went down on one knee and reached for the girl's hands with a rush of guilt. These children were all someone's sister, daughter, son, or brother. Their deaths would make those who loved them cry just as much as she'd cried for Tanais. "It's me, Timareta," she said. "I thought Mikkos had taken you all to Athens. Don't be afraid. We'll get you out of there."

Timareta stared at her, wide-eyed. Then a look of relief spread across her grubby face. "I remember you! What happened to your hair?"

"It got burnt. What are you trying to say, Timareta? Have you seen Annyla? Did the Alchemist take her? She's about my age, with curly red hair, wearing a white and orange robe..."

The girl shook her head. "You got to listen!" she said fiercely. "He did stuff down here. He said the people who came to rescue us would find a surprise, except I don't think he meant a nice one—"

Even as she spoke, a muffled boom came from the other end of the tunnel. Lysippe whirled, and the Amazons sprang round with their bows and axes raised, eyes searching the shadows. The captives screamed. Only Hero didn't realize what had happened. He was still peering into the darkness beyond the bars, calling for his friend.

Lysippe put a hand on his elbow. "Hero!"

He didn't look at her. She forced his head round. "Hero! She's not here. Something bad's happening. We have to find the key!"

At last, Hero noticed how everyone was staring back down the tunnel. He paled. "He's got her with him, hasn't he? If he's hurt her, I'll— I'll—" He shrugged off Lysippe and raced back the way they'd come.

"Wait!" She called after him, but it was no use. Even if the boy had been able to hear her, she didn't think he'd have stopped.

The Amazons braced themselves against the bars and tried to bend them with their bare hands, but it was no use. More booms shook the rock, and a bitter smell drifted out of the darkness. Trickles of dust and small stones fell from the roof of the tunnel. The captives screamed again and scrabbled more desperately at the bars.

Oreithyia pulled Lysippe under her shield, and they raced back along the tunnel. Smoke hung in the junction where they'd split up earlier, fizzing purple and green in their torch flames. As they ran through it, they met the priests running in the other direction.

"It's a trap!" shouted the Megabyxos. "The Alchemist isn't down there. Get out, quick!"

"Where's Hero?" Lysippe hung back, peering into the thick, green smoke. She thought she saw a human shape trying to hold up the roof.

"Run!" Melanippe tried to drag her up the steps after

the others, but Lysippe twisted out of her grip.

"We can't leave Timareta and the others down here!" she shouted. "Hero's deaf! He can't hear the rocks falling."

Oreithyia turned, the gryphon-shield still raised. "We have to leave them, daughter! The oreads will stop them getting crushed, but if we don't get out of here, we'll be trapped as well. Then there'll be no one to dig them out."

Oreads, Lysippe thought with a shudder, realizing what she must have seen in the smoke. Amazons who have died in here.

The Megabyxos was almost at the top of the steps when a blinding flash lit the tunnel ahead. The priests stumbled backwards, sending the Amazons staggering back against the walls. Rocks the size of urns bounced down past them, filling the tunnel with rubble and dust. Lysippe lost her footing and rolled down several steps. She curled up as small as possible, covered her head with her arms, and shut her eyes. Every breath, she expected a large rock to hit her, but they all missed. The echoes seemed to go on forever, rolling away into the earth.

Finally, it was over. Lysippe sat up carefully and blinked around. All was thick, dark, ringing silence. She tested her limbs. They were stiff and sore, but everything seemed to work as it should. She explored slowly, touching the walls of her rocky prison. It was just big enough to kneel in. When her ears recovered, the only sound she could hear was her own breathing.

"Mother?" she whispered.

No answer.

"Melanippe?"

No answer.

"HELP!" she shouted. "I don't want to be an oread! Please don't let me die in here! I want to be with Tanais, in the sea—"

There was an ominous creak. She held her breath, terrified her shout had disturbed the rocks and would bring down another avalanche.

But laughter tinkled around her. *"You're not going to transform yet, silly. You've still things to do in the world. Open your eyes."*

Lysippe had thought her eyes were already open. She blinked in surprise. An oread crouched beside her, pushing at the rock with her glittering black arms. As she pushed, the rock creaked and moved until Lysippe had enough room to stand. The oread's hair sparkled with ruby lights, and her face and body were angular as if sliced from dark granite.

"I remember what it was like to be alive," she said. *"Not much fun, except for the fighting. Call the gryphon. It's almost big enough to take us from the world now, and soon I can rejoin my mother."*

"You're Smyrna's daughter!" Lysippe eyed the oread, remembering how Smyrna had claimed she'd been murdered. But there was no sign of a wound on the sparkling body. "Where's my mother and her tribe?" she asked, suddenly afraid for those she loved. "Where's Hero? What happened to Timareta and the other captives?"

"Don't worry. They're all still breathing. So is the mortal priest, though we pushed the rock close to him. He's sweating a bit. He doesn't like close spaces."

Lysippe couldn't help a little smile at the thought of the Megabyxos' fear. "The gryphon hasn't gone, then?"

"Of course not. You still haven't finished what you came here to do, have you? Be quick about it. The gryphon's above us now. We're nearly ready to fly."

Remembering how the creature had enlarged the crack in the cliff on the island, Lysippe raised her face to the rock with a surge of new hope. "Dig, gryphon!" she called. "Dig!"

She must have been buried closer to the surface than she'd thought. There was a trickle of dust, followed by an avalanche of small stones. Then dazzling light pierced her prison. A shadow blocked the light as the gryphon's golden eye peered in at her. The eye withdrew, and the creature carefully enlarged the hole with its scarlet claws until she could climb out.

Lysippe emerged into a glorious sunset that had painted the sea the colour of fire. She supposed the air must still be full of smoke to turn it so red, but after the Alchemist's foul caves it smelled like all the sweet things she'd ever known. She breathed deeply as she admired the full-grown gryphon. Its tail was still flaming, curled high over its back like a torch. As the rocks tumbled away oreads, exposed to the sunlight for the first time in hundreds of years, glittered and sparkled their way into the creature's luxurious mane.

One by one, as they were uncovered by the gryphon, the trapped Amazons, captives, priests, and finally the Satrap, staggered out of the depths shading their eyes. But apart from the Amazons, no one seemed able to see the gryphon or the nymphs on its back. They exclaimed instead at the sunset and talked in hushed tones about the miraculous earthquake that had freed them, convinced that Artemis had shaken the ground to save their lives.

Blinking and spitting out dust, Hero staggered across to Lysippe. "I thought we were done for! Are you all right? Is everyone alive?"

Lysippe gave him a cold look. "No thanks to you!" she said. "It was a trap. You led us straight into it."

"No, Lysippe!" Hero's eyes were wide and hurt. "I didn't know what he was plannin', honest! Where's Annyla? Have you seen Annyla?"

The freed captives were running down through the avalanched rocks, leaping and cheering. A short way off, on the peak that overlooked the city, the Megabyxos and the Satrap were pointing down the hill and speaking in low tones. Lysippe followed their gaze and saw two figures stumbling through the rubble of the distant Temple. The larger one was dragging the smaller one, who kept falling and had to be jerked up again.

"The Alchemist has got her," Lysippe said, her words tight.

The Amazons gathered round. "It'll take too long to

catch our horses," Melanippe said. "The gryphon will be quickest."

Her mother thrust the shield at her. Melanippe handed her a bow and quiver, and pushed a little dagger through her girdle. Her eyes widened as Lysippe slipped the shield on her arm, but she didn't waste time asking how she'd learnt to use it.

"We'll meet you at the Temple," Oreithyia said. "Go!"

Hero frowned as Lysippe ran to the gryphon. He almost followed, then blinked and took a step backwards. His gaze lifted until it reached the creature's magnificent blue and red wings, and his mouth fell open.

Lysippe did not wait to enjoy his reaction. As she settled herself in the hollow of the gryphon's neck among the glittering oreads, she clutched Melanippe's bow with sweaty palms. *This time,* she promised herself. *This time, if I get a chance, I'll kill the Alchemist.*

The gryphon landed on the bank of the Selinus and curled its tail over the water. There was a blue sparkle as Smyrna flowed up through the flames to take her place with her oread-daughter and her oceanid-sisters.

"Thank you, young Amazon," she said, her tone gentler than before. *"Now hurry, or you'll be too late."*

Lysippe had considered asking the gryphon to help her rescue Annyla. But as soon as Smyrna was on board and Lysippe had dismounted, the creature took off again and glided towards the sea to collect the oceanids.

Clutching her bow and trying not to think of Tanais, Lysippe raised the shield over her head and ran towards the blackened remains of the Temple. The Alchemist had drawn quite a crowd. The citizens were still angry at the way he'd tricked them on the beach and surrounded him with their salvaged weapons, muttering dangerously. But they were held back by the Alchemist's wild eyes and the sword he flashed near his captive's throat every time someone moved. Annyla lay bound to the remains of a fallen column, her arms and legs stretched around its girth and another rope tied around her neck to keep her quiet. Pale streaks in the dirt on her cheeks betrayed the fact she'd been crying, but she seemed to have passed through fear and stared silently at her captor while he unwrapped the three pieces of the broken gryphon egg. Waiting nearby, laid out with chilling precision, were a crucible, a brazier, copper tools, packets of powders and a vial of green liquid.

While the crowd watched in fascinated horror, held immobile as if under some spell, the Alchemist heated a mixture of powder and liquid in the crucible and stirred it, creating coloured sparks that blistered his face and must have been how he'd lost his eyebrows and lashes. Carefully, he picked up a piece of the egg in his tongs, dipped it in his potion, and approached Annyla.

He made a small slit in her tunic and placed the fragment on her trembling stomach. She let out a whimper of terror and closed her eyes. The crowd moaned in sympathy. But nothing happened, and everyone held their breath while the Alchemist repeated the stirring and dipping and balanced the two smaller fragments on her eyelids. No one paid any attention to Lysippe as she climbed on to a blackened stone and softly set down the shield. She selected an arrow, nocked it to her bowstring and raised the bow. She took aim at the Alchemist's broad back and tried to recall the hatred she'd felt when she'd seen him stab Tanais with his sword. But her hands trembled, and before she could loose the string the Alchemist moved behind the column, putting Annyla between him and her arrow. She lowered the bow in frustration.

"Behold the Philosopher's Stone that changes worthless metal to gold and wards off death!" the Alchemist cried, his eyes glittering and his silver hair reflecting red as he raised his sword to the dying sun. "The Stone is broken, but I've studied the ancient texts and they say the blood of an Innocent of Artemis, shed here in her holy sanctuary, will mend it. Then I'll be your immortal King!"

The crowd muttered louder.

"Let the little priestess go!" someone called. "That's no more a magic stone than I'm Emperor of Persia!"

The Alchemist whirled to see who had spoken, brandishing his sword. Lysippe dropped the bow and snatched up the shield again before he saw her.

"You'll be the first person I test it on, once it's mended!" the Alchemist threatened, pointing his sword at the man who had spoken. "We'll see who doubts then."

"Your army's defeated, Alchemist!" another man called. "The Megabyxos won't stand for it."

The Alchemist laughed. "The Megabyxos is finished. He's buried in a tomb more secure than any priest deserves, along with the Ionian Satrap. I'm your ruler now."

Lysippe seized the opportunity to slip through the crowd and crouch beside Annyla's column. Quietly, using the dagger Melanippe had given her, she sliced the rope that bound the girl's neck. Annyla stiffened and let out a moan of fear. "Shh!" Lysippe whispered, lifting the egg shells from Annyla's eyes and raising the shield a little so she could see who it was. "I'm going to cut the other ropes. Follow me."

"*Lysippe!* He told me you were dead!" She feared Annyla's relief would give her away. But the young priestess slipped silently off the column, dislodging the final piece of egg, and joined her under the shield.

The crowd gasped as she disappeared from view, and the Alchemist whirled back. He stared at the severed ropes in disbelief, squinted around the base of the column, and bellowed with rage. "Slave! I see you!"

"Run!" Lysippe shouted, tugging Annyla after her.

She could see the priests and the Amazons, hurrying up the Sacred Way. But Annyla was too weak from her captivity to run, and the Alchemist already had some of his powder in his hand. She dragged Annyla behind the blackened stone where she'd left her bow and fumbled for the dropped arrow. The Alchemist laughed and sprang after them. Thinking of Tanais' webbed hands and their mother's ruined eyes, Lysippe aimed the arrow at his heart and saw him pause. But before she could shoot, the sun slipped below the horizon and the light left the sky.

Enormous wings beat overhead. Everyone ducked as an unearthly shriek split the air. Out of that darkness fell a star, trailing flame, straight towards where the three of them were frozen like a sculptor's frieze. Annyla screamed and ducked. The Alchemist's eyes glittered in triumph as he raised his face to the sky. Lysippe flung aside the bow, leapt on the stone and cupped her hands above her head. The star landed in them, surprisingly gently. As its fire faded, warmth and strength flowed into her, filling her with a vast joy. For an instant, anything seemed possible. Bringing Tanais back from the sea... conquering the Macedonians... riding Northwind across the world at the head of a great army...

Then the Alchemist was there, his sword at her throat.

"I believe that's mine," he said. "Drop it, slave."

Lysippe stared into his lashless eyes, unafraid. "You're not an Amazon. It'll turn you to ash."

The sword pressed harder, drawing blood. "I'll take that chance. If a child like you can handle it safely, it'll hardly harm one with my knowledge and skill."

Lysippe smiled. "If you want it, then take it!" Still with a curious sense of calm, she threw the egg at him.

He could have let it fall. But his greed got the better of him. He dropped his sword and plunged after the egg. As his hands closed about the still-glowing shell, a look of total surprise crossed his face. He shuddered once. Then his body crumbled before Lysippe's eyes and blew away on a gust of wind. The egg dulled as it bounced twice, coming to rest against Lysippe's foot. She stared down at it, numb.

Annyla stared, too. "A new Sanctuary Stone!" she breathed. "Pick it up, Lysippe, quick! Before someone else touches it."

But no one else seemed interested in what had happened to the star after it had disintegrated the Alchemist. They crowded forward, poking the ash where he'd stood to make sure he really was dead this time, while above them the gryphon spiralled unnoticed out of the world carrying Smyrna, her daughter, and the other nymphs to the land beyond the sky.

"Artemis has punished the Alchemist for defiling her Temple," the Megabyxos announced firmly, arriving breathless at the ruins with the Amazons and the Satrap close behind. He looked hard at Lysippe, daring her to contest this. "The goddess has returned to us. Great is Artemis Ephesia!"

Lysippe could not speak. She gathered up the new egg and clutched it to her breast, while all around her the crowd took up the chant, which grew in volume until the hills echoed with their voices.

"GREAT IS ARTEMIS EPHESIA!"

Smyrna speaks...

We are free! After all these long years, it is... indescribable. And my daughter is with me, as I shall shortly be with my own mother and her mother before her, all the way back to the First Mother Harmonia. Soon we shall leave this world with all its memories, good and bad. But before we do, there is time for questions. Will the Amazon who holds the new egg wield it in revenge, as I would have done? Or will she find another use for it? She is a child no longer, and it is her decision.

I hope for a happy ending. Yet the further we ride, the clearer I see that our time on the earth can never be truly happy. Those who are left behind when the gryphon flies will always find something to fight.

But that is as it should be. It is what makes us Amazons.

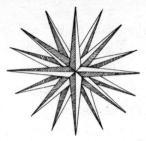

Chapter 19

NEW YEAR
You would not find out the limits of the soul,
even by travelling along every path.

That summer, the Ephesian New Year marked a special celebration. Not only was it the city's first festival since the fire, but the Megabyxos had decreed New Year's day an auspicious time to lay the first block of marble in the foundations of the new Temple of Artemis, which was being built upon the site of the old Temple, more glorious than before.

Lysippe must have been the only person not at the foundation stone ceremony. She sat alone on the beach by the harbour, staring out to sea. Northwind nibbled reeds behind her, surrounded by avalanche debris from the Alchemist's caves. The bay was very calm and clear. She could see the white sand sloping down into the turquoise shallows, and a shoal of tiny fish darting in and out of the rocks beneath. A burst of laughter and music came from the other side of the hill, making the little horse raise his head and prick up his ears. Lysippe sighed. Rather than cheering her up, the sounds of celebration only made her feel more alone.

She'd messed everything up. The night the Alchemist died, she had run down to the harbour and thrown the new egg into the sea. She'd called and called for Tanais until her throat was sore and her voice hoarse, but her sister hadn't come, and now she didn't even have the egg. It must have rolled down between the rocks in the night. Or maybe the gryphon had come back and taken it away. However it had happened, when she woke after a sleep brought on by sheer exhaustion the egg had gone, and no amount of searching from boat or shore could find it.

Everyone else in Ephesos was far too busy to notice her misery. A few days after the Alchemist's death, a small force of Persian cavalry arrived to investigate the rumoured Macedonian invasion, only to find there was nothing left for them to do. Seeing the devastation, the officer immediately ordered his men to lay aside their weapons and help the citizens and their slaves restore their city. On his advice, the new houses were being built further around the hill so that if there was another fire it wouldn't spread so quickly, and he and the Satrap were discussing the possibility of a city wall. There was plenty of cash to pay the builders, since upon hearing of the tragic fire and the way the brave citizens of Ephesos had repelled the Macedonians from their shore, the Emperor himself had sent his personal commiserations and a generous amount of Persian gold for the rebuilding project. The bees were back in their hives. The priests and priestesses had been given temporary quarters by grateful citizens, and the Amazons were heroes. As for what had happened on the evening the Alchemist had died, everyone agreed the goddess had intervened and blasted him from on high for daring to defile her sanctuary – and if anyone thought they'd seen Androklos' flying lion with a hundred or more sparkling nymphs clinging to its mane, they kept the tale to themselves. It was well known that those who claimed to see nymphs were driven out of their homes by their wives and labelled mad by everyone else.

Perhaps I'm mad, Lysippe thought. Perhaps that's why I thought I saw a gryphon's egg fall from the sky and kill the Alchemist...

"Lysippe! You can't sit down here moping all day."

The shout made her jump. She turned to see Hero and Annyla clambering over the tumbled rocks to reach the sand. They were dressed in their best tunics, and Annyla had flowers woven into her hair. A twist of orange silk around her neck concealed the rope burn, and copper bracelets with little bees dangling from them hid the marks on her wrists. Since the night the Alchemist had tried to sacrifice her, she'd started having vivid dreams and was gaining a reputation as a local oracle. Hero had changed, too. Although he still teased Annyla, calling her his sweet Melissa, he walked taller. It was as if the Alchemist's death had done more than free him.

"We thought we'd find you here," Annyla said breathlessly. "*Please* come up and join the celebrations, Lysippe! There's all sorts of wonderful food, and the Megabyxos is actually smiling for once. He's changed, you know. Melissa Aspasia thinks he had some kind of vision while he was trapped in the Alchemist's caves. And he's told everyone the Alchemist masterminded the fire, so you don't have to worry about people being nasty."

Lysippe closed her eyes. "I have to stay here in case Tanais comes."

Hero planted himself in front of her, arms folded. "You can't go on like this, Lysippe! It's been a month, nearly. She's gone. Accept it. She's happy. I bet she's up there right now in some fantastic world, lookin' down on you and thinkin' how silly you are."

"No!" Lysippe refused to accept this. "She wouldn't have gone without saying goodbye. Tanais wasn't completely transformed... you don't understand."

Annyla joined Hero and slipped her hand into his. "Shall I tell her?"

"You'd better, or all the food will be gone by the time we get back."

Lysippe looked at them in frustration. "Tell me what?"

Hero pulled a face and said, "Annyla had a dream. About your sister."

"Oh, no..." Lysippe stared at them in disbelief. "It won't work! I can't believe you'd be so cruel—"

She broke off as a sound she hadn't heard since the night the Temple burnt down echoed round the hills.

The Sanctuary Horn.

Annyla and Hero exchanged a glance. Lysippe's heart gave a peculiar little leap. She stared at her friends again, then at the twin-peaked hill that hid the city and the site of the new Temple. Just another refugee from some skirmish up the coast who hasn't heard about the fire, said the logical part of her brain. But her legs moved of their own accord, splashing out of the water. She whistled for Northwind, and the little horse came trotting down the beach towards her, kicking up puffs of sand. She ran to meet him, vaulted on to his back while he was still moving, and urged him into a gallop.

Hero and Annyla ran after her. "Hey, wait!" they called. "Wait for us!"

But Lysippe barely heard. As the horse rounded the last bend of the Sacred Way, she saw a priest standing on the slopes of the Sacred Hill beyond, blowing one of the bronze horns that had been saved from the fire. A huge crowd pressed around the old gate of the Temple, where the foundation stone had been laid earlier that morning. In their midst, Lysippe glimpsed the white and orange robes of the Melissae. They were carrying a litter that bore a dripping, greenish body with sparkling hair.

Lysippe rode through the crowd, ignoring the shouts of protest, and flung herself from Northwind's back in mid-gallop. She staggered, recovered, and fought her way through the brightly-clad citizens who surrounded the litter. "Get out of the way!" she cried, wishing she still had the gryphon egg so she could make them all disintegrate. "Let me see her!"

"Don't push, girl!" someone muttered. "Stay back with the other women. It's a refugee from the sea. Probably one of them Macedonians – he might be dangerous." Then they recognized Lysippe, and the crush parted like waves before a trireme's bows. "It's the Amazon princess!" they whispered. "Let her through."

She reached the litter and flung herself over the limp body. "Tanais!" she cried. "Tanais! Oh... speak to me!"

"Lysippe?" The whisper was very faint. Her sister's eyes didn't open, but she feebly pushed something warm and round into Lysippe's hands. "Here... take it... it's yours."

Lysippe clutched the gryphon egg, staring at her sister's body, afraid to blink in case it turned out to be a dream. But Tanais didn't vanish. She was alive and out of the sea. *Alive.*

They had no words. Silently, they clung to each other, forcing the litter-bearers to stop.

After what seemed an age, sounds and smells penetrated their private world and Lysippe remembered they weren't alone. From a far-off place, a hand touched her shoulder. "Lysippe."

She turned to see Oreithyia and the other Amazons behind her. Their mother was squinting at Tanais' half-transformed body, and Lysippe was suddenly glad Oreithyia still couldn't see very much – although her eyes were healing, she claimed it was like seeing the world through alabaster. Melissa Aspasia arrived and shooed the crowd back. She instructed the priestesses to set down the litter on the foundation stone and rested a hand on Tanais' forehead. She pulled open her eyelids, felt the blood pulse in her neck, ran her hand over the green and blue scales on Tanais' arm, and wonderingly touched the healed wounds on her chest.

At last, she looked up with a little smile. "She'll live."

A sigh rippled through the crowd, and Oreithyia closed her wounded eyes in gratitude.

Lysippe touched Aspasia's arm. "I'm really sorry about your Temple, Melissa. I'll make up for it, I promise."

"I know you will, Lysippe," Melissa Aspasia said gently, glancing at the egg Lysippe had twisted into a fold of her cloak for safety. "But let's make your sister more comfortable first, shall we?"

Lysippe clasped Tanais' hand again. The scales were rough where they were drying out, but the flesh beneath was warm and smooth. She became aware of Hero and Annyla behind her, out of breath after their run along the Sacred Way, trying to see over her shoulder.

"I knew it," Annyla breathed. "I saw this in my dream."

"Will she stay like that?" Hero wanted to know. "What made her come out of the water?"

Lysippe showed them the egg.

Oreithyia, not seeing this, smiled. "Tanais' father was

a Scythian, not a god like Lysippe's, so really Tanais is only half-Amazon. Maybe that means she can only ever half-transform, and the sea rejected her. Or maybe Lysippe's love brought her out of the ocean. However it happened, it's a miracle. The First Mother has given me my daughters back." She groped for Tanais' webbed hand and hugged Lysippe with her other arm. "I'm so proud of you – both of you. And I've some good news, too. I was waiting until I was sure before I told you, but Melissa Aspasia just confirmed it. You're going to have a new sister."

Lysippe stared at their mother in disbelief as she realized what Oreithyia must mean. All that time Tanais had been transforming in the ocean and she'd been waiting hopelessly on the beach, their mother had...

"It happened the night the gryphon flew and the new egg fell to earth," Oreithyia continued with an embarrassed little cough. "I dreamt I slept with a god, exactly like the night you were conceived, Lysippe. There was a falling star that night, you know, except we never saw where it landed... it's good to know there's another tribe of Amazons somewhere in the world strong enough to hold a gryphon's egg."

Lysippe transferred her amazed stare to the other Amazons.

"Just me, Lysippe," Oreithyia said gently, giving her another squeeze. "I think I must be the only one of us with enough pure Amazon blood to get pregnant that way. So our quest is over. There's no question of us going to fight for the Macedonians now. We're going home."

The story was already spreading back through the crowd, changing as it went. "The Amazons are the daughters of Artemis!" ... "No, they're the daughters of nymphs!" ... "The princess and her sister are immortal!" ... "No, their father was a god, like the father of the Macedonian Queen's son..."

There was more, but Lysippe stopped listening at this point. "When Queen Olympias hears of this, she'll be back for the real egg," she whispered. "She'll never leave us alone." A horrible vision of her tribe, hopelessly outnumbered and brandishing axes, galloping to meet the Macedonians and dying on the points of their long spears, came so vividly that she gasped. She felt for the egg beneath her cloak, and suddenly knew what she had to do.

At the dark of the moon, Lysippe, Tanais, Hero and Annyla crunched across the foundations of the new Temple, unseen by the handful of guards who patrolled the site. The Amazon shield with its gryphon design wasn't quite big enough to hide them all, but the men were not expecting intruders. Aside from the paving slabs that had been laid over the past few days, there was nothing as yet in the new Temple for anyone to steal.

The rubble had been cleared, the ashes raked, and a new foundation of sheep's fleeces and charcoal laid over the marshy ground. Salvaged fragments of the old columns were stacked neatly on the plain at the foot of the Sacred Hill, waiting to be recycled. Even on such a dark night, they shone faintly in the starlight.

"Here," Lysippe whispered, lowering the shield to get her bearings. Tanais, who was still rather weak after her time in the sea, sank on to a slab of newly-cut marble and stared about her. "I still can't believe the whole Temple's gone. I feel awful when I think you did it all for me."

Annyla smiled at Hero. "There were a few other things going on at the time... I reckon Herostratus would have burnt it down, anyway, in the end."

Hero scowled. "Just get on with it, before someone sees us."

Lysippe pulled the egg out from under her cloak and stared at it. In the dark, the golden swirls on its surface glowed with a light of their own. She could almost hear it whispering...

Seeing her face, Tanais snatched the egg from her and dropped it into the charcoal. "That'll do," she said. "Bury it deeply, little sister. We don't want any of the builders digging it up again by accident."

"They won't," Annyla said. "They've finished the foundations now, and the Megabyxos has blessed them with the blood-sacrifice. They're sacred."

"They will be soon, you mean," Hero said. "Hurry up, Lysippe."

Lysippe used the sharp end of the shield to dig down beneath the charcoal, while Hero and Annyla tugged the fleeces aside. When the hole was deep enough, she rolled the egg gently over the edge and watched it drop into the shadows. Her heart gave a little tug of loss. But before she could reach into the hole and pull it out again, Hero kicked a shower of charcoal down on top of it, and Annyla and Tanais pulled the fleeces back. To her relief, the whispers stopped.

They carefully smoothed over the place until it blended into the rest of the foundations, and Tanais pressed her hands to the charcoal and closed her eyes. The scales on her skin were not so noticeable in the dark. Every day, she looked more human and less oceanid. Only her hair remained strange, with a glimmer of green at the ends.

"I feel sad for the little gryphon," Lysippe said, watching her.

"It's the right thing to do, little sister. Since you used the egg to bring me back from the dead, it's going to need a few centuries to recover its powers. It'll hatch the next time it's needed, and then we'll ride the gryphon from this world together. Meanwhile, it'll protect everyone who seeks sanctuary here, for years and years to come."

Lysippe nodded. Tanais was the first person she'd told of her idea. Their mother had wanted them to take the egg back to Scythia and use it to build a great tribe of Amazon warriors. She said Melissa Aspasia had a theory that those Amazons who dreamt they lay with a god actually self-fertilized themselves, and thought that contact with an object from beyond the stars, such as a gryphon's egg, might trigger such a change in their bodies. This would explain why Queen Oreithyia had become pregnant the night the Alchemist died – and she thought she could probably get pregnant that way again, if she kept hold of the egg. Annyla had at once released Lysippe from her promise to return the Sanctuary Stone to the Temple and said of course the Amazons must take it with them – she'd no idea at the time that it was so important to them. But Lysippe pointed out that Oreithyia hadn't been in actual contact with a gryphon's egg before she'd given birth to her, and neither had the Macedonian Queen before she gave birth to her son. In the end, they'd all agreed that Lysippe was right, and that she should bury the egg where it would be safe.

Lysippe straightened her shoulders and took a deep breath. "I just wish I could hear what the little gryphon is trying to say."

"I think it's too young," Tanais said, getting to her feet. "It's like baby-talk. Give it a few centuries to grow, and maybe it'll make more sense."

"Come *on*, Lysippe!" Hero said, hopping from foot to foot. "If the Megabyxos finds us here, we'll be in trouble – or I will be, at any rate. You three will doubtless get off with a warning. You realize most of the city's already forgotten you and Annyla were with me when the fire started? I'm the one who's going to go down in history for burnin' down the Temple! It's a good job I made that second copy of the Philosopher's Stone – at least I can flog it to some unsuspecting alchemist to fund my exile, when the good citizens of Ephesos decide to ostracize me." But he grinned, as if he didn't mind being infamous. The grin turned soppy as Annyla wound her arm around his.

"Herostratus!" she said firmly. "You might end up as history, but Lysippe and Tanais will be legend."

"Ah, a prophecy!" Hero said, teasing now. "And the Macedonian Queen? What do you prophesy for her, my sweet Melissa?"

Annyla smiled. "With such an amazingly accurate copy of the Philosopher's Stone in his crib, naturally her precious little Alexander will grow up to believe himself the son of a god and set out to conquer the world, just like the Oracle said."

"Ha!" Hero snorted and leant closer to nuzzle her hair. "And us? What do you see for us? Could a priestess of Artemis accompany a rogue like me into exile, do you think?"

Lysippe and Tanais exchanged a smile as they tactfully left the two friends together in the shadows to finish working out their future.

"I never asked you," Lysippe said, gazing up at the stars. "What's it really like to transform?"

Tanais smiled. "It's nothing to be afraid of, little sister, but I can't describe it. It's something you have to experience for yourself, and I think it's different for different people, like what you feel when you kill a man. But maybe you won't have a violent death. Maybe you'll go straight to the other world with the gryphon."

"I didn't kill the Alchemist – I would have, though, if he hadn't disintegrated first."

"I know you would have. But I'm glad for your sake that you didn't have to."

"I keep wondering what he saw when he touched the egg, before he died."

Tanais threaded her webbed fingers through Lysippe's straight ones. "Thank the Mother that's something we'll never know! There are *some* good things about being an Amazon."

"Like living without men?" Lysippe said, looking speculatively at Tanais. She wasn't sure if her sister was old enough to carry a child, or even if she had enough Amazon blood, but she couldn't stop thinking of the Macedonian Queen, only a few years older, and how Tanais had nearly transformed.

"Not me!" Tanais said with a laugh. "Not yet, anyway. We'll have enough trouble teaching our new little sister to ride and fight. I suppose I'll have to take her on Sunrise's withers—"

"No!" Lysippe said at once. "I'll take her on Northwind. He's quieter."

Tanais looked as if she were about to argue. Then she laughed again. "We'll share the teaching, then. I saw Melanippe and a few of the others eyeing up the unmarried Ephesian men, so I expect there'll be more than enough young ones around soon to keep us both busy." She slipped an arm around Lysippe's shoulders. "Come on, sister, we've been fighting long enough. Let's go home."

GUIDE TO LYSIPPE'S WORLD

Lysippe and Tanais came to Ephesos in 356BC, when the city was a distant part of the Persian Empire. Athenian (Greek) rule in the Aegean had broken down, and tyrant kings were busy seizing power for themselves. The most powerful of these was King Philip of Macedonia, who paved the way for his famous son Alexander "the Great", born on the very night the Temple of Artemis burnt down.

At the time of this story, the city of Ephesos was situated on the plain and the sea reached inland as far as the Temple of Artemis. Later, the city was rebuilt further around the hill and the bay silted up. The ruins seen at Ephesos today date from the Roman era.

The quotes in the chapter headings are from the works of an Ephesian philosopher called Heraclitus, who was famous for his obscure riddles, translated by Richard Geldard and used by kind permission of Lindisfarne Books.

agora   Market place, the centre of the city.

alchemist   One who practises the ancient art of alchemy. The alchemist's dream was to find the Philosopher's Stone that could change worthless metal to gold and give eternal life.

alchemy   The ancient study of chemistry, closely linked to philosophy.

Amazons   A legendary race of female warriors who were supposed to cut off one breast and live without men. They lived in cities around the shores of the Black Sea, but were driven into exile by the Greeks, whose myths say that the first Amazons were children of the war-god Ares by the naiad Harmonia, born in the glens of Phrygia.

In this story, the last Amazon tribes live a nomadic existence on the Scythian steppe – a theory borne out by recent discoveries of Amazon graves in Kazakhstan on the Russian border. To keep the connection with myth, Amazons who die a violent death transform into nymphs.

amphora   Storage jar for wine, oil, etc.

Anatolia   "Land of the Mother Sun" – what we now call Asia Minor, which includes Turkey.

Artemis   Greek goddess of the hunt and ancient mother-goddess of Anatolia. She was worshipped in different forms in many cities.

Artemis Ephesia   Mother-goddess and Mistress of the Animals worshipped in the famous Temple at Ephesos. Her sacred creature is the bee.

Ekatomvion   First month of the new year in the Ephesian calendar. July/August.

gryphon   A magical creature, half-eagle and half-lion, with a flaming tail. Gryphons are associated with Artemis. They are fierce guardians of the dead and of treasure, and normally eat horses. In this story, they have a symbiotic relationship with the Amazons, who are the only ones who can see them properly and touch their eggs without being burnt to ash.

Gryphon Stone/ Sanctuary Stone/ Philosopher's Stone	Black and gold "Stone" that falls from the sky with the power to make people immortal and transform things. The Greeks call it the "Philosopher's Stone" and believe it turns worthless metal to gold. In the Temple of Artemis, it is known as the "Sanctuary Stone" and is supposed to protect people who claim sanctuary in the Temple. The Amazons call it a "Gryphon Stone" and believe it is the key to their lost strength.

In this story, the Stone is a gryphon's egg, which will hatch if hot enough, but otherwise remains dormant. Amazons can hear it whispering. |
Hades	The Greek idea of where souls go after death. Hades is a shadowy place under the ground with no distinction between heaven and hell.
himation	Decorative women's cloak, worn over a long dress or "chiton" (tunic).
hydria	Large, three-handled jar for collecting and storing water.

Megabyxos Chief Priest of the Temple of Artemis in Ephesos. His duties include managing the Temple bank and performing sacrifices to the goddess.

Melissae Priestesses of the Temple of Artemis at Ephesos. Their duties include tending sick and wounded refugees who come to the Temple seeking sanctuary. Melissa means "honey-bee".

mercenary A soldier who fights for money, rather than for his own country. This means mercenaries often switch sides, fighting where the pay is best.

nymphs Ghosts of Amazons who have died violent deaths and haunt the places where their blood was spilt. They are bound to those places until the gryphon hatches to carry their souls from the world. The Greeks believed nymphs were rural deities who sometimes helped women with childbirth and acted as Artemis' handmaidens. Not everyone can see them.

There are various types, according to where the Amazons died/transformed:

dryad – tree-nymph
naiad – river-nymph
oceanid – sea-nymph (sometimes called a nereid)
oread – cave-nymph.

oracle Priestess who speaks directly with the gods and answers people's questions about the future. There were several oracles in ancient Greece, the most famous being at Delphi.

ostracize Exile from society. Greek city states were ruled by a democracy, and very unpopular men could be voted into exile by writing their name on fragments of pot called "ostraca".

pediment Triangular area at the front of a Greek temple, above the columns and under the eaves, often decorated with sculptures or statues. The pediment of the Temple of Artemis in Ephesos had four Amazon statues and three windows.

philosopher   A thinker/scientist who tries to make sense of the world. There were many Greek philosophers with different views, most of whom wrote their thoughts down. The scroll mentioned in this book was written by Heraclitus of Ephesos, who had a reputation as a riddler. Today, only tantalizing fragments of his work remain.

silphium   Stalks of a cure-all plant that grew on the North African coast.

Skeroforion   Summer month of the Ephesian calendar. June/July.

steppe   Grassy plain.

Thargelion   Summer month of the Ephesian calendar, named after the festival of Artemis' Birthday. May/June.

trireme   A long, narrow warship with three banks of oars for fighting at sea.

unguent   Sweet-smelling paste or lotion, used on the skin.

THE
Seven Fabulous Wonders
1

THE GREAT
PYRAMID
ROBBERY

Magic, murder and mayhem spread through the Two
Lands, when Senu, the son of a scribe, is forced to
help build one of the largest and most magnificent
pyramids ever recorded. He and his friend, Reonet,
are sucked into a plot to rob the great pyramid of
Khufu and an ancient curse is woken. Soon they are
caught in a desperate struggle against forces from
another world, and even Senu's mischievous ka, Red,
finds his magical powers are dangerously tested.

000 711278 5

THE
SEVEN FABULOUS WONDERS
2

THE
BABYLON
GAME

When Tiamat, the adopted daughter of a perfume maker, touches one of the ancient dragons – the sirrush – who patrol the inner city of Babylon, her luck starts to change. Could it be that some kind of magic gift from the sirrush is helping her win at the Twenty Squares Club?

But someone has noticed Tia's change of fortune and, when a mysterious secret is uncovered in the hanging gardens, Tia and her friend Simeon get caught in a power struggle. For Tia's magic gift is the key that could save the city from its unpopular king – or destroy it altogether.

000 711279 3

Visit the booklover's website
www.fireandwater.com

THE SEVEN FABULOUS WONDERS

forthcoming titles...

December 2003: Book 4
The Mausoleum Murder

The Mausoleum at Halicarnassus is one of the most magnificent tombs ever constructed. But its life-like statues conceal a terrible secret dating back to the curse of King Midas...

July 2004: Book 5
The Statue of Zeus at Olympia

Alexander the Great is targeted by the Persians in this tale of treachery at the Olympic Games. But daring to offend the King of the Gods on his home ground during such a time proves to be a costly mistake...

April 2005: Book 6
The Colossus of Rhodes

For years this titanic figure guarded the harbour entrance on the island of Rhodes and kept watch over its people. Then a fatal prophecy foretells doom and destruction...

January 2006: Book 7
The Pharos at Alexandria

In the days of the last Egyptian Queen, Cleopatra, the citizens of Alexandria fight for independence against the mighty Roman Empire. Their great lighthouse is the key to control of the port, but do they dare awaken the spirits of their ancestors...?

COMPETITION

Katherine Roberts
has written about the
Seven Wonders of the World.
What do YOU think
the Eighth Wonder
should be and why?

FABULOUS PRIZE

The winning entry will be published in the back of
Book 4: *THE MAUSOLEUM MURDER*, out in
December 2003. Plus, the winner will have the
opportunity to meet and interview Katherine Roberts.
The interview will be featured on the HarperCollins
web-site, www**fire**and**water**.com, and on Katherine's own
web-site, www.katherineroberts.com.

Send your entry (no more than **200** words) to:

8th Fabulous Wonder, Children's Publicity,
HarperCollins*Publishers*, 77-85 Fulham Palace Road,
London W6 8JB.

Competition open to UK residents only.

Terms and Conditions:
1. Closing date 30 June 2003.
2. Proof of postage is not proof of receipt.
3. Winning entry will be notified by 31 July 2003.
4. Travel expenses to meet Katherine Roberts included in prize.

Katherine Roberts

I spent my childhood on the beaches of Devon and Cornwall, searching rock pools for weird creatures. My first stories, featuring some of these creatures with added magic, were told to my little brother at bedtime when I was eight. But it was another twenty-two years before I dared send anything to a publisher – initially short stories for adults, followed by my first children's book *Song Quest*, which won the Branford Boase Award in 2000. In the meantime, I went to University to study mathematics, worked as a computer programmer, exercised racehorses, and helped in a pet shop. I also learnt to fly a glider, morris dance, and ski down black runs... all these experiences creep into my books in fantastic ways!

The Seven Fabulous Wonders series grew out of my interest in ancient myths and legends and the creatures that inhabit them. Rather than re-tell the familiar tales, I wanted to explore what happens when legend meets history, and especially the gaps in-between that nobody knows very much about. In this series, you will meet seven extraordinary young people who lived in a time when magic and reality were closer than they are today – a time that gave birth to the fantastic fiction I so love to write.

Katherine Roberts, Ross-on-Wye
www.katherineroberts.com